VIOLENT CHAOS

BAY RIDGE ROYALS
BOOK FIVE

HEATHER LONG

Violent Chaos/Heather Long – 1st ed.

ISBN: 978-1-956264-84-5

For my subconscious.
You really are so much smarter than I am.
You are also an asshole, but apparently we like that.

SERIES SO FAR

FOREWORD

Dear Reader,

Welcome to Violent Chaos, this is officially book 5 of the Bay Ridge Royals. If you have not read Shamelessly Loyal, Battle Lines, Deceptive Truce, or Wicked Surrender, please set this aside and go grab them. This series is best read in order.

All of that said, what do you *need* to know? Let's talk, previously, for the Bay Ridge Royals...

So much happened in Wicked Surrender...

So much.

Let's start with the TL:DR: Ezra tried to fall on his sword for everyone—again. Bodhi focused on protecting Lainey *and* the men in her life, because her people are now his people. Milo returned, having told King to fuck off, and reunited with Lainey. Adam and Lainey finally took that step into lovers and Ezra was invited to play. Following a near miss ambush, Bodhi helped Lainey fend off attackers and then later joined her in the shower. In the end, the guys went to save Ezra from himself while Lainey went to deal with her sister only to be kidnapped.

Got that?

For those who would like more details, we picked up in Wicked Surrender where Deceptive Truce left off including learning of the threats made by Wallace Graham to force Ezra's hand in agreeing to the public announcement of his engagement to Oksana.

Bodhi took charge to get Lainey out of the ballroom, leaving Milo and Adam to worry about her. Bodhi also took care to deal with any potential threats, including Karagiani who tried to keep Lainey there.

Then once in the car, he took her to his place in Virginia several hours away where she could deal with her emotions in private. They grew closer, including Bodhi admitting his interest in her. While she needed care and not sex, he curled her up in bed with him. Later they went to a sex club in DC called the Underground to snare some information.

Back on Long Island, Adam pursued Ezra when he took off from the party to find out what the hell was going on. Ezra fled to his cousin's place in Connecticut. Dominic "Nicky" Walsh is a cousin on his mother's side, he is also working on getting Ezra out of the arranged marriage. It turns out, he also has history with Milo in that Ezra sent him to help Milo get a deal years earlier when Ezra set him up to take a fall for a crime as ordered by King.

After the talk with Nicky, Ezra and Adam broached the subject of Ezra's kiss as well as Ezra's determination to sacrifice himself. Adam recognizes that he has a lot of work to do to regain Ezra's confidence and faith. He also recognizes that while he doesn't know what to do with Ezra's desire, he's not put off by it.

He's determined to figure it out. One way or another.

Milo talks to his sister, Ivy. She's upset that he's gone to live with King in order to protect Lainey and Andrea. She also wants to do something to help, but he doesn't want her anywhere near King. The man's interest in the daughter he never wanted rubs Milo the wrong way.

After returning Lainey to New York, Bodhi left her with her grandfather until she was ready to go back to her apartment. Then he offered to drive her. He also had a conversation with Leopold Benedict when her grandfather insisted that they "talk as men do." It was both hilarious and sweet.

Once back at her apartment, she discovers Adam waiting for her and Ezra is upstairs asleep. They came to the apartment after leaving Nicky's place. Adam recognizes that Bodhi is interested in Lainey, but he's refusing to back down. If it means he has to share her, then he will.

They end up having sex and he is more than staking his claim. Ezra comes in to watch and Adam teaches him a little bit about what it means if he wants Adam to claim him too. They end up sharing Lainey between them. It's just another step on the road as they try to discover what can be.

After a day spent in bed together, the three are trying to work out the new balance. But Adam and Lainey are both worried about Ezra. Milo shows up, having told King he wasn't playing this game anymore and he reunites with Lainey. Ivy calls as he and his mayhem are about to have sex, and Milo pulls the big brother card, graphically telling her what he plans to do to Lainey. Then he tells her to get one of her seven boyfriends to entertain her.

Adam takes Ezra back to his apartment to give Lainey and Milo time. King shows up to make a proposition to Lainey, whether he is aware that Milo is there or not is unclear. King also tries to tempt Lainey with some information on her family. She's not biting.

Later, at dinner with her grandfather, Lainey learns he wants her to marry Milo, preferably, but marry someone before her inheritance kicks in to protect her. With her 21st birthday so close, he's concerned. In the meanwhile, Ezra shows up—drunk as hell—having slipped away from Adam. Leopold isn't thrilled, but Lainey hustles him out of there and takes him back to her place.

They are ambushed outside of the apartment. Ezra is too drunk to fight and goes down. Lainey does her best to defend him and uses a baton that lets her break a couple of arms. Bodhi shows up as the tide starts to turn and he is more than happy to deal with the rest.

After they are all down, he immobilizes the survivors, carries Ezra inside, then leaves Lainey to take care of him and herself while he handles cleanup. When he does join her, he finds her in the shower and he is more than happy to tend to her injures and her. They have sex and once they are curled up in bed, Ezra eventually crawls in on her other side.

The five of them work together to interrogate the survivors. They don't know who they are or who sent them. Ezra is certain it's his father which leads to him slipping away to give himself up to protect Lainey, particularly cause his drinking could have gotten her killed.

The four of them go after him, but Andrea messages from Lainey's apartment. She's left school and wants to visit. Unwilling to take Andrea on this fight, the boys drop Lainey off at home. She's armed and security cameras show the outside of the apartment and the hall is safe.

Once Lainey is up and in her apartment, she's ambushed again. This time, they succeed. When she wakes up, she's in an unfamiliar room and she's naked.

This brings us to Violent Chaos. Whew... right, here we are. As always, I have fallen so deeply in love with these characters and I cannot wait to see what happens next.

As stated previously, *this* series contains some spoilers for 82nd Street Vandals, there's no way to get around that. If you do decide to check out 82nd Street Vandals, be sure to start with *Savage Vandal*.

For a little housekeeping. Bay Ridge Royals is a why choose romance with characters exploring and coming to terms with their evolving sexuality including a possible bi-awakening, identities, and relationships.

TWs: Mentions of SA. Kidnapping. Intimidation. Car accidents. Threats of violence. Discussion of trafficking. Smuggling. Be kind to yourself, this is a dark romance series.

Thanks for checking out Wicked Surrender, I can't wait for you to get to know them.

Happy reading.

xoxo

Heather

P.S. Human voices only. All the work involved in this and all my novels from the stories themselves to the covers, to editing, to the audio are human-produced materials and voices only.

BAY RIDGE ROYALS

Main Characters
Elaine "Lainey" Benedict
Milo Hardigan
Adam Reed
Ezra Graham
Bohdi Cavendish

The Families
Benedict
Reed
Graham
Adley
Clifton
Marlowe
Cavendish

PROLOGUE

BODHI

BODHI

THE DAY ISLA DIED

"Mr. Cavendish," Mr. Fitz said, pulling my attention from the assignment. "Collect your things."

It was hardly my first time to be sent for discipline, yet somehow, I doubted this was anything I did. Still, I packed away my books, slung the book bag strap over my shoulder, and made my way to the front of the room. Mr. Fitz held out a small square of paper with my name on it. The orange slip was a summons to the front office.

"Have a good day, Mr. Cavendish."

"Thank you, sir." I pushed open the door and strolled out of the literature class. The only thing I enjoyed was the Chaucer bits because the older English was amusing. I didn't have to wait too long for the office to find out what this was about, however: Counselor Donnaghan waited in the hallway.

He was both my academic and disciplinary advisor. While I wasn't fond of him, I respected him. He didn't lie to me or generally pander to the family name. "Mr. Donnaghan?"

The soft sigh he exhaled told me everything. I almost didn't need the explanation he braced to offer me. "I was going to take you to my office for this, Phillip." It was definitely bad news. "But you already know."

"My mother?" It was a guess. It might have been my great-grandmother, though she wasn't as elderly as the title suggested.

"I'm afraid so, son." He put a hand on my shoulder. It was an offer of comfort and support.

A myriad of reactions spilled through me, as though a stopper had been pulled and they fell through me and then away again.

"I am very sorry, Phillip. So very sorry. There's a car coming to pick you up. I was told the service would be private, so you won't have to worry about any public spectacle."

A frown tightened my brow as I compartmentalized the data.

"Do you want to go back to your room to pack anything?" That question registered faintly, and I shook my head once.

"No, sir. Thank you." I was on autopilot.

Mr. Donnaghan frowned, and I could practically read his desire to get me to talk in his expression. He didn't pursue it. Instead, he walked me through the school to the administration buildings and then to the ellipse. We weren't there long before a car pulled in. The driver was just another of the faceless masses who served the family anonymously.

"If you need anything," Mr. Donnaghan told me, "anything at all, just call."

"Thank you, sir." I wouldn't need anything. I wouldn't call. This was a family matter.

A private matter.

I would take care of it myself.

THE DAY I MET HER

"Phillip, son, I'm sorry," Leopold Benedict told me. "I wish there was more we could do for you." He and his wife seemed very kind. They'd attended the private funeral, though they'd sat far away from the family. My father had only offered him the barest form of civility.

That intrigued me. It was only *after* the funeral and after I began to dig into Mother's death that I found out Mr. Benedict had been visiting her. A year later, I found out about the letter. A letter he refused to give me. A promise he'd made to her. A promise he wouldn't break.

I respected the concept, I did.

But I wanted the letter.

If he wouldn't give it to me, I'd break in and steal it.

The Benedicts owned multiple properties. I worked my way through the ones in the city and on the coast before Der Sonne. Der Sonne's security was impressive, but it had the same blind spots so many wealthy homes had.

Staffing.

Getting in wasn't the problem. Benedict's butler was a cagey one, and I gave him a wide berth. It was late in the evening, the family was out at an event, and the staff was

3

scarce. It shouldn't have surprised me to find the letter secured in a safe. It took some actual effort to get it open.

The code, though, was on a business card tucked into the back of a painting of his wife. I put the card back once I had the safe open. I ignored everything else except for the stack of letters and other papers. I could barely mistake my mother's handwriting for anything else.

I returned the rest of the papers unreviewed. Benedict was entitled to his privacy and his secrets. This secret, however, was mine. Sliding the envelope into my jacket, I cleaned up and headed for the door. A shuffle of a step pulled at my attention as I left Benedict's office, and I locked eyes with a tiny little pixie on the stairs.

The heart shaped face beneath the cloud of dark hair and wide eyes was a punch to the throat. She tilted her head, studying me then the library then back to me. I put a finger to my lips and she grinned. The sheer trust in that smile didn't belong to me. Shouldn't and yet—I recognized the desire to never betray it.

When she mirrored the action, putting her finger to her lips, I winked and then made myself leave.

Oddly enough, that image imprinted itself in my brain, and I started keeping a distant ear and eye out for my little pixie.

Particularly when she never betrayed me.

Ever.

THE DAY I SAW HER AGAIN

"Phillip." Surprise decorated her voice, and it echoed the mild shock rippling through my system. The fact Graham and Reed were here didn't surprise me, even though they kept circling her like a pair of jackals intent on keeping everyone else away.

"Elaine Benedict," I greeted her, crossing the room to kiss her on each cheek. Better to let everyone know they were not going to be messing with her. I liked the Vandals. PPG had reminded me of Lainey B, and now I knew why. They were friends. It was hard to hide or ignore. Not that I had any desire for either.

I also liked Freddie, and he trusted most of the people in this room. Acceptable endorsement. Still, as the conversation broke down the upcoming fight, I kept an eye on all the players.

Lainey B was wading into this war.

That meant the rules had changed.

ONE

MILO

"**T**hey aren't on Long Island," Adam said as he leaned between the seats. We'd just watched Mayhem head into her apartment building. On the one hand, I hated leaving her here. On the other, I was grateful for Andrea's interruption. Taking Lainey into potentially violent situations would never be my first choice.

"Where to then?" Bodhi asked, and like I had been, he stared at the building for a long moment before switching his attention to Adam.

"Looks like an adjunct building near the County Clerk's office in Queens."

"Great," Bodhi said. "I haven't been arrested in a while." But he pulled into traffic smoothly.

"It'll be faster if we head to 53rd," Adam argued abruptly. 53rd was behind us if I was measuring it right.

"Not this time of day. The FDR to the parkway. Fewer

lights." Absolute confidence underscored Bodhi's retort. I believed him. So did Adam, apparently, because he didn't argue.

"What do we do if he's already married when we get there?" Because at this point, it had been hours since he left the warehouses in New Jersey. He'd had easily an hour, maybe two, lead on us between when he left, when they found his note, and our making our own way back to the city.

Not for the first time, I wished I knew Manhattan and its boroughs like I did Braxton Harbor. I was working on it, and I was getting better. Better, but still not as well as I needed to know it. Especially since it looked more and more like this was where I was spending the rest of my life.

A twinge expanded in my side at the thought. As uncomfortable as it was to admit to myself, it was also the right thing. Where Mayhem was—well that was home now.

Adam grunted. "We get him a divorce. Then I beat his ass for being a goddamn martyr."

"So the only ones around here who get to do that are the two of you?" Bodhi's question lumped me in with Adam and I frowned.

"Excuse me?" Adam snapped.

"No," Bodhi said with a shake of his head. "I don't think I will."

"He means you throwing yourself in the fire to work for Waldemar and get Ivy out—or working for King to protect Mayhem." Hard to miss the facts.

Adam snorted. "You too because you left Lainey for King to protect Andrea."

"Yep." I wouldn't argue this. Leaving her sucked. But protecting her sister? Finding a better way to take down

King? Doing everything I could to secure the future? Yes, I would take those hits.

Not responding right away, Adam glared out the front of the vehicle.

"You don't have to like what he did," Bodhi commented. "But it's better to think about why he did it."

"I still don't like you, Cavendish," Adam retorted after a beat.

"I'm shattered." The deadpan response pulled a real smile to my face, and I shook my head.

"Asshole." Despite muttering, there was almost a ghost of a smile in Adam's voice.

Bodhi just shrugged. "Yep."

The drive seemed to be interminable, yet it wasn't more than thirty minutes from leaving Mayhem to when we arrived at the building where Adam had tracked Ezra. According to the tracking data on his phone, Ezra was still inside.

That was something.

Based on the location, I expected the glass building on Kew Gardens to be closer. It wasn't a long walk, but the Grahams didn't strike me as strollers. Either way, Bodhi pulled down into the public parking behind the building.

"Radiology, fitness club, law offices, and the office of the District Attorney," Bodhi said before we got out of the car.

The DA? I shot him a look.

"Like I said, been a while since I was arrested." The faint amusement didn't offer a lot in the way of comfort. I had zero intentions of being arrested.

"Metal detectors?" Adam pulled out a gun and holster, then slid it under the seat of the car.

"Probably." At Bodhi's suggestion, I did the same. When he didn't disarm similarly, I eyed him.

He pulled out a card from his wallet. The flat, white keycard had no discernible marks. "If you have one of these, you don't have to go through the metal detectors.

One of us would be armed.

"Can we go now?" Impatience marked Adam as he slid out of the car. We'd hardly been dressed for "business" when we were at the warehouse. Still the sports coat Mayhem had tossed me worked well enough despite my jeans. Adam and Bodhi were both in dark slacks, and button downs with their own suit coats.

It was like there was a dress code the elite subscribed to along with their Fox and Hound magazines or whatever the fuck it was they read. For some reason, the idea of that magazine summoned the image of Mayhem in her riding gear. I had zero objections to how those clothes fit her.

Shaking my head, I raked a hand through my hair, then looked at the pair of them, then focused on Bodhi. "Following your lead."

Adam snorted but checked his phone one more time before sliding it away. "They are probably on the fourteenth floor. They have attorneys here. There's also a walkway that will take them right across the street to the courthouse."

"One crisis at a time." Bodhi stared at the doors to the annex where the elevators waited. The parking was below the building. Exit was going to take us a minute. He gave himself a little shake, then his chin lifted and his eyes narrowed. The change was subtle but present.

The arrogance that eddied in the air around him was an energy many tried to achieve but seldom accomplished. Power wreathed him. Power. Privilege. If I had any doubts about him belonging to this world, they were utterly eradicated.

Mayhem wore that same power when she walked into a

room, and she shed it easily when she was no longer on display. Without a word, Bodhi strode toward the elevators and we followed in his wake like a pair of bodyguards. Kind of funny considering Adam belonged as much as Bodhi did.

Inside, Bodhi bypassed the metal detectors and waved us through. No one questioned him. Hell no one gave him a second glance. Even when security gave me a once over, they accepted that Bodhi belonged.

Walk in like you owned the place and let everyone defer to you. As much as I didn't mind old-fashioned fights, I'd rather skip them when we had this much security. The fact the building was also home to the District Attorney's office didn't bode well if this went sideways.

At the elevator, we managed a car on our own then we were on our way to the fourteenth floor. No conversation or body language to betray us. There were cameras everywhere.

Faith, I reminded myself. Whatever we had to do, we would. Then we'd deal with the fallout. Though, if the fallout was excessive, it might be me kicking Ezra's ass. The closer we got to the fourteenth floor, the tenser Adam seemed to grow.

I slanted a look at Bodhi. Unlike either of us, he leaned against the back wall, arms folded like he didn't have a care in the world. He caught my gaze and lifted his chin toward Adam before he nodded.

Yeah, he saw it.

I tapped my ear once then nodded at Adam again. Bodhi looked thoughtful, but he dipped his head once as the elevator halted.

Right, he'd get Ezra. I'd cover Adam.

Not waiting for either of us, Adam strode down the hallway. Where power had cloaked Bodhi in the parking garage, it rippled in waves off Reed. Pure fury fueled his steps. I really didn't envy Ezra on this one.

He may have actually pushed the man too far. The hallways were wide, paneled in wood, and decorated with art. Unlike most generic office buildings, this one appeared to have some personality.

Sullivan, O'Conner, and Yates was located behind a pair of glass doors with gold-plated handles. The receptionist's desk was empty, but the doors pushed inward for us. It was a weekday. Still early in the day for the receptionist to be gone for the day.

Adam circled the desk then depressed a button that unlocked the doors leading deeper into the office. I moved as his shadow, aware of Bodhi falling into step with me. The rhythm of motion I recognized.

When we'd gone after Bradley Sharpe, I'd worked with Adam and Ezra. Bodhi had gone in on his own, but Ezra, Adam, and I stuck with Mayhem. That had gotten Ezra shot.

Hadn't stopped the jackass from doing his best. The issues we had—they were going to take a while to work out. But what—or should I say *who*—we had in common made it paramount that we *would* work it out.

Inside the law firm itself, it smelled like coffee, printer cartridges, and hints of tobacco. There was leather cleaner and soap too if I wasn't mistaking it. While the center of the room contained a network of cubicles, there were no people.

Despite the personality reflected at every desk and the variety of larger offices visible through the open doors, no one was here.

I gripped Adam's shoulder to keep him from plowing

forward. He hesitated a beat, swept the room with a look, then glanced at me and beyond me to Bodhi.

"They've cleared out witnesses. Not an uncommon practice." In the large, empty room his hushed words seemed louder than I cared for.

"Gun," Bodhi said as he pressed a Sig Sauer into my hand. I checked it then nodded. The only doors that were closed were the ones at the far side. So not only had they removed witnesses, they'd moved everything to the room the farthest from the public.

"This is a bad idea," I said as Adam focused on that door.

"Yep," he said, then spared me a faint smile. "Still doing it."

"Didn't say we weren't."

At my comment, he frowned briefly and his gaze locked on mine. Did I mean it? Could he trust me? Yes, I meant it. I would have his back.

Another nod. "Thanks."

"Bond later, work now," Bodhi ordered, and I caught the faintest flicker of Adam's smile as he faced forward again.

"We're charging in," Adam said.

"If there are guns, drop," I told him. Cause he would be going first, that meant Bodhi and I would be a second or so behind him.

A second was a long time when guns were pointed at you. These guys didn't move with me like we had all our lives. I could take a room like this with the Vandals without breaking a sweat. We understood how the other thought, fought, and moved.

I didn't know Adam and Bodhi yet. I was learning. So were they.

For now, verbal cues and suggestions were just going to have to do.

Four strides from the door, Bodhi went a little wider. "I got left."

Three strides from the door. I nodded. That left me right.

Two strides. "Get Ezra out first," Adam ordered.

He might not want to go.

Didn't matter, we were there. Adam pushed the door inward without knocking. The hum of conversations flooded out like alley cats tumbling one over the other as they bit and scratched.

"What the hell are you doing here?" I didn't know the man but he looked enough like Ezra to pin him as the father. The bride-to-be was here and she looked terrified. Across the room from them a man rose who looked like some of the guys I'd spent time with in prison.

Identifying the threat, I pointed my gun at him. "Take a seat. Nothing for you to concern yourself with."

His eyes narrowed, but he kept his hands where I could see them and the tattoos on them.

"Guys..." Ezra said. "What are you...?"

There wasn't time to answer him because the body-guards with the man across the table moved. So did the ones near Graham Senior.

I put bullets in the shoulder of one of the men charging me, then another in a knee. They went down even as the discharge from Bodhi's gun told me he'd dealt with the others.

"You're leaving," Adam ordered Ezra as he approached him. Like everyone else in the room, Ezra was in a suit. Yeah, I was definitely underdressed for this anti-kidnapping attempt.

The fact we'd fired guns inside the building hadn't been lost on me. From the moment the guns discharged, the clock counted down our need to get the fuck out of here. The girl next to Ezra tried to grab a hold of him but Adam snapped a single look at her.

"Don't."

She withdrew her hand like it had been stung.

"Adam—" Ezra began but Adam gripped his arm and hauled him toward us. Graham Senior lurched forward and all hell broke loose. The bodyguards weren't the only people armed. Ezra's mother let out a scream as his father charged.

When Adam thrust Ezra at me, I shoved him behind me then blocked the knife that appeared in Graham Senior's hand. The screaming from his mother was ear piercing. Particularly when the fiancee joined in on the shrill noise.

"Be quiet," Bodhi said, the command sliced right through the sound. I twisted Graham Senior's arm until the knife fell from his hand and then shoved him away. Adam didn't let him get far before he delivered a sharp uppercut. The man staggered, but it was Adam's next blow that sent him crashing into the top of the table.

"No," Ezra shouted and cut around me to intercept the bodyguard with the shoulder wound. He got between the man and Adam. "Enough—everyone just *stop*!"

"We're here to rescue you," Adam snarled at him.

"I didn't ask for you to rescue me," Ezra snapped back. Really not the time for a lover's spat. "I have this under control. Mr. Do—" He didn't get to finish the thought as the bodyguard surged forward to snag the fiancée, but Ezra blocked him and shoved him backward.

Adam dragged him back, all but throwing Ezra behind him as he put himself between Ezra in the rest of the room.

"Goddammit—"

"Enough," I said, cutting him off. "You want to bring her with us, we'll take her. But you're leaving."

Ezra swung a look at me.

"You can leave on two legs or over my shoulder. Don't really care which." I'd made Mayhem a promise, and I intended to keep it.

He scowled at me, but the occupants of the room seemed frozen in a violent tableau. Ezra searched my face then behind me. He must have been looking at Bodhi.

"Now, Graham," Bodhi ordered. "They need to get medical care for their people."

"Go," the girl said abruptly and Ezra looked at her.

"Oksana..."

"No, you have proven to me that my father will negotiate." She spared her father a look. "I have already disappointed him many times, but I think he and I can do something with this." Whatever she said next was in Russian or something. Ezra answered her but she sliced a hand through the air then evaded him as she circled the table back to her father.

"Fine, she stays. We're going." Adam turned, all but manhandling Ezra out of the room, trusting me and Bodhi to guard his back. I backed up until Bodhi nodded with his head to the door, then I was out.

Adam had Ezra halfway to the elevators. We really needed to go.

"Gentlemen," Bodhi said. "I trust this issue will remain between us."

"Of course," the other man answered. "Until next time."

"Don't let there be a next time," Bodhi warned. "I'm not feeling friendly."

Then he closed the door, and I pivoted to watch it as he

headed toward me. We split our attention behind and ahead.

At the elevator, Ezra was glaring at Adam. Sweat dotted his face and there was blood on the sleeve of his jacket. I didn't get a chance to ask because he dropped as the elevator doors opened.

TWO

LAINEY

Awareness crawled through me again like a half-crippled hangover from a bad night of binging with no water. My mouth tasted like ass and my head pounded. Scraping together my focus, inch-by-inch, I forced my eyes open.

The shadows of the room I'd awoken to the first time hadn't changed. The air was still chilly and the cold sent a shudder through me. Then a second. Sitting up abruptly, I gripped the edge of the sofa—good, not a bed.

My head swam like I'd been caught in the agitation generated by a storm aboard a yacht. The lurching threatened my stomach, but I breathed in through the nose and out through the mouth.

I'd had exactly one real hangover in my life, and I disliked the experience so much, I'd refused to ever indulge that much again. This wasn't *me*.

Memory dripped through me. Fragments landed with a splash.

My apartment.

Andrea.

Someone grabbing me.

Each piece sent out a ripple to chase after the others. The attackers had been *in* my apartment.

How?

They hadn't been visible in the hall.

I dug my fingers into the fabric, head swaying as I kept my breathing rhythmic and tried to deepen it. Clarity was necessary. My vision was as fuzzy as my tongue. In a minute, I would stand. If I could find water, that would help.

Attackers.

In my apartment. Irritation raked through me, dragging the razor wire of fury after it. Andrea's phone.

Whoever *they* were. They'd had *Andrea's* phone. I'd given them the passcode to the apartment and the alarm code. Lifting my head, I studied the room around me even as another shiver hit.

I was freezing, but I'd been freezing for a while because I barely noticed until I shuddered. They'd stripped all of my clothing off. What wasn't numb, ached. So I couldn't really tell if they'd done anything else.

I touched two fingers between my legs and they came away dry. Not that it meant much, but I'd take it. First thing's first. I needed clothing of some kind. Sooner or later my captor was going to show up and I had zero intentions of being naked when I faced off with him.

There were enough disadvantages in my current situation. Shelves lined the walls. They didn't have anything on them. In fact, the more I studied the room, the more the lack of any items or decorations struck.

Bare walls.

Barren shelves.

Thin, gossamer like curtains over shuttered windows. Absolutely useless and yet there they are.

I'd been dumped into a closed room.

It took me far longer than I cared to admit to make it to my feet, but I kept my breathing even as I began a search. There was a water closet tucked into the corner. Not a bathroom, just a water closet. Maybe this room was meant for a gathering space and not a living one? I had no idea.

The water worked on the sink, and the mirror was in shadows. The light cracked on, but the brightness made me flinch away. I was seeing spots for a solid minute after turning it off.

I splashed icy water on my face, and that helped to clear more of the cobwebs away. I rinsed out my mouth before I drank handfuls of the water. The ache in my throat seemed to intensify before I swallowed enough to soothe it.

After drinking, I shook the water off my hands. There wasn't even a single hand towel in here. I began a methodical search of every nook and cranny, starting with the bathroom.

There were coverlets on the furniture in the room but very little else. The sofa I'd been lying on had been uncovered, but there were two high-backed chairs and another chair tucked into the corner.

When my search yielded nothing else, I shook out the first coverlet and ignored the little poof of dust. A little folding and judicious tying turned it into a toga. I used the second one to make a cloak of sorts to cover up more.

The stale air, now littered with dust, made my nose itch. The sheers over the windows were no obstacle, but the shutters were.

They were locked together.

The louvers were also locked down. At least they wouldn't move with any tugging or pushing. But the louvers were slats, which meant if I could jam something in there, I could possibly wedge them open to see where I was or even break some slats off.

I continued my search, looking for possible weapons. The closest thing I found was an ugly bust of a head that was made out of brass. It was the only thing left sitting on a shelf and tucked into a corner like someone had forgotten it.

Measuring the weight against my palm, I carried it back with me to the sofa. Three doors in the room. One that was locked and presumably led to the exit. One to the water closet.

The third was also locked, and I wasn't sure if it was an exit to outside or to another room. None of the doors were on the wall with the windows. Age and disuse seemed to hang in the air. I got myself another drink, formulating and discarding a half-dozen ideas.

At least I could think now. The longer I was on my feet and moving, the more clarity I gained. Of course, movement also increased the thunder of my headache. Among the other irritations, the lack of a clock or some way to even tell what time it was added to my aggravation.

Daytime was a guess, but that was only because the shadowy light creeping in around the shutters added to the gray gloom. Even that was beginning to vanish. I finally turned on the light in the water closet and faced away to let my eyes adjust.

The light sliced across the room, bisecting it and deepening the shadows around the edge. It reminded me of that creepy film *The Others*. I'd never been fond of ghost stories.

It was completely dark around the edges of the shutters

when a release of tumblers on the door alerted me to a new arrival. I closed my fingers around the bust. It wasn't much, but it could definitely hurt if I got the chance to land the blow.

The door pushed inward allowing a man I didn't recognize to enter. He scanned the room then me. "Stay seated," he ordered.

A second man followed him. The light from the hall backlit them both, and I couldn't really make out more than the paneled wainscoting behind them. Another detail to add to the catalog I was creating.

The second man carried a huge tray. The smell of stew, fresh bread, and even cheese, hit me like a truck. My stomach growled.

The tray was placed on the table. There were two carafes on the tray as well as a mug, a glass, and silverware.

Well, how very nice of them to provide me with weapons. As eager as I was to lift up the silver-domed lid to eat, I didn't move. I kept my gaze on the two newcomers. I had no idea who they were.

Then a throat cleared and pulled my attention to the still open door. My stomach plummeted and rage exploded like oxygen fed into a backdraft of a fire. I hit my feet.

"What the hell is going on, Harper?" It came out far more croaky than I cared to admit, but staring at Harper Reed, I didn't give a damn.

Adam and Andrea's father.

My mother's husband.

My stepfather.

The man my grandfather downright loathed.

"Leave us, gentlemen," Harper ordered with a faint smile. Still dressed in a suit, he looked like he could have just arrived from a board meeting.

The men withdrew, and they closed the door but not fully. The faint crack meant they could hear us and probably respond if I attacked Harper.

Rising, I faced him. It also put me closer to the tray and the array of weapons they'd brought me. If any of that food was hot, the burn would be to my advantage. My stomach cramped and grumbled again.

The obnoxiousness of the noise would have embarrassed me in any other situation. Currently, I didn't give a damn about decorum.

"I'm sorry for the accommodations, Elaine, but this room is ideal for keeping your presence quiet."

"You mean my incarceration?" I raised my brows. What else did you call a locked room you wake up in *naked*? "Where is my mother? Where is Andrea?"

He chuckled. "Please, have a seat. I would have had food brought to you sooner, but I was attending to other matters. I'm sure you're hungry."

"Starving won't hurt me." I continued to stare at him. "Where is my mother? And Andrea? I presume it was you who gave those men Andrea's phone?"

Another faint smile touched his lips. "Your ferocity has always entertained me. Perfectly poised, but your grace is no disguise for the powerful woman beneath."

It took every ounce of my discipline to blank my face. Disgust curled through me. "Are you arriving at a point soon? Or do you have more meaningless drivel to share?"

Harper Reed was not my friend. Nor was he my family. Despite his and Mother's rather heavy-handed tactics over the years, I'd kept my distance. He was terrible to Andrea when he remembered she existed.

And Adam...

My stomach dropped again. The guys had to know I

was missing by now. They would have found Ezra, hopefully saved him. Now they would be looking for me.

"It's fascinating," Harper said, rubbing his jaw almost thoughtfully. "You and your mother—raised by the same people, yet you are so wildly different. You have a strength and a determination she lacks. It will make bedding you fun, I'm sure."

I didn't vomit. "Over my dead body."

"It won't come to that… but for now, you will stay here and you will eat your meal and you will behave."

"Will I?" I dared him.

"You will, because you care about Andrea. I know where she is and you don't. Your behavior and choices will have immediate ramifications for her."

I hadn't thought it possible to be angrier. "You're threatening your own daughter?"

"She is more useless to me than my son at this point. She will never inherit. Nor will your mother. I thought it possible to persuade Leopold, eventually, but he has effectively cut off every possible avenue. In two days, you will turn twenty-one."

"So what?" I spread my hands. "Do you think I'll just sign it over to you?"

"Of course not, you are far too stubborn. That part of your nature will help. You see, it won't be long before I'm properly widowed. Then we wait a reasonable if scandalous amount of time to be married. You will find your accommodations improve after the wedding, but I will take care of all your business interests."

Was he insane? "Why would *anyone* believe that? And I'm *not* marrying you." Widowed? What had he done to Mother?

"It doesn't matter who believes it or not, you stupid

25

little girl." He smoothed down his tie. "You see, once the papers are filed and the ring is on your finger, everything that is yours will also be mine. Nothing your grandfather does will be able to block me again."

He was insane. "I don't inherit everything in two days."

"Of course not, but once our marriage is secured. Leopold can go the same way as Melissa, then everything will be ours, my dear. Now—eat. I'll be back to see you in the morning."

Shock held me prisoner.

"And remember," he said when he opened the door, "every infraction, every misstep, every choice you make that fails to obey me—Andrea will pay for." His smile held not one iota of warmth. His blue eyes were empty and devoid of a soul.

It was like talking to a demon.

Or making a deal with the devil.

The door closed behind him, and I sat abruptly.

He was going to kill my mother, or he already had. He was threatening to hurt my sister if I didn't obey him, and once I had—he would kill my grandfather.

Glancing at the tray, I stared at the silverware and then back at the door.

The only way out of here was over his dead body.

CHAPTER

THREE

ADAM

The drive to the hospital was interminable. I couldn't find a wound anywhere on him, but Ezra was down like he'd gone blackout drunk. The lack of alcohol on his breath was even more concerning.

"How much longer?" I demanded.

"We're there," Bodhi said, swinging into the ambulance bay, where we were about to get yelled at. But I was shoving open the back door, and Milo was out to give me a hand.

A security guard was already coming down the ramp, but a pair of nurses followed. "We need help," I said, pitching my voice to carry. "He collapsed, and we don't know why."

"The car can't stay," the security guard cautioned, but I wasn't the only one ignoring him. Milo and I had Ezra almost to the doors when the nurses returned with a gurney. We lifted Ezra up and got him on.

"Go with him," Milo said. "We'll park and follow."

"I need to call Lainey," I said.

"I got it," he told me. "We'll call her. Go on, we'll find you guys in a few."

I should've thanked him, but Milo was already striding back to the car, and he'd barely closed his door before Bodhi was pulling out of the bay. Sticking close to the gurney, I stayed with Ezra all the way to an ER bay.

"Did he take anything?" One of the nurses was asking as she pushed up his sleeve. I'd already stripped off his jacket, but they were cutting the rest of the shirt off of him.

"I don't think so," I told her. "Not willingly anyway."

There were bruises on his chest. Fresh ones layered over older ones. His knuckles were also bruised.

He'd been going to the fight clubs.

Aggravation blew through me like a hot desert wind. Ezra seemed determined to drive me crazy or get himself killed.

Maybe both.

I pulled out my cell phone and fired off a message to Lainey before I sent a second message to my doctor. I wanted our physicians looking after him. People I trusted.

The acknowledgement that the doctor was on his way arrived.

The whole time the nurses kept moving, they were getting vitals, hooking up IVs, but this was just saline or so she said. Another nurse came in and took several vials of blood. A doctor followed, and he was listing off a series of tests he wanted done.

"Dr. Rambeau is on his way."

The doctor who was doing a physical exam and study glanced at me. "Family?"

"Yes."

He nodded. "Does he have or has he had a substance

abuse problem?" He lifted Ezra's right eyelid and shone light in it. My stomach dropped at the size of his pupil. It was fat, like it had blown. The second one was just as bad.

"Alcohol," I told him. "He drinks. A lot. Too much sometimes. But I didn't smell any alcohol on him or his breath."

"What about other substances? EKG, and get him on a cardiac monitor..."

My blood ran cold, but I shook my head. "No other substances. He did the occasional edible. But he wasn't a fan of coke or other harder substances."

He'd experimented once. Really didn't like the effect it had on him or his judgment. Said he'd stick to alcohol. I believed him. I'd never been tempted. There were too many ways it could go wrong, and I didn't need another set of problems.

"Blood pressure is low, heart rate is slow..." The doctor was staring at the monitors, then he moved over to where another machine was spitting out a slow roll of paper. "Someone get me a urine sample."

How the hell were they...?

They answered the question by cutting off his pants, and then they were threading a catheter up his urethra. Grimacing, I pressed a thumb to my lips to keep my objections to myself. It took almost no time before they had urine filling a bag.

Thankfully, they covered him up, but there was something brutal about how helpless he looked. Eyes closed, head back, and his whole body so brutally still. An alarm went off.

"Bradycardia..."

I fell back a step, tracking every single thing they did as the doctor moved and a second doctor joined them. They were doing a rush on blood work and urine. Ezra didn't so much as twitch.

He hadn't opened his eyes since he collapsed in my arms. Movement to my right pulled me from my study, and I glanced at Milo. He had his arms folded and stood like a silent guardian.

"Bodhi's on his way to Lainey's." The way he said that, his voice pitched low and his expression taut registered under the cloud of worry crowding me.

I frowned and cut a look at him. "Why?" I was already pulling my phone out of my pocket. I hadn't been paying attention to it if she responded. I just wanted her to know we had him—even if his condition was still in question.

She hadn't responded.

My eyes narrowed. The message was unread too.

I hit call and put the phone to my ear. It rang once then went straight to voicemail. I hung up and repeated it. Still voicemail.

Dr. Rambeau appeared. There were so many people in the room now, it practically hummed with the conversations. None of the medical staff looked happy. The more alarmed they grew, the more my stomach knotted. Whatever the fuck was happening wasn't good.

"No answer," I told Milo then switched to Andrea's, but before I could press call, the chaos in front of me unraveled.

"Asystole!"

Ezra flat-lined.

A hand locked down on my shoulder, the fingers digging into me as they kept me both still and on my feet. The sound around me faded as I zeroed in on Ezra's face. He wasn't moving.

Someone was doing CPR on him, their hands pumping his chest while someone else put a breath bag on his face. She squeezed a breath into him in between pumps.

"Epinephrine," Dr. Rambeau said and they were unlocking a cabinet and pulling out a shot. All the oxygen backed up in my lungs. The pain clawing inside of my chest threatened to rip my ribcage open.

Ezra could not die.

He couldn't.

I would fucking kill him if he died.

"Epinephrine in," a nurse said and everyone paused for the longest three seconds of my life.

Then a blip hit the screen. Followed by another. I was sure they said something, but it took everything I had to not double over.

Milo kept me on my feet, and I didn't even realize I was leaning on him until his words penetrated.

"Are they doing a tox screen?" He was asking. "We didn't see any sign of drugs. But he collapsed as we were leaving—whatever caused it could have been given to him there."

"You're thinking poison?" Rambeau asked him.

"Maybe pharmaceuticals. I know there are a lot of them if misused…"

"We're doing a full tox panel, but we need an idea of what we're looking for or we can't test for it."

"Stuff you give old men, maybe," Milo suggested and I dragged my attention slowly off Ezra after I made sure his chest was rising and falling on his own. If we had more privacy, I'd go over there and put my hand over his heart so I could feel it beat.

"Old men?" Rambeau asked, his eyes narrowed and Milo shrugged. Throughout the whole conversation, Milo was keeping me on my feet.

"Just a suggestion."

"We'll take care of it," Rambeau said before he gave me a look. He wanted my permission.

"Do everything," I told him. "I don't care what it is. They keep asking me about substances like cocaine."

"Slow heart rate, low blood pressure... if it's not recreational and it is pharmaceutical, it could be beta blockers. I'll order the tests."

Then he was on the move again.

"You good?" Milo asked after another long moment. It dragged my attention to him, and I tried to straighten. It took a lot more effort than I cared to admit, but I did manage it.

"Thanks," I said, and it came out rough. "For what you told the doc too."

"No problem," Milo said. "We'll figure this out."

Right. I stared down at my phone. Fear had chased most of the thoughts out of my head. Acid burned in the back of my throat. Fear was not something I was accustomed to. Not anymore. It threatened to choke me out.

Lainey.

I was calling Andrea.

She was with Lainey.

I called my little sister's phone. It rang four times. Then it went to voicemail. Fresh apprehension unfurled within me. I called it again.

Four rings.

No answer.

And again.

Then I dialed Lainey's apartment. There was a direct number that I rarely used. But it just rang.

Ringing with no answer.

I snapped a look at Milo. "Cavendish is on his way?"

Milo nodded. He checked his phone. "He's still thirty minutes out."

Thirty minutes.

A hell of a lot could happen in thirty minutes. Later in the day, traffic was heavier. I looked up the contact for the front desk for her building.

"Milton, this is Adam Reed. I need you to check on the Benedict apartment. She's not answering and I'm concerned."

"It will take me a few minutes."

"I'll wait," I told him. "Go look. *Now*."

Someone was back with test results. Milo had shifted so he was between me and everyone else. He was also between Ezra and the opening. The man was guarding us—the realization settled in my bones. Whenever I glanced at him, he met my gaze and there was a kind of rough comfort having him there.

He didn't offer platitudes or some kind of false hope. I appreciated that. Right now, there were no other options. Ezra needed to be fine, and I needed to know where Lainey was.

More test results were back, and I was still waiting on the doorman. In the meanwhile, Milo checked his phone then shook his head at me. Cavendish wasn't there yet. The waiting was hell. I should have killed Wallace Graham when we were there.

Damn them all.

Every single one...

"Mr. Reed," a nurse said from the opening, and I leaned slightly to glance around Milo. The man could be a roadblock if he wanted to—it was kind of impressive.

I raised my eyebrows at her and she gave me a tight smile.

"You are Mr. Reed—Adam Reed?"

"Yes." I braced myself for whatever she had to say next.

"We have another patient that just came in...she might be a relative."

Fresh panic hit me. I glanced at Milo. His expression had tightened to something forbidding.

Yeah. Me too.

"Stay with him?" I didn't think I needed to ask but if Lainey was also here, he was going to want to see her too.

He nodded.

"Take me," I said to the nurse as I followed her out. I was still waiting for the concierge for her building to get back to me.

She hurried across the increasingly crowded and active emergency room to another room. Like Ezra's, this one had four walls and a door with a window in it rather than curtains offering privacy from the bay next to it.

When she pushed open the door, I stopped cold at the woman laying there in the bed.

"Female, late forties, unresponsive..." One of the other nurses ticked off. "We've been trying to reach her husband but he isn't answering."

Melissa Reed was pale, almost gray-faced and not moving. She looked worse than Ezra.

What the fuck was going on...

"Mr. Reed?" The concierge said into the phone. "She's not there."

CHAPTER
FOUR

EZRA

My head pounded like I'd gone on a three day bender. My mouth tasted like ass and my tongue seemed fuzzy. All around me machines beeped, people talked, and wait—was that Adam?

I opened my eyes. Well, I tried to open my eyes. My eyelids resisted, they seemed glued shut. The sheer amount of effort it took to peel them apart threatened to exhaust me. Still, bit by bit, the light began to invade until I was squinting.

My vision was filled by a rather attractive nurse leaning over me. Normally, I would take a moment to admire the breasts in my face. Unfortunately, they weren't the breasts I *wanted* to see. They also didn't belong to the woman I loved. When the nurse withdrew, however, my gaze clashed with Adam's.

"You son of a bitch," Adam said, his voice a raw snarl with fury. "Don't you ever fucking do this again."

Great, I was excited to see him. *But now I'm in trouble...*

Story of my life. I opened my mouth to protest and defend myself. Except, I didn't recall doing anything fun enough to end up in the hospital.

Why was I here?

I tried to put the rattled pieces together—but they didn't make sense. They were in too many pieces that didn't belong. It was like someone mixed up a bunch of different puzzles. The last time I was in a hospital, I was here for Lainey. I wasn't here for Lainey now right—

Son of a bitch.

Even as one thought collided with another, the harsh reality crashed into me. I was supposed to be meeting with my dad and the Dovzhenko family. I'd left Lainey with Adam and the other guys while I went to fulfill my father's desires. I'd marry Oksana. Take the deal, and protect them.

So how did I end up *here*?

"Mr. Graham?" The voice belonged to an older doctor who pulled my attention from Adam's blazing blue eyes. Oh, he looked familiar. The doctor—I knew him. Rambeau. Doctor Rambeau. He'd pieced me back together a couple of times and set my arm when it had been broken. Once upon a time, he'd also dug some bullets out of me. He was one of ours.

"What?" I didn't really want to agree to anything when I didn't know what the hell was going on. "Why am I in a hospital?"

"Because you passed out," Adam said before the doctor could explain. "You collapsed when we came to get your ass from that stupid wedding. You were trying to commit yourself to that girl."

That girl. Oksana. They followed me? Memories spilled through me, bursting through the foggy dam. Gunshots.

Cavendish? Hardigan? They'd come with Adam. They'd all come.

No sooner did that elation bloom than it exploded with a sickening pop. They'd threatened my father.

Dammit.

Dammit.

Dammit.

"You stopped me?"

I didn't really remember if they stopped me or not. *You followed me. You came to get me.* A traitorous voice whispered in the back of my mind. *Adam came.*

He stared at me like I'd grown a second head. "Of course I fucking stopped you. Look —"

Dr. Rambeau held up his hand, and the pair of nurses that were still in the room with us split their gazes between me and Adam. "Gentlemen, I will leave you to discuss this in a moment. I need to get Mr. Graham's vitals, and I need to ask him a few questions. Mr. Reed, if you would step out."

"No." Absolute finality marked that syllable. Adam didn't look away from me once throughout the doctor's speech.

Yeah, Adam wasn't going anywhere. "It's fine," I said, and made myself look at the doctor. "He can stay. He's my emergency contact anyway." Him and Lainey both. "Just tell me what happened, doc—I didn't even have a drink today." I would fucking kill for one right now, though.

"I'm still running your tox screens, Mr. Graham. My concern is the low blood pressure and sluggish heart rate."

I frowned. I didn't really have any response for that.

"Have you had any issues with your cardiac health? Racing heart? Fainting spells? Blood pressure dips? Anything you might have noticed."

I shook my head. "Pretty fucking healthy."

"His liver is probably pickled," Adam said, with a bold smirk in my direction.

Asshole.

"We're still running your urine, and there is some bloodwork we're waiting on. A lot of the common culprits have already been dismissed. Based on Mr. Reed's description and your symptoms, we're testing for beta blockers. You haven't been experimenting have you?"

Beta blockers?

Even as I turned that over in my head, I appreciated the doc's lack of judgment in his tone or his expression. He seemed to be genuinely just looking for answers. Part of why we liked him so much.

The only person I know who took beta blockers was my grandfather. That miserable old bastard died a couple of years previously. Could definitely tell he'd raised Dad. Still... he'd taken beta blockers.

I'd had water in the room. Water—and juice. Would my father have given me beta blockers? Had he actually tried to kill me?

"How long till I can get out of here?"

"You're not going anywhere," the doctor said before Adam could vocalize his own objections "We need the rest of the screens. We need to make sure your heart is stable and your blood pressure is steady. At the moment you run the risk of a serious heart attack, and that's the last thing you want."

No, the last thing I wanted was my father going after Lainey, but I'd talk to Adam so we could deal with it and him.

Impatience crept through me. "How long is that gonna take?"

"It'll take as long as it takes," Adam said, and then he locked his eyes on mine again. His patience had officially run dry. He wasn't waiting for our discussion anymore. It radiated in every nuance of his posture. "Doc if you don't need him for anything else, can you give us some privacy?"

A small, cowardly part of me wanted to ask the doctor to stay. I'd been avoiding this conversation for weeks. If we didn't have it, he couldn't look at me with the disappointment that seemed to shine in his eyes. More, he couldn't reject me and call me the fool a thousand times over.

I knew who I was.

And what I'd done.

If only I could take it back...

"Keep it moderate, gentleman," the doctor said. "He still needs to stay calm, and continue recovering. If you can maintain your tempers, I'll allow the conversation."

Holy shit. I stared at the doctor with a whole new level of respect. Very few people ever told Adam no. In fact, I could count them on one hand.

"I got it," Adam said. "But he and I need to talk. It's important."

That sobered me almost as effectively as waking up in the hospital. It took the doctor and the nurses a couple more minutes before they left, but soon there was just me and Adam alone with the soundtrack of the machines. At least my room had walls and a door.

It offered more privacy. After they were out, he drew the curtain across the door. Another layer of privacy. Then Adam came to sit on the edge of the bed, close enough that I could touch him. He stared at me for a long time. Maybe he didn't want to do this either.

Maybe we could just go back to who we'd been...

"What were you thinking?" The question held so much

39

emotion and meaning. He sounded aggrieved, exhausted, furious, and—confused?

"You know what I was thinking. He's threatening you, he's threatening Lainey. With everything else going on, and now somebody attacks her and tries to kidnap her—" I shook my head. "I know those guys weren't talking and didn't know who hired them, but they worked for him. It's his M.O. That means he's never gonna stop. He's already killed to show me he'll do it. You and I both know what he's like."

I couldn't risk her. I wouldn't risk either of them.

"Why won't you trust me to protect you?" The volume of hurt in that single statement silenced me. Why would he...?

"Adam, you can't just be the only one who fights. You're not the only one with blood on the line. Don't you have *your* father to deal with? King? Whoever this mysterious woman is that you're working with? Fuck knows I've got mine. If I married Oksana, it would take one of the boots off our necks."

"It doesn't take the boot off of any of us if it puts the boot only on you."

I wanted to argue with him.

"Unless you want to marry her," Adam said, tilting his head, and everything in me rejected the very notion.

"No," I said. "I don't want to marry her. I barely even like her. I mean she's a kid. She's stupid sometimes. Not all the time—I feel bad for her. She's got a life worse than we do. And the only value she has to her family is based on who she can marry. Which means she has zero freedom and zero options. I'm kind of afraid if I say no, they'll kill her."

She seemed to think it was a real possibility.

"Then we just kidnap her — reach out to Fletcher, get her a new identity, and move her the fuck away."

"That's what Nicky and I were working on. But she rejected the deal with the FBI."

"This wouldn't be a deal with the FBI. This would be a deal with the Network and I'm not asking her."

Adam didn't bring up the Network often. If at all. He worried about his cousin being a part of it, and at the same time—he was proud of him. What I knew about the Network...? Well, I knew not to fuck with them, that much was true.

He gripped my hand, and it shut me up on every level. His skin was warm where his fingers laced with mine. I was suddenly aware of every callus. The blazing ferocity in his gaze pinned me in place.

"Will you please stop running away?" I couldn't believe he was even asking that question at the moment.

Is he really holding my hand?

"I don't know how not to." The admission spilled out. I didn't know how *not* to run. My whole life had been running. Running from my father, from his expectations, from his demands and his cruelties. Running to Adam, then running with him to school, then for King and finally for Lainey. All I'd done was run and juggle and try to do it all.

"You asked me for something," Adam said. "You know what, correction: you kissed me. Then you asked me why I didn't see you. You asked me why I never saw you. Now I have a question for you..."

My heart sank. What the hell did he want to ask me? Did I even want to hear this question? But even as the fear clawed its way through me, I slapped it back. Adam was sitting right here. He was holding my hand. He came to save me.

Fucking listen to him.

"What's your question?"

"Do you *want* me to see you?"

That line held so much meaning, almost too much. The depth of it threatened to drown me. "Can you?"

"Been seeing a hell of a lot since you kissed me."

Heat flushed my face. My cheeks were hot. It'd been a long time since anything embarrassed me. Wasn't even sure what to do with it.

"I don't know. I wanted you to see me for so long. But I didn't think you were interested in guys." There was always a bit of shame that I thought about him and he didn't seem to notice. At all.

"I don't think I was interested in guys either." Adam shrugged. "To be honest, I don't think I was interested in anyone who wasn't Lainey."

Laughter rippled through me. If that wasn't the truest fucking thing ever. I snorted as the humor escaped me. Adam's obsession with Lainey was a visceral thing. "Yeah, I get that. I'm kind of into her myself."

I downplayed it, but instead of pulling away or chastising me, Adam squeezed my hand.

"Oh, I know how into her you are. Enjoyed the hell out of sharing her with you."

That confession stunned me more than any other.

"So what you're telling me," I said, fighting to contain bits of hysterical laughter that were trying to spill out. "All I needed to do was hit you upside the head with something and demand to know your feelings?"

Adam shrugged. "I didn't know that *I* was what you needed. I don't even know if I'm capable of giving it to you."

My heart sank like a stone.

"And I'm not saying I won't, I'm not even saying I'm

42

unwilling. I just don't know if it's possible. And after you kissed me—I've been trying to talk to you about this. All you've done is run."

"I don't wanna make you do anything you don't want to do," I told him. "It's kind of why I kept it to myself. It's kind of why I wanted to keep my distance. I never meant to kiss you."

"So let me get this straight," Adam said, putting another hand over mine, so he was cradling my hand between both of his. "You kissed me out of frustration, but if that hadn't happened, you would never have told me. You would've done what? Kept wanting me without saying anything? Then spent the time with me, sharing Lainey and saying nothing else?"

"Maybe?" Really didn't know what else to tell him because frankly it was the only thing I had left to do. "I didn't plan to have sex with Lainey. Not the first time—but I wanted her. I still do. I love her." Those words came as easy as breathing. "I've only ever loved two people. You and her."

I threw myself out there and Adam's eyes offered me a glimpse of real hope. So I dug my fingers into his hand, holding on.

"I thought you'd left us. Yes – I know you were trying to figure shit out and take down King. I get it. The problem is that I love you and you keep going out on your own, not involving me. Taking *risks*. Nearly dying. Then I'm left over here waiting and wondering and hoping and then dreading. It kills me. It kills me to think if you're out there and I can't do anything to help you. I was ready to kill Liam to find you."

Frankly, I owed Liam, because he took me to Adam to prove to me he was alive.

"I get it," Adam said. "But you know how I am. You know how I feel about people who fuck with what's mine."

Always the asshole. I snorted. Then his words registered. "Wait..."

I stared at him, and he raised his eyebrows.

"You're calling me yours."

"Yes." Then before I could even respond, he pressed a finger to my lips. "As much as we need to finish this conversation, as much as we may need to talk about this for hours, days, weeks—however long it takes—we have a lot to figure out, you and I. We have even more to figure out with you, me, and Lainey. I want to figure that out."

The last sentence gave me a boost I hadn't known I needed.

"But we have another problem right now that's a little more immediate. But understand, if you try to run, you better get much better at it. Because I *will* find you, and when I do, I will beat your ass for taking off."

The absolute possession in those words offered me the greatest comfort I'd ever received outside of the open acceptance in Lainey. "I believe you."

"Good." Then he pinched the bridge of his nose, and all at once his exhaustion became visible. He was so tired and weary.

Worried.

Fuck. "Where is Lainey?"

Now the look on his face terrified me.

44

FIVE

LAINEY

I had no idea how long I've been in this room. I couldn't tell if what little light seemed coming through the shutters was the building lights or the sun. Restlessness invaded me. The room was cold, so pacing helped.

I didn't eat the food. Frankly, after everything, I didn't trust him not to drug me. I could drink water straight out of the tap. Still, I worked on finding other items I could use as weapons. I had the silverware, and I'd already hidden it away, and I had the knife handy. Not that I thought they'd leave when and if someone came to collect the cold meal.

Aware there were likely cameras in here, I fought to keep my expression neutral. Movement kept my muscles warm. At the same time, his plan circled in my head.

Get rid of Mother—I suppose that would take time. Even a man of his position couldn't just have someone killed. No, he'd need to make it look accidental.

Disgust turned in my stomach. Honestly, I didn't know

why it surprised me that he would threaten her. He'd been inordinately cruel to Adam's mother. For as long as I could remember, he paraded my mother around—his mistress—in front of her and everyone else.

Everyone knew.

They just didn't comment. Whether it was to "protect" Emily's reputation or feelings, I had no idea. Open secrets were simply accepted. Most men had mistresses. Many of the wives had lovers of their own. Everyone danced the dysfunctional society dance.

We'd all done it. From the day Andrea was born, her father was no secret. She carried his name.

Andrea...

Where was she? What had he done with her?

Whatever happened, I couldn't stay here. I wouldn't be used as leverage against anyone. Nor was I marrying that son of bitch. Could he make it happen? Politically? Legally? Probably.

But I wasn't going to allow it.

Pretty Boy or Adam would find me. They would likely tear the city apart to look for me.

Or Bodhi. He had his ways, and I trusted him to hunt. If I had a tracker anywhere in my clothes or jewelry, I doubted it had made it this far. It explained why I was naked.

A shudder passed through me at that memory.

Ezra...

I closed my eyes as pain fisted in my chest. Trapped here, I was no help to Ezra. What if they weren't able to get him away from his parents? Or that ridiculous marriage—

What was it with everyone and marriage? The contract was legally binding, but thankfully women were no longer bound forever to their spouse because they couldn't inherit or own anything.

Around and around, my mind chewed on every single thought. I made myself stop. The endless questions pecking away at me like a flock of birds in a horror film. Each one punching up the panic that I refused to let free.

Deep breaths.

Deep, regular breaths.

Solve the problem, I told myself.

Solve the problem.

What did I have?

How could I use it?

Identify the options.

Snapping my eyes open, I swept the room.

The faint light through the shutters never shifted nor changed in angle. Was I at Waltham Corners? Or somewhere else?

The makeshift toga outfit was cute and all, but I needed shoes. If I was in a house of any kind, that meant rooms with clothes.

If not—well, maybe I could get a drop on a guard.

Putting a pin in that, I focused on the room. First problem.

Escaping this room.

I eyed the door, then collected the butter knife. The doors were older, sturdy. But the locks were old-fashioned. Fat keyholes and all that.

It would take some effort to wedge the knife in. However, when I was getting started, my gaze landed on the hinges.

The hinges *inside* the door.

The hinges I could get to...

A little thrill went through me and I diverted back to the meal tray. The butter dish was silver, and heavy. It also had flat sides. If this was going to work, I needed to move fast. I dragged a chair over to the door, climbed up and used the knife to wedge against the bolt then hammered it with the butter dish.

It wasn't quiet and it took a few practice swings to get it right. I damaged the wood on the door—not that I cared—but the first bolt came out.

Panting I went to work on the middle one. The more noise I made, the sooner they were likely to show up. No way in hell was I staying here though. It took what *felt* like forever to get the second bolt out.

The third went faster. Either I'd gotten more practiced at it or it was just looser. I didn't care. Once it was out. I used my knife as a wedge and pulled the door open.

Braced for a guard to end my flight before it even started, I froze in near shock when the hall appeared empty. It was dark in the hall. A single, dim light illuminated the stretch of carpet lining the path between a half dozen closed doors.

I didn't recognize the pattern of the carpet, but I did the runner. This was Waltham Corners. I had to be in the closed wing. Once upon a time, Jason and his wife had lived here with their son.

But after Fletcher escaped, Jason and Sable moved out. The wing had been closed pretty much since. I tried to picture the layout in my head. It had been a long time since I'd been anywhere near these rooms.

I left the door ajar and checked the handle to the first room I came to. Locked. The next one—also locked.

Great, how many skeletons was he hiding up here?

A shiver traced up my spine at the very thought. He could have anyone locked away in here. Who would know?

"Good job, Lainey," I muttered to myself. "Freak yourself out."

Okay, so not to be the girl in the horror movie. I needed to find a way out, shoes, a phone, or all of the above. Knife firm in my hand, I checked every single door as I moved down the hall.

They were all locked.

As tempting as it was to knock and check to see if there were other prisoners, I skipped that. I could come back with weapons and backup. Then we could find out what was behind the doors.

At the end of the hall was another door. It was right next to the single hall lamp that cast weird shadows behind me. Ignoring that thriller effect, I crossed my mental fingers and turned the knob.

The door opened easily. My anxiety collided with elation. Instead of opening to the outside or to another room, I'd revealed a stairwell, with steps.

Steps.

Third level. The attic.

Waltham Corners had rooms on some of the uppermost floors. Knife in hand, I descended the steps only to find the door at the base was locked securely—from the outside. The hinges were also on the outside.

Hand pressed against the door, I fought to control my breathing. When Mother stayed here when I was young, she'd also had a suite on the third floor of the other wing.

We'd used the servants' stairs—just like these—to get to and from them. Adam had given me shit once about going back up to the servants' quarters.

Weird, the words still had some sting all these years later. Except, it was what he'd said after that...

"...if you must come and go, use the outside entrance. At least then we don't have to deal with you."

Outside entrance. There'd been stairs near one of the side gardens, tucked behind tall, skinny pines to disguise it.

We could come and go discreetly.

I couldn't remember where that entrance had been. It was off a sitting room, I thought. Mother had a sitting room and two bedrooms. One for me when I was visiting. Later for me and Andrea. Then the other for her.

Pressing my ear to the door, I strained to listen. No sounds penetrated the old wood. They probably wouldn't. Most of the doors were over an inch thick and real wood. They were built to insulate for warmth and for sound.

Frustration swelled up.

Fine. I could beat on the door and alert them I was free. Maybe one of the maids would let me out. Or maybe it would be one of his goons that grabbed me at the apartment.

Yeah, I didn't want to risk that. Not yet.

So time for plan B.

I retreated back up the stairs and to the room where he'd been holding me. I'd searched the room plenty. There was nothing I hadn't found. So I tested picking up the chair I'd used. It was heavy and awkward.

Still, I dragged it over to the shuttered windows. The first swing had me staggering off balance. The second was just sad.

But the third one impacted the shutters themselves and bits of wood flew off.

Better.

My arms burned, but I was breaking these shutters.

Then the windows.

An exit was an exit.

SIX

BODHI

R eed's arrival did nothing to assuage my concerns. Hardigan showed up with him. "Graham?"

"He'll be fine," Hardigan said. "We left a couple of bodyguards babysitting him." The faint twist to his smile held no humor.

Agreed. I'd find it humorous later.

"What do we know?" Reed asked, scanning the apartment. The anger littering his tone had gone cold. Her purse was on the floor, along with her phone, her keys, and her gun. She'd never had time to even get it out. I hadn't found her knife. There were droplets of blood, however, not enough to indicate a severe wound.

Right now, I wasn't sure whose favor that fell in. But any wound done to her was going to be visited on her captors three times over.

"It had to be a team, and they had to be inside the apartment, because the ambush didn't happen in the hall. There's nothing on the cameras, before, during, *or* after.

They turned off the exterior camera after we were already on the road and after she would have come up here."

Keeping it clinical was something I could offer. I wasn't divorced from my emotions, but I'd learned how to separate out my personal feelings to get the work done. Once I had her back, I would let the worry and the fear in.

"She let them in," Reed said with a kind of dawning horror. Then his expression flattened to pure furious.

"That was my supposition," I told him. "The message from Andrea."

Her sister.

It was the perfect trap.

"She gave them the code." Milo curled his hands into fists. I respected the violence. More, I respected the control. "That's why they used Andrea's number."

Cloning a number wasn't that hard. Reed had his phone out and he put it on speaker. The number rang once then went straight to voicemail.

He placed a second call. This time the person who answered sounded groggy. Had it grown late? I'd spent the day examining every inch of her apartment, the hall, the entrances and exits.

The team that took her was smart and they were clean.

"Mr. Reed?" The woman sounded very confused.

"I need to speak to Andrea. She's not answering her phone."

"Mr. Reed, it's—"

"I don't care what time it is." The authoritarian note in his voice shut the woman up. "This is an emergency. Get her. Now."

"Yes, sir. Please hold." The woman's drowsy voice sharpened and the three of us waited even as Adam began to pace. Restless energy crackled through the room. All we needed was a target.

The only reason I hadn't already gone was because I didn't know where to look specifically. The last thing I wanted to do was waste time. She had to have been taken down to the garage through the private elevator by someone with the awareness to circumvent security.

We were upgrading her apartment to add cameras to the interior. Or she could move into my apartment. I had them already.

Time seemed to drag, but I wasn't the only one checking my watch.

"It's taking too long, isn't it?" Milo asked finally and Adam nodded once.

After another full three minutes, the woman returned. "Mr. Reed." She sounded remarkably more awake and upset. "Andrea is not in her room, nor is her RA sure of where she is."

"Where the fuck is she?"

"I—we don't know. Security is sweeping the grounds as we speak, and we are rousing the students. I checked with the main office to see if she was checked out by family, but there's nothing. We will do absolutely everything..."

Reed wasn't listening anymore. He ended the call and his gaze struck Milo's.

"I don't think King would have grabbed her from the school," Milo said. "If he did—then he would have her phone. However—he's made it very clear he will honor the deal he made with you. Even when he came by here to make her an offer of his own."

"Excuse me?" A vein pulsed in Reed's forehead.

"Save it," I told him. "If you don't think King is the problem, then we leave him for another day. I want to know who else would have access to your sister or the ability to clone her phone. If she's not on campus, then she either left of her own free will or she was taken."

"Clearly," Reed gritted out. "Andrea wouldn't have taken off. She's not like Lainey. Lainey booked herself transport cross-country and disappeared on a whim. But she always had a plan and a reason. Andrea's—she's far more sheltered."

"Sheltered or obedient?" Milo asked and the pair shared a rueful smile which answered that question. Lainey B would not be controlled. Not by anyone. "Fine—I stand by the idea it's not King. This doesn't feel like him. He's—a dick and I don't trust him as far as I can throw him."

"Ezra's family didn't have time to lash out," Reed said, picking up the thread from Milo. "Wallace threatened to have her tortured and killed to get him to agree to that damn engagement. But there was no time between our arrival there where he was going along with their asinine plan and when someone had to have struck here."

Had he?

I made a mental note. Wallace Graham could be dealt with.

"Fuck," Reed continued. "Lainey's mother is in the hospital. Andrea is missing. She's missing."

"Why is Melissa Reed in the hospital?" I asked.

Reed shook his head. "They weren't sure, they were trying to reach my father but—"

He stopped. The way his head jerked up and fixed on me told me everything I needed to know.

"What about your father?" Milo asked.

"Hang on," Reed said, before he dialed another number. "And let's head for the car."

He was already striding out of the apartment and I was right behind him. Milo was with us.

As the elevator opened, Reed said into his phone, "Where is my father? Do you have eyes on him?"

There was a beat.

"Explain."

Milo hit the parking garage level and he folded his arms. Even in the elevator, Reed couldn't stand still. His foot tapped out his agitation.

"Not acceptable. Track him down. Melissa Reed was in the city and now she's in the hospital. I want to know where all of them are."

He ended the call as the elevator doors parted in the parking garage. I'd been down here to inspect. If they'd taken her out through one of these levels, I hadn't found it. The operation had been clean and smooth.

Too smooth.

Too clean.

They'd been prepared and they knew the location.

"Where are we going?" Milo asked as I unlocked my car. He was already sliding into the front passenger seat and Reed glared at the vehicle then us before he climbed into the back.

"Waltham Corners," he answered. "The men I had watching my father lost him in the city this morning. We all watch each other, so the only way they lost him is if he deliberately gave them the slip. Add Andrea to this and Melissa in the hospital..."

"What are you thinking?" Milo asked as I pulled out of the slot and opened the private gate to exit the secure parking section.

I didn't need to know what he was thinking. I'd already arrived at the location. Lainey B was about to come into the first third of several billion dollars. Her grandfather hadn't claimed her sister and he'd disowned her mother.

Reed wanted her money.

To get it, he would have to control her.

The pathetic act of a desperate man.

An entire generation of desperate men.

I only half-listened as Reed spoke to Milo about their respective fathers. I had disliked the Reeds for a long time.

A very long time.

Lainey loved this particular Reed.

Well, she loved two of them. The sister made sense.

I wasn't so sure of Adam—*yet*. But I could see his value.

We were ten minutes out from Waltham Corners. The temperatures outside had dropped well below frigid. The ice on dark roads glistened from the headlights.

"You still haven't found her?" Reed was pissed. "I'm sending private security there. You will let them take over the investigation."

Milo shot me a look. I didn't try to interpret it in the dark or make any assumptions. Reed was being pushed from all sides at the moment. Graham in the hospital. Lainey taken. His—their sister missing.

We had to find Lainey. Find the sister. Keep Ezra alive.

In that order.

"How much security should we expect?" Milo asked into the silence after Adam ended his call.

"Considerable," Adam said. "Only about a third of them will obey me. The rest are on my father's payroll. If we get lucky, we won't have to fight any of them."

"We're not going to be that lucky," I informed him.

"No," Adam said. "We're not. Take the next right, then follow it around to the lake road."

"Rear entrance?" Most of the estates out here had more

private approaches and access points for family and friends. While secure, they were usually wound through the woods or along the lake's edge in order to provide more privacy.

"Yep. Unmanned gate. But once I use my code, it will let them know I'm on the property."

"Have a different code you can use?" Milo asked him.

"If they haven't changed it."

I didn't really care about being quiet. I cared about getting to Lainey B. She'd been taken hours earlier. She was resourceful and capable, but a person capable of taking audacious action such as kidnapping her from her apartment, using her sister—in theory *his* own child—to bait the trap?

No, the sooner we got her away from him the better. The only thing I needed to know was how much pain to inflict before I killed him. Whatever Adam decided, Harper Reed was going to die. Today.

Tomorrow.

Next week.

He'd touched what was ours

I slowed at the gate and rolled down the window. The keypad glowed green as it recognized the motion of the vehicle.

Adam gave me the number. I entered it. There was a distinct pause. For a moment, I thought the code would fail, but the keypad flashed and then the gate opened.

"First time in his life, Hamilton has been useful for something." He sat back as I accelerated my way along the winding drive toward the house. The green of the labyrinth appeared, illuminated by my headlights and then movement had me slamming on the brake.

A chair flew through the air and impacted against the drive, shattering it.

"The fuck…" Milo had a hand braced against the door then leaned forward like I did as glass showered down and then another chair came tumbling out.

Floodlights suddenly flashed to life around us and I got a good look at a long leg followed by a gorgeous body climbing out of the windows on the third floor dressed in a —toga.

"I'm going to kill him," Adam swore.

Not if I got to him first.

SEVEN

LAINEY

My arms burned from swinging the heavier furniture at the shutters, then at the thick-glassed windows afterward. It took forever to break the damn things. Once I flung one chair through, I used a second to knock out the larger jagged chunks. I was probably gonna end up with some scrapes.

I'd heal.

The cold air rushing in the window actually felt pretty good against my flushed skin. Toga or not, I was climbing down the outside of the house. If I remembered the way it was built right, there would be enough handholds and footholds for me to at least make my way to the ground floor.

The driveway being right out there wasn't great. I didn't want to jump too far and risk breaking my legs, my arms, or my neck. Stone rasped against my palms and abraded my knees as I slid along it.

As good as the chill felt at first, the updraft under the toga was *not* pleasant.

"Mayhem!" Of all the voices to hear right now, Pretty Boy's was not the one I expected, but I gripped the wall and glanced down.

Oh, that was a mistake.

It was one thing to intellectually recognize how high up I was. It was something else entirely to see it up close. Trying to ignore the sensation of falling, I found Pretty Boy there below with Adam and Bodhi.

Relief spilled through me, along with a little bit of hysterical laughter. It was dark out here, except for the floodlights. The air was icy, and the guys were all in coats and looking amazing.

Even their fury looked good.

"I'm coming down," I told them. I mean, obviously. Still, I made it to the corner of the building ignoring the way the stone roughed against my skin. The rusticated stone offered me places to grip with my fingers and toes.

The stones might have been squared off when they were shaped for the wall, but they were placed and set uneven. I'd climbed up one of these walls when I was younger on a dare.

It had really pissed Adam off back then.

Still, shimmying down the icy wall with my fingers and toes getting number by the minute was not a good time. My nose was starting to run from the frigid air. I clamped my teeth together when they started to chatter.

"Jump," Bodhi ordered and I hesitated to check where I was. I'd been moving steadily down the corner of the building. I was still a couple of stories up.

Bodhi and Adam were not far below me.

"Jump," Bodhi repeated. "I will catch you."

I believed him and I was having trouble maintaining my grip. But I didn't want to hurt him either, so I tried to shimmy a little lower before I let go and pushed off so that I would fall.

Bodhi grunted as I collided with him, and he staggered back a step. Adam and Pretty Boy both caught him to keep him from going down.

I twisted against him and wrapped my arms around him. As desperate for the contact as I was the heat, I held onto him and reached out to both Pretty Boy and Adam with my hands.

"We got you." Pretty Boy started rubbing my hand as if aware of how cold it was and Bodhi let out a little hum of disapproval as he leaned back.

Adam, however, went from relieved to furious. "It was my father, wasn't it?"

I could try to soften it for him. It wasn't Adam's fault. Wait, they were here— "Where's Ezra?"

"He'll be fine, Lainey," Adam said, stripping off his jacket to wrap around me even as Bodhi turned me toward his car. "Is my father still here?"

Shivers broke through and I shuddered again. "Yes," I told him. "He is...he's—definitely lost his mind. But he said something about dealing with Andrea, and I want to know where she is."

"Take her to the hospital," Adam was saying to Bodhi, but I shook my head even as Pretty Boy opened the door.

"No." My teeth chattering was not a good look or a good sound. "I want to be here. This is my fight too."

Bodhi slanted a look at me, then down the length of me then back to my eyes. "Did they hurt you?"

"Chloroform," I admitted. "Or something like it. They

were waiting inside. They put something over my mouth and nose. It tasted nasty. I woke up here—naked."

"Naked?" The fact all three of them said it in the same deadly soft tone should not dip me in fire, but it did.

"Yes, hence the toga," I told them, then I focused on Bodhi. "I want to be part of this. I need to know where Andrea is. The sick bastard planned to marry me as soon as he got rid of my mother so he could get his hands on my grandfather's money."

Money.

At the end of the day, it came down to something as banal as money. Mother was never going to believe me, but I was far more concerned about Andrea. At least Mother was an adult.

Bodhi's arms were like bands of steel around me. Emotion seemed to drain out of his expression as he looked at the house.

"You sure?"

"Yes," I told him. "I'm very sure. I need this."

"Let her stay," Adam said, and of the three of them, he was the one I least expected to back me up. "She has every right to see this through."

"Agreed," Pretty Boy said. "But let's get her somewhere warmer..."

"And shoes if you have them," I murmured. Not that Bodhi had released me; if anything, he just curled an arm under my knees and carried me like a bride around the car to set me inside with the heaters blowing on me.

"Stay here for a moment." He brushed his knuckles to my cheek, and I didn't miss the way he inspected my hands and my legs before he headed to the back of the car.

Pretty Boy filled the gap. As much as I just wanted to crawl from lap to lap for a little while, we couldn't afford to drop our guard. He wasn't. That was exactly why he was there.

Guarding me.

The one keeping his distance though worried me more. Adam paced back and forth, his shirt sleeves rolled up and I didn't think he was even aware of the icy air.

Bodhi was back with a bag that looked familiar. At my raised brows, he said, "You're not staying in your apartment again until we add interior cameras and revisit all security measures. I packed things for you to take you to my place."

The simplicity of the delivery robbed it of a dictatorial command.

"I would prefer you were safe, and you have the right to feel safe in your home."

Hard to argue with that.

"You know what... I'm not even going to fight you guys on this. I'm too damn annoyed they got to me and I'm the one that gave them the code to let them in."

"Don't worry, Mayhem. We'd have all done the same thing. It was a smart trap." Milo shot me a sympathetic look, but the tightness in his jaw reminded me that I wasn't the first woman in his life to disappear.

I wanted to comfort him, but we didn't have time right now.

Later, I promised myself.

Later, I would make this right for all of us.

When I opened the bag I found shoes, underwear, leggings and a sweater.

"Phillip," I exhaled. "I love you."

"Thank you," he said. "But they're just shoes."

There was a downbeat and then an upbeat, and my lips began to twitch.

Milo was the first to chuckle, but Adam joined him

albeit briefly. I dragged on the leggings, and stuffed my feet into socks then Uggs.

They were warm. When I tugged the toga loose and shrugged out of the jacket, the guys covered me from all angles and then I was stuffing myself into a sweater.

Dressed.

I was definitely warmer.

I was also angry.

"I don't suppose anyone has a gun I can borrow..."

Milo held out my baton, and I shot him a smile.

"We've got you covered."

And I would have them covered. Bodhi put the bag back in the car, then they shut off the engine and left it parked in place. The chair was broken on the drive and no one had come out to see anything.

This wing of the house wasn't supposed to be occupied.

"It's a flaw in security," Adam muttered as he led the way around the back. My hand was in Milo's, and Bodhi moved behind us like a shadow.

"Harper probably ordered it," I said. "He locked me on the third floor with every other room locked. He didn't want anyone to know I was there."

Did I think security would have let me out? Maybe. Would Harper have let me out? Unlikely. Whatever was going on with him, the man had lost his damn mind.

We stepped inside via the library. It was the same one where I'd reunited with Bodhi when we'd all confronted Ezra and Adam learned that Ezra and I had become lovers.

Emotion clogged my throat as we passed through. The guys didn't even slow down. I supposed it didn't mean as much to them, or maybe we just had more important things to worry about.

I was definitely firm on the latter.

We left the library and followed the long hall past the ballroom and headed toward the other wing. The wing where Harper and my mother lived. Where Andrea had rooms when she was home. Where Adam used to have rooms...

I honestly didn't know if he ever bothered to come out and stay here for more than a night anymore. I definitely didn't attempt it.

Ahead was the grand foyer to Harper's side of the house. Between the clothing, the boots, and the movement, I'd grown warmer. I'd also gotten angrier.

A man appeared. "I'm sorry, Mr. Reed. Your father doesn't want to be disturbed."

The man's gaze skipped past Adam to me and he actually paled a fraction. Taking advantage of the guard's distraction, Adam hit him so hard, I flinched. The crack of knuckles to jaw was audible. He followed the first blow with a second, then a third. The man went down with the fourth.

It was Bodhi who circled us and flipped him onto his stomach then bound his wrists to one of his ankles behind his back with zip ties.

"Stay with me," Pretty Boy said, squeezing my hand once. I had my baton in my free hand. He had a gun in his. A little unfair, but I'd work with what I had.

"Mr—"

The new arrival didn't even finish his comment before Bodhi was on him. Three more men arrived. Bodhi had his nearly down and Adam slammed his fists into the new arrivals. Milo joined, but he wielded the gun as a weapon.

I caught the guard going for his own gun with my baton. I had to let go of Milo to do it, but I drove the guard back until I caught him square across the face.

Blood spurted from his broken nose.

But he was down, and now I had a gun too.

Much better.

I turned to find all three men staring at me with equal amounts of mad fury, lust, and something else. I lifted my chin.

"Save it for later, boys. We have an appointment and I *really* want to keep it."

My gaze clashed with Adam's, and for the first time, I saw the darkness of guilt slide through his eyes. This was *not* his fault.

As much as I wanted to savage that blame he was shouldering, we needed to corner Harper and find out where Andrea was.

Now.

"One sec." Adam went back to the first man he took down, then fished through his pockets until he pulled out a phone. I stared at the man for a beat then nodded.

Head of security.

"There are four more on site," Adam said, then tossed the phone to Bodhi. "Want to make sure they aren't a problem for us?"

"With pleasure." He murmured, then fixed a look on me. "Stay with them. No more disappearing."

"Do my best."

"All I'm asking."

Then he was gone.

Milo and Adam secured the rest of the downed guards before we headed down the hall toward Harper's office.

If he didn't know I'd already escaped, he was about to find out.

EIGHT

ADAM

S ending Cavendish to deal with the rest of security meant I didn't have to think about them anymore. Based on what I'd seen of his actions at the Sharpe estate, he would dispense with security swiftly and with prejudice.

Milo moved Lainey between us as I headed down the hall toward my father's private office. I rarely ventured in to visit him in his personal domain if I could help it. There was something about his office that had left me cold since I was child.

Maybe it was the fact my mother never went in there. Maybe it was due to the idea that every single time I'd ever faced my father's wrath—it had been in that room.

Or maybe it was just that the room represented him and I loathed the man.

Loathed him and his brothers. How I got a sibling, a mother, and a cousin I loved from a father and uncles I hated, I would never know.

Some luck had to be seen to be believed.

"Exits," I said over my shoulder. "There—" I motioned to a set of doors that would take them out onto a terrace. "There." The next set opened onto a sitting room that opened onto a drive. My father used that for business guests that he didn't want out in the house.

"And there," Lainey finished for me, pointing to a wall that disguised a door. You had to know it was there. "You press the paneling. It takes you to another hall and from there you can make your way out."

I shot her a grateful look. We should probably have given Milo a better rundown on the location. We would have—if my father hadn't forced our hand. Taking Lainey crossed every goddamn line.

When I tracked my gaze to meet Milo's, I flicked a look to Lainey then back to him. He nodded once. She came first. It was why Cavendish was clearing out security to keep them from coming at our backs.

If everything went sideways, Milo would get her out of here. Cavendish and I could clean up.

"Stop it," Lainey said, bumping me with her hip. "We're doing this together."

Like me, she kept her voice low, but it didn't rob her of her ferocity.

"You'll indulge me," I told her, shooting a look ahead before pulling her into an alcove. Milo moved with me, both of us blocking her in. I put a hand on her cheek. There were no visible bruises. But I'd seen the bruises on her hands earlier. The scrapes.

My fierce little warrior was more than capable of protecting herself. Didn't mean I wasn't going to protect her.

"I will, will I?" Always provoking and daring, but she raised her eyebrows at me, as if telling me to prove it.

"Yes," I said with a single nod. "You will indulge us. You got taken. You hate that for you and you know damn well we do. So for a little while, you will indulge all of us because Milo will throw you over his shoulder and carry you out of here if we think it's necessary."

She huffed out a little scoff, but it wasn't one of disbelief. It was more of a resignation.

"Sorry, Mayhem," Milo offered. "He's right."

"I know he's right. Like I said outside, I will indulge this *for now*."

"Thank you," I whispered, then kissed her once. "Ezra's already tried to get himself killed. You two are going to be the death of me."

She covered my hand with hers. "He's really okay?" Fear flickered to life in her eyes.

"I promise. I have him under bodyguard watch too." We didn't have much time for this, but I needed the contact. I needed the assurance, and I needed to give it to her as well.

She leaned into my hand where it rested against her face. Amusement sparked to life in those rich hazel eyes of hers. Sometimes, I forgot just how much green lived there. At others, it seemed hidden. Like her smile.

"We'll have your back," she promised.

I drank in her nearness. Fuck knew, she'd always had my back even when I wanted to lock her away and she rebelled against me. "I don't deserve you," I whispered.

She pinched me and I damn near laughed. "That's my decision and not yours. Now, shut up and let's deal with Harper."

"Yes, ma'am." I winked and forced myself to let her go. Squaring my shoulders, I let who I was straighten my spine.

I was a Reed. While I hated most of my family, my mother raised me to believe who I was had as much to do with my actions as with my bloodlines.

It wasn't just Harper Reed's blood in my veins.

It was hers.

I strode forward, the weight of the gun in my palm a comfort it probably shouldn't be. The past decade and change, I'd made some hard calls. Some of them were brutal. Some of them were altogether too easy. I regretted none of them.

Not at the moment.

To protect what was mine? I'd do it again in a heartbeat.

At the door to my father's office, I tested the handle. It was locked. If I had a shotgun, I'd take out the lock. As it was. I glanced at Milo. Then we both looked at Lainey.

She shifted her stance and her grip on her gun. I holstered mine and Milo did his. We backed up a few steps then hit the door with force. The double doors buckled, part of the frame cracked, but they didn't give.

We retreated then rammed them again, both of us slamming our shoulders into the doors. The weight, the torque, and the force were enough to send a shock of numbness through my joint.

It took three tries, but the third slam of us crashing into the doors rocketed them apart, and we staggered into the room with Lainey striding between us, gun pointed at my father who was on his feet.

"Don't," she told him when he reached for his phone.

Phone.

Not gun.

Stupid old fool. He brought a phone to a gunfight.

I straightened, ignoring the pain shooting down my arm and the numbness in my fingers.

"How the hell did you get out of—"

"My cell?" She snorted. "You really are stupid if you thought I would just stay put cause you told me to."

He glared at her then at me. "I suppose *you* let her out."

"No," I said, even if I owed him absolutely zero explanation. "Lainey is not a fragile fucking flower. She is more than capable of waging war all by herself. If you paid attention, you might have realized your plan was doomed from the start."

Straightening, my father had the temerity to give me a dismissive look. "I practically set her at your feet. Gave you plenty of time to take control and you did *nothing*. Useless. Absolutely useless."

"Let me guess," Lainey interrupted. "You wanted me to get pregnant as a teenager."

"The when only mattered until now." Harper told her. "The who was more important. Your grandfather cut off your mother, but he would not be parted from you. *You* were his only hope of an heir, particularly after he rejected Andrea. She was as useless to me in this as Adam proved to be."

Disgust curled through me. "The only reason you got her pregnant was for the money." Andrea's birth had *hurt* my mother, no matter how she had tried to disguise it.

All at once, Andrea became all the things I'd believed Lainey was before. Yet, it was neither of their faults that my father was a monster.

"If Andrea had been a boy, I might have stood a better chance." The dismissive shrug enraged me.

"She's perfect as she is." It helped that Lainey glared at him with the same icy disdain.

For some reason, that amused him. His chuckle was one of thinly veiled contempt coupled with dark humor.

71

"Elaine," he said, focusing on her. "Your mother is dead—if she's not by now..." He checked his watch. "She will be within the next few hours."

The cold delivery floored me. The absolute lack of emotion in his voice bordered on psychopathic.

"Not that it should bother you. Alive or dead, she can't hold a candle to your wealth or the power you will control shortly."

"You think telling me you killed my mother will make your insane offer from earlier more attractive? Because that's a level of delusion too far."

I wanted to smile at her and offer her comfort. I actually had no idea how Melissa Reed was doing. She was at the hospital. I'd put security on her—a habit more than a necessity. Security to keep my father and his people away from her.

But he was right. She could be dead.

Instead of being dissuaded, however, Dad just shrugged. "I think you are far more rational than my son or your mother. You understand negotiation and benefits. As I told you earlier, every decision you make will have a profound impact on Andrea."

"Excuse me?" I narrowed the distance and grabbed him by his collar and hauled him right over the desktop. We were near equals in height, but I had muscle on him. Muscle and experience. "You want to leverage *Andrea's* safety?"

"You are too swayed by your own emotions," my father informed me. That cold distance in his eyes seemed to stretch to infinity. "Andrea is a bastard. I legalized her when I married Melissa. But that doesn't change the fact, she wouldn't be able to inherit by the terms of your grandfather's or your great-grandfather's wills. No, you have that distinct right—*for now*."

"You're talking in circles, Mr. Reed." Milo entered the fray, and it was taking everything I had not to strangle my father where he stood.

I would like to lock my hands around his throat and squeeze until the capillaries in his eyes burst and his face went red with his desperation for oxygen. I wanted to squeeze until his heart gave out entirely.

"Why don't you cut to the chase. We'll begin with where is Andrea?"

A good question. One we needed an answer to before I killed him. I would find our sister if it was the last thing I did.

"Do you really think I'll remove my advantage from the board by telling you?" Now, there was the arrogant domineering man who'd raised me. He sincerely looked down his nose at me, disgust seeming to ooze from every pore. "My negotiations will be with Elaine and they will be over our marriage. You two gentlemen are welcome to leave."

"You speak like a man who thinks he has options," Cavendish interrupted. For once, I was really fucking glad he was there. Emotion didn't sway him and even as I held onto my father by his shirt, I was fighting every instinct that said to beat him down.

Beat him and not stop until I had his blood all over my hands.

Harper Reed was a detestable man, but he was still my father.

"I always have options." When Father put his hands over mine to try and peel them off of him, I gave him a hard shake.

"Don't," I told him. "Where is Andrea?"

73

"I already told you the terms for the discussion," he said as if he were still in control.

"How much plausible deniability do you need, Adam?" Cavendish circled us and went to the desk. He pulled open a drawer and stared at something. "Also, I need his hand."

"Go to hell," my father snapped and Cavendish just smiled.

"I don't need it to be attached," Cavendish offered and Milo took a step forward and he gripped my father's arm before he could flail and slammed it down on the desk.

"Knife?" It was almost conversational.

"Do we need a specific kind?" Lainey asked. Fuck, I loved her.

"Sharp is usually preferred. Or at least larger for chopping purposes." None of our knives were that big. "Bones are a bitch."

"There is a sword collection on the second floor." At Lainey's suggestion, my father actually paled.

"I'll cooperate," he said, and disappointment sort of popped within me. "Then you'll let me speak to Elaine."

"You might want to cooperate with us," I told him. "We're not cooperating with you. Your time for being in charge is officially over."

Milo and I lifted him up and moved him around the desk to where Cavend—Bodhi stood, and that was when I saw the palm scanner.

Oh, good to know.

Hand down on the scanner, I held it in place. The computer came back online and the cameras.

"If you want to take charge of him," I offered and Bodhi nodded. Then he punched my father so hard, bone actually crunched and he went down.

Milo caught him briefly then dropped him onto the carpet.

"Damn," I muttered as they dragged him to a chair and lashed him to it. I wished I'd done that.

"There's time," Lainey said, and at her soothing tone, I met the rough sympathy in her gaze. "Andrea first."

Andrea first.

"I'll check on your mother."

She gave a little shrug. "Mother made her bed and chose to lie in it with him."

I nodded once and sat down at his desk and started going through his files.

"We need to decide what you want to know, because we're not keeping him around to lash out."

That was the moment I accepted what I wanted.

I paused mid-keystroke and spared a look at my father.

Yes.

I wanted him dead.

After tonight, he would be.

NINE

LAINEY

Bodhi finished securing Harper to his chair while Adam seemed focused on the computer. A combination of adrenaline and unease flooded my system. My hands ached. My feet were still protesting their cold. At the same time, I was wrapped up in the warmth of the three men working together.

The only missing piece was Ezra. I worried at that absence like I would a lost tooth. He should be here. The problem was, he had to want to be here and not—

"Hey," Pretty Boy stroked along my arm as if to let me know he was there before he wrapped his arm around my middle. As capable as I was of standing, I leaned my back against his chest.

Eyes closed, I drank in his nearness and soaked in the strength of his embrace.

"I'm alright," I murmured, as much to soothe myself as to comfort him.

He pressed his lips to the crown of my head then my

temple before he sighed. "Are you lying for me or for you?" The lightness in his voice couldn't quite disguise his concern. Not that I wanted him to hide it from me. We'd had to be apart too much over the last few months.

Frankly, this "kidnapping" had been salt on a wound I hadn't realized was still open.

"A little bit of both." Admitting it cost me nothing. "Worried about Andrea." Terrified really. "And Adam."

At the mention of his name, the man in question frowned at me. "I'm fine."

"Liar," I told him cheerfully enough, and he pursed his lips.

"I will be fine," he corrected and that made me smile for real as Pretty Boy gave me a light squeeze.

"Better." I mouthed the word more than said it before adding, "Me too."

Bodhi left Harper to cross to me. "Let me have her for a moment."

The absolute lack of testosterone-fueled antipathy in Adam's brief look at the request or Milo's response when he pressed another kiss to my head before letting me go buoyed me. Aware of the weapons I was still holding, I kept the gun pointed away as Bodhi cupped my face. He searched my gaze.

"Injuries?"

"Pride," I admitted. "Worry for Andrea."

"Physical injuries," he corrected with just a hint of reproach. For some reason, the corners of my lips curved. He rarely, if ever chastised me. Sometimes, he would correct or inform, but he never seemed to get angry.

Right now?

He was angry.

It shimmered in the coolness of his eyes. "Pretty Boy," I

said, surrendering the gun to him and my baton. He took them easily, and it was my turn to lift my hands to Bodhi's face.

Rather than mirror his action, I showed him my palms. The white scrapes from the stone across them. They were a little raw and sore, but my injuries were negligible.

"You saw my legs," I reminded him.

He nodded once. Then his gaze drifted down my body. "You said you woke up naked."

"As far as I know, they didn't touch me. I'm not sore. There's no ache and no evidence of contact."

He nodded once.

"And I don't—feel violated other than they got me in my apartment and took my clothes. *That* annoyed me."

Some of the ice in his gaze seemed to break apart. "Anything else?"

"No? I mean I was cold. That was frustrating. I'm a little hungry. But I didn't trust the food not to be drugged, so I wouldn't eat it."

While it was Bodhi holding me and asking for the answers, I didn't miss the way Adam's shoulders dropped or the relief in Milo's long exhale.

They'd been worried about me.

"I promise, I'm fine. I'll be finer still when we find Andrea and I see Ezra. But you three are the best medicine a girl could ask for."

"Especially the shoes?" There was the barest hint of humor there, and I grinned for real.

"The shoes were the second best gift of the night." Then I pushed up on my tiptoes and brushed his lips with mine. I kept it light, easy, and gentle. The teasing little nips earned me a far firmer kiss as he wrapped his hand around my throat.

The gentleness of his grip summoned tears to burn in my eyes. He stroked his thumb along my pulse point. My heart leapt at the contact. When he licked a path across the seam of my lips I parted to him and drank in the taste of him.

Tension seemed to drain out of his muscles. His stance remained rock steady; he was definitely the one keeping me on my feet while he devoured my mouth. Finally, he lifted his head. The lightest scrape of his teeth over my lower lip sent an exquisite shiver through me.

"Don't disappear again," Bodhi told me. "I don't like it."

"Do the best I can," I whispered. "Thank you for coming to find me. All of you."

"Always," he promised. Forehead pressed to mine, he studied me and the air in the room seemed to lighten.

Or it did until...

"I think I might vomit," Harper commented. "Is Cavendish why you couldn't seal the deal, son?"

Rolling my eyes was better than giving any kind of weight to Harper's words. Bodhi straightened. Phillip was in there, but the man holding me right now was every bit the dangerous killer he'd proven to be when lives had been on the line.

I trusted him utterly. I curled my toes in the Uggs. He nodded once.

"Shut up," Adam said over his shoulder. "The only thing you know about women is marrying them for clout, money, or fucking them for your own pleasure. Which amounts to very little."

"It's alright, Adam, he fooled our mothers. Not us." I had my hands against Bodhi's chest as I locked gazes with Adam. The corner of his mouth quirking, Adam nodded. "Do you want to ask your questions first?"

Because it was his father.

With a sigh that seemed more performative than actual, Adam leaned back in his chair. "I thought I'd let Bodhi and Milo begin, actually. Age before beauty after all."

I didn't laugh.

It was an absolute battle of wills to keep a straight face.

Thankfully, Bodhi stood his ground, blocking Harper from seeing me as Adam gave me the drollest of stares.

"Don't worry, Lainey can go whenever she wants," Bodhi said. "Beauty and brains will always take the lead."

Heat scorched through me. Not the most appropriate time for this. Not in the slightest. Still...

"I really only have one question."

Adam nodded slowly as did Bodhi.

"We'll get your answer, Mayhem." Pretty Boy slipped my gun back into my free hand and then my baton before he pressed a soft kiss just behind my ear. "Thank you for being safe."

I smiled, pivoting to brush a kiss along his jaw. "I promised."

I had promised him to be as safe as I could be. He studied me for a long moment, seeming to need to memorize my face. Not that I had any objections. I adored my pretty boy so damn much.

"Yes, you did." He nodded once, then slanted a look past me to Bodhi. I couldn't interpret the look, nor did I try. For this to have a chance of working for all of us, I had to trust the boys to work out their issues with each other. They needed to find trust and common ground.

We needed to be a team.

Adam drummed his fingers once, but his attention wasn't on the computer screen though he appeared to be looking at it. If anything, I'd bet he was watching his father. Then his gaze clashed with mine.

Need clawed through me. Need to soothe the tension in his face and the muscle ticking in his jaw. He was furious. Yet, he kept a tight leash on that anger. The amount of control he could exhibit when it came to ruthlessly suppressing his emotions should scare me.

So much of this should scare me.

But these men did not.

I craved their brutality, their violence, and their loyalty. I craved *them*.

They were perfect for me in so many ways. Even beautiful, broken Ezra. His wildness hid a damaged heart. A heart we needed to fix.

"Agreed," Bodhi said abruptly, settling whatever the silent conversation was and he brushed a kiss to my forehead before he headed over to where Harper sat. Pretty Boy followed him, and I trailed after, but rather than go to where Harper glared at all of us, I slid up onto the desk.

The perch put me close to Adam, and when he settled a hand on my thigh, I leaned down and met his kiss as Harper let out a yell.

"You basta—" The word choked off to a gurgle as I traced my fingers down Adam's cheek. The low scream from Harper grew in intensity as he struggled.

His shriek sliced through the room following a very distinctive *snip*. The shriek became a howl, but I didn't slow my kiss with Adam. Instead, I dueled with his tongue, and when he dragged me off the desk and into his lap, I kept my arms wide so the weapons didn't touch him.

When he sank his teeth into my lower lip, I tasted a hint of copper and opened my eyes. No, it wasn't taste. Copper scented the air.

"That was your pinky," Bodhi informed Harper. "Stop sniveling and pay attention. I won't explain this more than once."

"I'm bleeding."

"You won't die," Pretty Boy informed him in an idle tone. "Not yet. But we can cauterize it."

"You can—can—no!" All at once, Harper flailed as Milo retrieved something from the fireplace. I'd half-forgotten there was one in here. Adam slid his hand under my sweater, and traced his fingers against my skin as we watched Bodhi grip Harper's arm and keep him still.

It didn't matter how much he flailed, when the hot poker touched his skin—it scorched. The smell was horrific. Copper. Meat. Searing.

"Breathe through your mouth," Adam whispered in my ear before he nipped the lobe. I tried to block my nose and followed his instructions.

It definitely helped.

Harper sagged in the chair abruptly and there was an odd—

Oh.

He urinated on himself.

I wrinkled my nose.

"Chickenshit," Adam muttered.

"Don't worry," Bodhi said, almost cheerful. "We have smelling salts."

Not five minutes later, they woke him up and Harper jerked his gaze around from Bodhi to Milo then to me and Adam.

"You're really going to allow them to do this?" The demand was laughable.

"You forced your wife to watch your affair with my mother for years."

"You flaunted her in front of everyone, but my mother had more class in her toe than you ever have." Adam took my lead and flowed with it.

"You kept my mother on a string, determined to make sure she always came back to you." I shook my head.

"You don't understand..."

"I'm sorry, what part of, you are going to kill my mother, then marry me, and rape me until I'm pregnant did I misunderstand?"

Bohdi didn't have to tell Milo anything, he just braced the left hand and they snipped off his ring finger.

That was two fingers down.

Harper's screams were hoarse, but I just focused on the slow caress of Adam's fingers against my skin.

"You little bitch."

Milo punched him, and I had to bite my lip to keep from laughing.

"Watch your mouth when you speak to her," Pretty Boy informed him. "In fact, stop speaking to her entirely."

"Yes," Bodhi said. "Good plan. Where is your daughter Andrea?"

"Go to hell," Harper spit.

"Hmm, you first. Middle finger next."

"Wait—"

They didn't wait. They just cut it off. Adam shifted in the chair, keeping me in his lap as they asked Harper twice more.

He had no fingers on his left hand when he passed out again.

"Stubborn," Pretty Boy commented.

"Everyone breaks," Bodhi said, moving over to check a bag he'd carried inside. It was— "Gardening tools," he said, when he held up a little hand rake. "Someone left them out and I locked the rest of the surviving guards in the gardener's shed."

Oh.

I bit my lower lip. "Do we have time to tear it out of him?"

"We'll find her," Adam promised. "He probably just had her moved to one of the vacation properties."

Only he didn't sound so sure about that.

Three hours later, Harper had a finger and a thumb left when he finally broke. Venom painted his voice and his expression when he said, "You'll never find her. I closed the sale on her last week. She is well and truly gone."

CHAPTER

TEN

MILO

Harper Reed broke in pieces. It took us most of the night, but we got the whole of the story out of him. He poisoned his wife and sold his daughter — fucking sold her. What the hell was wrong with these people?

Cold, cool actions were not foreign to me. My own father was a raging piece of shit. He walked out of my life when I was seven and spent the last ten plus years trying to destroy me. Now? I had no idea what it was he thought he wanted, but I was done with letting him control my life or anyone else's.

And they were men like Harper Reed. If not for the fact that Mayhem had been right there, vital, alive, and full of her own anger — I don't know what I would've done.

When she delivered that line about what Reed wanted from her — it took everything I had *not* to kill him. I suddenly understood on a deep and visceral level why

Adam sat out the torture. The entire time, Adam kept his focus on Mayhem. She was grounding him in the present.

She grounded us all here.

It wasn't something she should've had to do, and yet I knew without a shadow of a doubt that she belonged in this conversation. It might have taken me a while to recognize that the best way to protect Mayhem was to involve her, but there was no unseeing it now.

The man *took* her. He *sold* her sister. He tried to kill her mother. Fuck, he might've already killed her mother. We didn't know how she was doing. Frankly, Lainey hadn't asked, not that I blamed her. The hardest part of all of this was recognizing how much we *could* do. In Braxton Harbor, I knew the rules and who made them. I knew how far to push it.

It made wading into everything here an ongoing challenge. On the upside, I had Mayhem. She came with Adam, Bodhi, and even Ezra.

Bodhi was the one taking point on this, and he seemed quite aware of what he could do. He also had no problems with pushing that envelope. I liked the man before. I even respected him previously. But today? Today, I saw his real value.

There wasn't a rule he wouldn't bend, break, or rewrite to help Mayhem. The cold look that filled his eyes when she detailed Reed's plan had echoed the violence in my soul. He didn't kill Reed, no, he just continued to take him apart.

Patient.

Effective.

Now, Harper Reed was dead and we were rolling the body up into clear plastic. Despite taking him apart, finger by finger—all of his toes, then his teeth, and eventually his dick, Bodhi hadn't made much of a mess.

Cauterizing everything really did work.

We taped up the body, and I stole a look to where Mayhem wrapped around Adam. He had his face buried against her throat. She stroked his hair lightly, but her gaze was on us.

"We still have to deal with the guards." Her soft reminder gave us all pause.

Guards.

That many bodies could create a number of problems.

"Adam," Bodhi said, turning to them. For the first time since we'd ended Harper, Adam lifted his head to look at us. "You said some of them were your men. Do you want to verify if any of them are out there, or should I just deal with it?"

He blew out a slow breath. "I'll deal with it. We have enough to bury. If my men are out there, they can help us deal with the others."

We had no other choice. I recognized it as they had to have. Witnesses were dangerous. Even if I didn't give a damn about myself, I wouldn't let any of them be used against Mayhem.

"I don't suppose you know which guards took you?" Bodhi studied Mayhem with an almost hopeful look. It wasn't funny, and at the same time, amusement speared me because her smile was damn near apologetic as she shook her head.

"I wish I did, but I never saw their faces."

A grunt of disappointment. "It's fine. We dealt with the real problem."

The corners of Adam's lips twitched, and he shook his head. "That shouldn't be funny."

"It's not funny," Bodhi said firmly. "It's unfortunate, but not funny."

89

He was so deadpan in the reaction, it reminded me of Rome when he just stated facts bluntly no matter how uncomfortable. Mayhem, however, let out a soft laugh, and the husky nature of the chuckle wrapped around me and saved my soul.

The darkness of her world was deep. Yet, it did not cling to her. She wasn't unaware, far from it; she recognized the depravity and the corruption. She just rose above it.

"Will you stay here with Milo?" Adam asked, his attention on Lainey now and not on me or Bodhi.

She tilted her head. "You don't want backup dealing with the guards?"

"He'll have me," Bodhi said in the same breath that Adam stated, "I'll have him."

Folding my arms, I waited them out. For her part, Mayhem tilted her head as if considering it. It was a little bit for show, but it was also a distraction. Because while Adam dipped his chin and seemed to wrestle with the kneejerk need to order her around, she studied him.

"Be quick," she said, as though settling it for herself. "I won't leave here without either of you. We still need to get Ezra."

That was another headache.

One headache at a time.

"We'll find her," Adam was saying, a reminder to all of us of the missing pre-teen. I still couldn't fathom the hows or whys behind that man *selling* his child. All at once, I wanted to kill him all over again.

Ivy's uncle abused her for years.

Adam's father sold his child, tried to murder his wife, and wanted to torture my mayhem.

Ezra's father? He'd murdered people to force his son to agree to wed, and then someone there poisoned Ezra.

What crimes did Bodhi's family name have hidden away? Or were those crimes like the ones that belonged to my father—the reason I was the man I was today?

Fuck all these people and their corrupt, gold-plated world. If I thought I could convince her to go, I'd steal Lainey back to Braxton Harbor and stay there. At least the dirty streets never pretended to be something they weren't.

"I promise you," Adam was saying. "We *will* find her." He pressed his lips to hers then lifted her as he stood. While I would have helped Bodhi with the body, Adam took care of it. The two left the room silently.

Mayhem glided over to me, and I wrapped my arms around her. I'd managed to clean up my hands. I probably should have showered before touching her again, and I would, but I needed the contact.

Craved it.

For the first time since we'd discovered she was missing, we were alone, and she was curled against my chest. I tucked my head down, savoring her nearness, but I didn't dare close my eyes.

I needed to be aware of everything and anything that moved.

"I'm okay," she murmured, and it struck me all at once that she'd been saying that for a couple of minutes. I was also holding on far too tightly. Forcing my grip to relax, I leaned back to study her.

After Ivy's uncle—after the hell he put her through—

"I never want to lose you," I confessed.

"You won't," she said, and something deep in my soul protested. How could she make that promise? Too much in life we couldn't control. I *knew* this. I'd lost control, been forced to surrender it. Prison to protect the Vandals, and I'd done it.

Fuck, I'd do it again.

"Mayhem…"

"Pretty Boy," she said, raising her hands to cup my face.

I stilled, focusing on this gorgeous woman with her eyes that seemed to glitter with all the secrets of the universe. Or maybe they were just her secrets. Whatever it was, I would die to keep them and her safe.

"You guys found me. I knew you would."

"That's why you were throwing chairs through windows when we got here." The dry tone was the right one. The corners of her lips curved even as she lifted her shoulders.

"I've never been fond of being told what to do. Or being locked in a room."

Good point. "Noted."

"Well, maybe if you lock me in the room *with* you." The offer went straight to my groin. Need for her vibrated through me. But not here. Not in the Reed house and definitely not with the stench of dead Harper Reed still lingering.

"I'll keep that in mind. Can I just—hold you for a minute? The chaos is coming for us, but I need you Mayhem."

She curled into me and gripped me so tight no doubt could exist between us.

"All I could do was focus on keeping Adam and Bodhi steady. I had no idea who'd taken you or why. They figured it out…"

"Okay, but you backed them up."

"I should have been with you." The admission cost me nothing. "If one of us had gone up with you—"

"Pretty Boy, Bodhi was driving. Adam had to go because of Ezra, and you went to protect them all. I was going up to my apartment to see my sister—" The catch in her voice gutted me. "We didn't see it coming. Not your fault. Not theirs."

"Not yours either," I stressed. "But you're going to have to deal with us being overprotective for a while."

"A while?" She raised her eyebrows. "A while? Have you met Adam and Ezra?"

She had a point. I hugged her again and held her close. "Well, at least you're used to it."

A laugh struggled out of her. The giggle was almost a little high-pitched and hysterical. Then another. And another. Before long, I was chuckling with her. She wiped the tears from my face and I wiped the same from hers.

We were almost composed before the other two returned. The minute Adam strode into the room, however, Mayhem cracked up laughing all over again.

The men paused, eyed her, then me, and I managed to keep a straight face. Barely.

"Time to go?" was all I said.

"Yes, we're getting Ezra then..."

Adam paused. It was daylight outside, we were all exhausted, and there was so much to do.

"My place," Bodhi said. "We'll regroup there."

"Are you sure?" Mayhem asked. "It's a lot to open your space to all of us."

"No," Bodhi answered her in a tone so steady, it was impossible to disbelieve. "It's not. I told you—they're yours. That makes them mine to look after. We'll get Ezra, if the hospital will release him. Your mother is there too."

"I don't want to deal with her right now." Lainey shook her head. "I don't have it in me to deal with that. Harper can't hurt her anymore and your uncles—" She spared a look at Adam.

"Jason isn't a threat. Hamilton won't be." Then he held out his hand to her and she flowed to him easily. Like me, he had a need to hold her and keep her close. Bodhi tracked all of it.

We all needed it.

"Hospital for Ezra, then Bodhi's place. You need to eat, Mayhem," I said. The decision was made. "Everyone needs rest."

"We need to look for Andrea too..."

"Already working on it," Adam promised. When Bodhi caught my gaze, I nodded. He took point, I brought up the rear. We put Adam and Mayhem between us.

For now, we would protect them and we would find her sister. One enemy down.

But how many to go?

ELEVEN

EZRA

God, the night passed in slow motion, despite the fact that I seemed to keep passing out. I spoke to several doctors through the course of the night. More than one was concerned, including Doctor Rambeau who had taken lead on everything.

Beta blockers. It would seem that I had taken, or been slipped, a massive dose of beta blockers. They ended up causing me to have a heart attack.

A heart attack.

What the actual fuck?

The whole concept was so utterly foreign to me that I wasn't sure what to do with the information. I needed to monitor my system. I would have to take other medication. I would have to have regular check-ups. None of which sounded like something I wanted to do.

My favorite piece of advice, however, was that I needed to stop drinking for a while. No drinking. No drugs. No partying. At least until my heart had time to recover.

The advice baffled me. What exactly did they think I was going to do?

Yet, even as that stubborn part of me wanted to lash out, there was a smaller, far quieter voice inside that reminded me, I drank too much, I partied too much, and I didn't usually give a damn.

I couldn't afford to not give a damn anymore. In the meanwhile, they wanted me to rest.

Rest.

Agitation and worry made that impossible. The two bodyguards Adam stuck me with before he left refused to leave me alone. I couldn't even close the door when I went to take a piss.

I could protest — news flash, I absolutely did – but they didn't give a damn. It made sense, and on some level, I appreciated the care. "Mr. Reed," they informed me cooly, "wants one of us with you at all times."

I couldn't even see the doctors or the nurses without them. I'd question that order, but why bother? Not after everything that had happened. Not when I could probably list what he thought might happen.

It had already happened, right under my damn nose. I'd walked into that meeting prepared to sign the agreements, the marriage license, and go see the justice of the peace to seal the deal.

Instead, Adam and the guys came for me. Damn fortunate, since I ended up in the hospital not that long after. Would I have survived if the beta blockers hit me and the guys *hadn't* been there?

Food for thought.

The one thing I did expect, through the course of the night, was a phone call. I didn't get one. I also half-expected my father to show up. If he did, I never saw him. I did send one of the bodyguards to check on Mrs. Reed—but they couldn't seem to find out anything. Rambeau, as Adam's doctor, however, was able to give me some information.

She was in a coma.

Fuck my life.

Lainey's mother wasn't the best person on the planet. She also wasn't a raving bitch or a lunatic either. Being a poor parent made her a worthless person. That said, I couldn't imagine that she deserved whatever had been done to her.

What would happen when Lainey found out? They weren't close. If anything, Lainey had grown far more distant from her mother than she already was. I could see exactly when the partition happened.

The day she married Adam's father.

None of that mattered. What mattered was Lainey.

Where the fuck were they?

No calls, no messages, nothing. I'd checked my phone easily a half dozen times. I'd sent a couple of messages to Adam. The fact he hadn't answered weighed on me. They'd gone to find Lainey.

Now, no one was answering.

I'd just gotten through my morning checkup and breakfast when the door to the hospital room opened. The pain around my heart seemed to expand, pushing all the air out of my lungs. Lainey stood in the open doorway, a mixture of tears and laughter in her eyes.

I probably deserved both, but I've never wanted to make her cry. Before I could say another word, she was across the room and then sliding onto the bed and wrapping her arms around me. She smelled like her. Felt like her.

I collapsed into her. Okay—the world was a much better place now.

"You guys can wait outside," Adam said to the body-guards. "Don't want anyone closing in to listen. Keep your eyes out for any other issues. While you're out there, reach out to your boss. I want another pair on rotation with you. Then I'm going to need another pair for follow purposes with vehicles."

That was extremely detailed and specific. Lainey and Adam hadn't arrived alone: Milo and Cav—Bodhi were with them. They drifted into the room like shadows.

How a man who was built like Milo and looked so damn dangerous managed to just blend in defied all understanding. As for Cavendish? He'd always been insane.

Just now that crazy was on our side.

Lainey leaned back, and all of my attention went to her. She seemed wan, stretched thin, and there were heavy shadows under her eyes.

"You look like hell," I said to her and she laughed.

"I look better than you."

Everyone, myself included, laughed at the declaration.

"That's not even a bet I would try to take," I told her. "But you're pale..."

I don't wanna insult her, but I was worried. She'd gone missing. What happened in the hours since they left her and they found her?

She glanced over her shoulder toward Adam, and he nodded. Then she looked at me again. That was another change. The connection between all of them—it had deep-ened. While it still felt like I was very much on the outside, they weren't the ones doing it.

They were including me.

What the fuck happened?

"Tell us how you are first," Lainey prompted me. "Then I'll tell you what happened. We're also going to check with the doctor to see if we can get you out of here."

"Hell yes," I said and almost wanted to jump up and get dressed right now. Based on the way, Adam was staring at me, it probably wasn't the best idea. So I focused on Lainey. "I got poisoned. Not really any other word for it. They said I had an overdose of beta blockers. And if the guys hadn't gotten me here when they did, I probably would've died."

Okay, in retrospect, I might've delivered that news with a little more care. Lainey blanched. She looked so stricken, I wanted to take it all back. Before I could react, however, anger swept through her eyes. A kind of pure fury I'd never seen in her before.

"But you're going to be okay?" she asked in a tone that demanded I agree with her.

"I will be, Kotyonok. No matter what, I will be. I've got some stuff to do, including medications and exercises and shit. Probably rest. He doesn't think the damage to my heart can't be repaired on its own, but I have to take care of it." The darkness in her eyes clawed at me. "I *will*," I continued, stressing that last word. "I know I'm not the best at it, but I have a reason to stick around now."

She flinched, just a little. I wanted to kick myself for saying that now. Why was I fumbling this so hard? Sobriety was really overrated.

"I always had a reason to stick around because of you," I promised. Maybe I hadn't *always* seen it, but she'd always been there. In my mind. In my heart. In my soul. "Do you think I can just get a little preemptive forgiveness for the next few days for saying or doing stupid shit until they clear my system of everything?"

"No," Adam said as he fixed a very firm look on me. "You

don't get latitude for any more stupid shit. If you even think you want to do it, you need to get permission. In fact, you're not allowed to think about it. *Ever* again."

Imperious fucker.

Lainey laughed and Milo just shook his head. Thankfully he didn't comment on how stupid I could be. I didn't need anyone to. I knew exactly how stupid I could be, and frankly I wanted to change the subject. Now.

"Did they say what was used to deliver the poison?" Oh, look, so did Bodhi. We were on the same page for a change. "Any needle marks anywhere? Something in your food? Something to drink? A patch on your skin?"

Once again, there was a great deal of specificity to that request. Unfortunately, I just had to shake my head. "I don't know, the doctor didn't say. They just came in and did another round of bloodwork. To see if they can get me out of here." I tracked my gaze to where Adam stood, stoic, with his arms crossed. "I wasn't sure they were going to allow me to leave even then." Especially if Adam wasn't back.

The smirk on Adam's face said no, I wouldn't have been allowed to leave. Admittedly, there was a small part of me that was really enjoying the possessiveness.

Very small part.

I needed to keep telling myself that, because otherwise, all that power would go to his head. As glorious as that image was, I couldn't afford to give him that much control —to surrender that much.

Not yet.

"Once we get the all clear, we'll go," Lainey said. "Bodhi has agreed that we're going to stay with him."

We were? And I cut a look towards Adam. Was *he* all right with that plan?

Adam merely shrugged. Like it was normal. Of course,

we would go stay with Cavendish. Cavendish who we couldn't stand. The crazy bastard who didn't threaten. Ever. He just—did. Sure, absolutely let's go stay with him.

Only Cavendish was now one of Lainey's lovers – which meant we had to be nice to him.

Right.

"Taking a minute there," Milo asked, a measure of amusement flickering around his eyes.

I looked up at him and shrugged my shoulders. I might need more than a minute. This whole situation was— strange. The fact he nodded once seemed to convey he got it.

He understood.

The hell of it was, I thought he really did understand.

Lainey distracted me, gathering my hands in hers. Couldn't really complain when my girl was sitting right there, holding onto me. She looked amazing despite the loss of color to her cheeks. Not even the anger in her eyes seemed to flush any pink to her face.

I still wanted to know what happened, I wanted to know who we were killing, and then I wanted to just hold onto her forever.

"Things change," Adam said. "A lot of things have changed over the last couple of years. We're all adjusting." His gaze fixed on mine, and I got the message. "It also means we need to keep talking, and keep working things out, and stop running away."

"And no more giving yourself up," Lainey added as her nails dug into my palms. Truthfully, she really was the only thing that could pull my attention from Adam. "I mean it," she said. "Ezra, I don't know what I would do if something bad happened to you. We need you. I don't know how all of this is going to work out, but I do know we need you to be a part of it. *I* need you."

She was impossible to argue with. Milo and Bodhi definitely didn't need me, but they weren't objecting. As much as I wanted Adam to need me the same, I wasn't sure we were there yet.

But Lainey wanting and needing me?

"I love you," she said, in a soft voice that arrested every argument on my tongue. "I know everything else seems so fucking impossible right now. Trust me, after the last 24 hours, it seems even more impossible. But that's why we need each other, why I need you. No more running, Ezra. If you run, we do it together."

"You don't know how to run." I almost wished I was joking. Lainey was ferocity incarnate. She dug her heels in and picked battles with people far beyond her.

For as long as I'd known her, she'd never let anything or anyone slow her down. Sometimes we could delay her, but she was still going to do what she wanted—what she needed to do.

She got on the bus and went across the country — with no one to protect her. And why? Because her best friend had a birthday, and she was going to go celebrate it with her. Then her best friend went missing and what did she do? She marched right into the Vandals territory to get them to help.

"So what I hear you saying is that you won't run because I won't run." Her smirk was absolutely adorable.

"Tell you what," I said. "Because I don't know that I can promise I'll never run again — largely because so far the odds are not in my favor. But if I do, I promise I'll come back. If you have to come looking for me..."

Bodhi coughed. "I'll pin you down and let her kick your ass. Not that she needs my help."

There was just a momentary bit of silence before laughter rippled through the room. For the first time in two years, not only could I breathe, I could let myself believe.

A knock at the door interrupted, and thank fuck, it was the doctor telling us that I could get the fuck out of here.

CHAPTER
TWELVE

LAINEY

H ands against the shower wall, I shuddered as Milo thrust so deep it pushed me up onto my tip toes. His hands were slick where they rested on my hips and his lips were hot on my throat.

Every glide of his cock through my folds had driven me mad. Pumping deep into me, lighting me up with shudders, he turned me inside out. I was torn between pressing back to meet him and pounding my fists against the wall.

"Fuck," I whispered at the end of a particularly hard thrust. "Pretty Boy..."

"I'm here," he promised, flexing his fingers against my hips as he dragged me back even as he pressed into me again. "Right here. Feel me."

How could I not? Thick, throbbing, and thrusting so hard, I couldn't focus on anything else. "I do," I whispered. I was drunk on him. Drunk on how he made me feel when he stretched me over him.

The trembling in my legs climbed to my arms and to my heart, then to my lips as the first keen of an orgasm burst through me, the pressure so intense that my legs threatened to buckle.

Milo didn't let me fall. He wrapped his arms around me, holding me tight as his hips pistoned, increasing the pressure even as pleasure burst through me. The scrape of his teeth alternated with the feathering brush of his lips as he left a trail of biting kisses along my throat.

"So fucking sweet for me, Mayhem," he whispered in my ear. His voice seemed as raw and shaken as I was. "So damn sweet. Watching you climb out that window last night..."

It had been hours. None of us had slept. Not while they dealt with Harper Reed and the subsequent cleanup. Not after when we went to get Ezra. The profound relief in finding him safe had left me battling tears all over again.

Damage to his heart.

I was going to kill Wallace Graham...

"Shhh..." Milo's voice wrapped around me even tighter than his arms. "Stay here with me."

"I'm here," I promised him again.

"Yes you are," he said, the scrape of his teeth grounding me again as he bit down on my earlobe. "You were so goddamn beautiful climbing down the side of the house, after breaking yourself out—you take my breath away, Mayhem. You keep taking it away."

I swore he said more but he slid a hand down my stomach to tease my clit. The lightest brush of his fingers jolted me, and my thoughts splintered.

One minute, he was deep inside of me and then he pulled out. I whined as reality crashed back in, but the sound didn't last long. Spinning me around, he was already picking me up and thrusting back in even as his mouth captured mine.

I rocked my hips upward eagerly to meet his, and then we were straining into each other. This position was even better; it let me dig my fingers into his muscles even as he devoured my lips.

The steady rhythmic thrust of his hips gave way to a jerkier motion, and the flutters of my pussy seemed to increase. Then he came in a rush, his breath hot on my lips and his dark eyes fixed on mine.

I drank in the sight of him even as I soaked in the feel of him. Dragging my hand up to his nape, I tugged him to me. He collapsed forward, his mouth landing on mine like a meteor falling from orbit.

Slow, loving laves of his tongue tangling with mine gave way to huffs of laughter as I lapped at his tongue, then his lower lip.

"No wonder he keeps calling you kitten," Pretty Boy murmured and his humor spilled over into me. The giggle that escaped had him leaning back to study me.

"He started calling me *Kotyonok* long before he ever kissed me."

"Hmm," he hummed. "Sharp claws and teeth."

I wrinkled my nose, but he wasn't wrong. "You like my nails."

"I love your nails," Milo whispered. "I love every damn thing about you, especially how you feel on my cock. I can never get enough of it. I could live buried inside of you, but it might get crowded with the other boyfriends."

Heat flushed through me at the declaration. I slid my hands through his wet hair, marveling at him.

"What?" He still had me pinned against the tile wall, his

107

half-hard cock still buried inside of me, though it was softening.

"You—make me happy," I told him. "Really—you accept them. Even if you don't really like them."

"I like Bodhi and Adam, for the most part. Ezra has some ground to reclaim." That admission seemed to cost him nothing. "But he doesn't get to treat you badly."

"He…" Defending him was right there, but I didn't want to make light of any of it. His choices over the past few months, not to mention some others of the past few years, had left their marks. "He doesn't want to hurt me. I know that he has, and, you know, maybe he will again."

I smoothed my hand down to Milo's chest, tracing one of the vines of ivy inked there over his heart. He wore his love for his sister on his skin, and it just made me love him all the more. The love he had for Em was something I treasured.

"I also know he loves me and that love has cost him." A reality I couldn't escape. It wasn't just his love for me. But also having to hide it, first from Adam, then from his family. Now it was out there and it came with its own consequences.

"You love him," Milo said, pulling me back to the present. "You love all of them. It's more than worth the risk. But he needs to be far more careful with your heart. I meant it when I said no one gets to hurt you."

"He doesn't want to hurt me." Cupping his face, I pushed upward to kiss him. My cunt was sore in all the right ways. I would be feeling him for hours yet. My pretty boy… "I love you too."

"I am a lucky bastard," Pretty Boy murmured before brushing his lips to mine. Eventually we had to get back to the actual shower. The tension locking my muscles eased, and the ache in my hands and legs from the climb seemed to have been soothed.

Even better, my craving for Pretty Boy had been sated—at least for the moment. I didn't think I'd ever get my fill of him. I ached for him sometimes, even when he was right there, and it was more than just sex.

So much more.

It was how he looked at me. How he listened. How he understood. Even when he didn't know what to think or how to feel, he never abandoned me, and I would never leave him.

"I love you," I whispered again, and the corners of his lips tilted upward. "I love you so much." Then I was repeating it as I peppered kisses to his cheeks. His laughter wrapped around me like a hug.

With Pretty Boy, I was safe. That safety had grown to include all of the men in my life. The four of them—so stubborn, impetuous, and focused. Each one of them was enough to devastate me, yet I adored them all.

Thankfully, they weren't forcing me to choose between them.

As reluctant as I was to relinquish this sweet bubble of bliss we'd created, the world wouldn't wait for us, and the men out there needed me. We had to find Andrea. We had to deal with the Grahams. Adam's uncles might be an issue.

And I supposed I should check on my mother. Then there was King...

I had wrapped a towel around my torso so I could pull a brush through my hair and the leave-in conditioner. Milo studied me from where he waited, arms folded and dressed again—more was the pity—but there was a knowing in his eyes I couldn't escape.

"We'll find her," he said. "I know he said he sold her, but he could have still been lying."

I snorted, not because I doubted Milo but because by the time Harper confessed, he'd been feverish with pain and ranting. I somehow doubted he even knew where he was anymore. "You don't believe that."

"No," Pretty Boy told me with that blunt evenness of his that I adored so much. "I don't. I want it to be true—for you and for her. Whatever happens, we'll find her."

How long would it take, though? Harper seemed convinced that he'd covered his tracks in addition to removing her. How he expected no consequences, I didn't know. Then again, he'd apparently tried to have my mother killed.

It left me to wonder if the illness Adam's mother suffered from for so long had been caused by Harper. Had she been killed as much by his neglect as by his mistreatment?

As lost in my thoughts as I was, Pretty Boy stayed with me until I was dressed in a pair of pajamas that left my legs bare and the oversized shirt hem skimming my thighs. It hid the pair of sleep shorts I also wore.

The slouchy socks finished the look. I couldn't adore Bodhi more if I tried. He'd packed my clothes. Despite how high-handed that might seem, he'd chosen good ones. Bodhi had installed me in his bedroom. The choice had not been lost on any of us. When Pretty Boy dropped his own bag in the room, Bodhi had just shrugged.

Ezra and Adam were across the hall. There was enough space to put them in their own rooms, but Adam had just put their bags in there before he and Ezra had gone back downstairs.

Whatever I expected Bodhi's apartment to be like, this

warm space with modern touches and wooden floors, not to mention a wooden circular staircase, had not been it. His living room included a loft library that looked down over the living space.

It was—exquisite. I kind of wanted to explore, but I had to save that for later. With Milo as my shadow, I descended the circular staircase to where Bodhi stood in the living room with Adam and Ezra. Well, Bodhi was standing, but Ezra sat in an armchair, while Adam glared down at him.

The tension crackled in the air, and Ezra darted his gaze from Adam's ferocious expression to me.

"What happened now?" I asked, slowing when I reached Bodhi. He lifted his arm and glanced down at me with a half-smile. Accepting the invitation, I leaned into him as he wrapped his arm around my shoulders.

The need to be close to them was like a fever in my system. Even with one hand against Bodhi's chest, I kept my attention on Adam and Ezra.

"Ezra wants a drink," Adam said, his tone too bland for the absolute fury in his expression. "I just reminded him that he's not allowed alcohol or drugs of any kind. He doesn't like the idea of a clean and sober lifestyle."

"That's not what I said," Ezra fired back. "I said that with everything going on, you should understand why I need a drink."

"No," Adam snapped. "N. O. Period."

I sighed because the mutiny on Ezra could be hot, but this wasn't really the time.

"Adam," I said and he whirled from Ezra to face me. The tension around his eyes softened as his gaze locked with mine. "He gets it."

"No, he doesn't," Adam admitted in an almost mournful tone, and I shook my head.

"He does," I said. "He's also not alone. Neither of you are. We need to eat—all of us. Then we need to plan. Because I'm not letting Andrea stay missing a single second longer than we have to."

Forgoing one battle for another, Adam straightened, then he dropped a hand on Ezra's shoulder. "Sorry," he muttered before crossing to me. Bodhi lifted his arm, and I flowed right into Adam. Wrapping around him, I held him tight and met Ezra's gaze over his shoulder.

For his part, Ezra dropped his gaze and made a face. Then he mouthed the word "sorry," and I nodded.

I meant what I'd told Pretty Boy. Ezra didn't want to hurt me. He didn't want to hurt anyone except himself. So we had to remind him that hurting himself would hurt us too. Until he got that message, well, we'd all fight and then we'd have to make up.

We'd probably fight again after that.

But I could handle it.

Handle them.

I blew out a breath even as Adam squeezed me tighter. I could definitely handle them.

Thankfully, they seemed able to handle me.

CHAPTER

THIRTEEN

BODHI

Food and drink went a long way around to settle everyone, even Ezra. Despite his litany of complaints, he was pale and a little shaky. Adam and Lainey weren't quite hovering. Still, they moved with him. One of them was always ready to catch him. I wasn't the only one keeping an eye on the trio: Milo stayed within range.

We wouldn't let him fall, still, I dragged a chair with me from my office to the private room. When the doors slid open for them, a shocked silence rippled over the group.

Ezra broke the uncertain quiet with a low whistle. "Cavendish—this is some seriously stalker-level shit."

I shrugged. Lainey glanced at the tangled web of strings connecting her photo to others. All of us were up there. But her attention didn't stay there. She drifted toward the other wall where I'd set up the network of everyone who had come in and out of my mother's life.

The numerous connections included members of my

own family, medical professionals, even her grandfather was up there. I'd scratched more than a few off. But there were others—and blank cards with question marks.

"What the hell is all this?" Milo asked as he tracked his gaze from the Lainey board to the one with my mother.

"A warning sign," Adam suggested. "Remind me to never piss him off."

"You've survived it once," I informed him. "I'm sure you will again."

That netted me everyone's attention. The corners of Lainey's mouth began to twitch, and she put a hand up as if to hide her smile. But she couldn't quite suppress her laugh.

Adam stared at me for a long moment, his expression unreadable. Then he shrugged. "Fair enough."

The acknowledgement unleashed laughter in Milo and even Ezra, who shook a little with his chuckling.

"Yeah, you sit down." I pointed him to the chair. To my enormous surprise, he actually obeyed me. I wasn't the only one, apparently: Adam frowned at him.

Lainey folded her arms as she drifted away from that board then propped her hip on the arm of the chair Ezra was seated in. Protective as hell, even right now.

"Where do you want to start?" She focused on me, and I loved her more. While I'd told her about my mother, she wanted me to take the lead on this. Reveal what I wanted...

"At the beginning," I said. "It's a bit of a tangled story, so I'll keep it to the facts. I'm saying this because it may be related to Andrea. She's not the first child the wealthy decided to get rid of."

As gentle as I made my tone, there was no escaping the tightness in her expression or the shadows moving in her eyes. My single regret was that I couldn't kill Harper Reed twice. His passing was not peaceful, nor was it painless. Still, killing him again would be nice.

"No," Adam said slowly, and Lainey snapped her gaze to him. "She's not. There are always rumors."

Yes. There were. Like the one about King being a member of one of the illustrious families.

"I know Em wasn't sold exactly," Adam said, glancing at Milo. His expression darkened.

"No," he said. "But we do know money passed hands." A muscle ticked in his jaw. "We also know that there were traffickers working in Braxton Harbor and elsewhere. People like Warrick who masked their dealings behind charity and philanthropy."

I turned that information over in my head. I had known about them. I'd also known that the Vandals had dealt with Warrick after his mother died. She'd been the true head of the operation. A gentle-looking woman, a grandmother, and picture perfect in every way.

How better to disguise a monster?

"We had human traffickers using the trucks for a while too. It was linked to the 19Ds—Diamonds. We dealt with it and with them." Milo hesitated, as though he were chewing on something distasteful.

"You still think King is tied into that." Adam seemed to understand where his mind was.

"My gut says yes," Milo admitted. "We didn't find anything that strictly tied him to it. Still, I know he was the reason I ended up going to jail. I don't know exactly *how* he set it all up, but I know he did. I know he targeted the Vandals. He wasn't supposed to, it was leverage against Liam but he made it clear to Liam he wanted to take over Braxton Harbor and he wanted the Vandals gone. That's not leaving them alone."

Adam's gaze flicked briefly to Ezra, before returning to Milo. Lainey's attention riveted on Milo and his was on his hands. I don't think they caught the glance.

I filed it away for later.

"So—the wealthy make their problems disappear by selling off their bastard children." Lainey shook her head. "And anyone else they want to get rid of. That should probably surprise me more."

Ezra put a hand on her leg and she covered it with her own. "Probably why your grandfather is so protective of *you*."

I frowned. Lainey's birth status didn't matter a damn to me but... Reed wanted to marry her because the Benedicts had made their own claims, they'd demonstrated her value and *no one* was allowed to treat her as anything less.

King was a bastard of one of the families. It might also explain his resentment beyond the fact that his son was in love with her. Reed wanted the Benedict fortune, something denied to Melissa, and by extension to Andrea. Though Lainey would never allow her sister to suffer for the sins of her parents.

"You look particularly cold and homicidal," Adam commented, his focus on me.

"Thinking about your father." It was true after all.

For his part, Adam actually laughed before he drained his coffee cup. "Yeah, that would do it." Blowing out a breath, he motioned to the boards. "Bring us up to speed?"

Agreed.

I summed it up as best I could beginning with my mother's incarceration at the various sanitariums and hospitals. I kept the stories from them, those private moments. Lainey was the first one I'd ever told.

The only one.

She would keep those tales safe.

Walking them through my investigation brought us to Pinetree and snared the attention of the other three. "That was how you met Freddie and Ivy," Milo said.

I nodded. "For a brief time... I thought I might have found my sibling in Freddie. But the age was wrong." Even with the age difference, I'd managed a DNA test. Mother had indicated another pregnancy before, one where they didn't let her keep the child. So I'd thought *maybe*? Turned out, we weren't related.

Friendship had softened that particular disappointment. I could be there for him and for PPG the way I couldn't be for my own brother or sister. They didn't seem to mind.

"Freddie might have liked it," Milo said and I shrugged. I would have liked it too. As much as I wanted the answers, I wanted to know they were safe. "Did you tell him beforehand?"

"No," I said with a short shake of my head. "He has enough issues. He didn't need to worry about mine unless the tie was actually there."

Milo nodded.

"I'd appreciate continued discretion in that area." In case they were wondering.

"Goes without saying," Ezra said, surprising more than me. "You probably needed to say it because I can be a dick and so can Adam, but Freddie's not bad. A little scary with the knife..."

"He's sweet," Lainey said, earning a chuckle. "Just don't be mean to Em."

"I would never," Ezra swore. "She's pretty damn scary these days too."

That earned a real laugh from Adam, and even Milo

began to grin, pride evident. PPG wasn't a broken bird anymore. She'd grown a lot stronger. That strength suited her. It was also why she wouldn't bend for King.

We might need her for dealing with him. She had a particular influence that might be an illusion the man perpetuated.

Turning my thoughts back to where we were, I wrapped up my hunt and the names still to be found. "As for this one," I said as I finished with my past. "I started building it when I realized the number of threats targeting Lainey. I wanted to know if there was a pattern."

"Did you find one?" Milo studied the board, arms folded and his expression dark. Milo Hardigan's colorful background made him an ideal ally in keeping her safe. He wasn't opposed to violence, but he didn't rely on it.

I flicked a look toward Ezra. Unlike some people. Then again, Ezra's father was abusive, so it made sense his son learned a lot of bad lessons.

Mine was remote, cold, and uncaring. But he'd only ever attempted to hit me once.

He hadn't appreciated my response.

"Yes," I said and Lainey blinked at me. "And no."

"Well, thanks for clearing that up," Ezra snarked. Lainey smacked his shoulder lightly. "Hey, I'm being nice."

"Uh huh." Her attention wasn't on him though; she split it between the board and me. "What did you find?"

"One we already know about..." I walked over and traced the string that went from her to Milo to King. Another went from her to Adam to King, then her to Ezra to King, her to PPG to King.

So many parts of the tapestry linked her to King.

"Wait." Ezra frowned. "Why is my father connected to King?"

118

"They all are in one way or another." I pointed to the board. "King took over the Royals, he didn't create it. Long before you or Adam were tapped, Harper and Wallace were also Royals, among many others traveling in your circle. It provided them with resources, support, and..."

"A network of connections to keep the wealth in their hands as well as other business deals." Milo rubbed his chin. "But if it was a closed circle, limited to the members of their families and I'm assuming the Sharpes, among others are also counted in this, how did Jeff Hardigan from Braxton Harbor, small time dope dealer, make his way up to lead a—whatever the hell the Royals are supposed to be?"

"A secret society," Adam said. "Only those in it should know it exists. But he doesn't run it like any society that I've heard of... except for the secrets and the tasks."

"Fine, but how does *he* do that—son of a bitch!" He rubbed his face with both hands and paced away. "You said your source indicated he might actually be related to one of the families."

"Exactly." I let that sit there for a moment, marinate in the quiet as they all absorbed it.

"That means you could be related to one of us." Adam blew out a breath and Ezra's eyes widened a fraction.

"Not sure I'm happy about it either," Milo admitted.

"That means Em would be related to us," Ezra said. "I like her."

The random comment punctured the air around them.

"And then there's this alleged third child of his..." Lainey pulled us all around. "Another missing kid. Bodhi's sibling." She locked eyes with Adam. "Our sister. Possibly Em and Pretty Boy's sibling."

"That's three," Ezra said.

"That we know of," I reminded him. "I don't believe in

119

coincidences. If it walks like a duck and talks like a duck, Occam's Razor says it's a duck."

"Just because you equate hoofbeats with horses, doesn't mean it can't be zebras." The comment from Adam surprised me. "I'm just saying we can't discount anything. Even the most outlandish theory might net us an answer or at least a direction to look in."

Thumbnail pressed against her teeth as though she were chewing it, Lainey rose and walked over to the board. She studied it without comment. I wanted to see what she saw, but I let her do it.

She was present for everything in her life, she might very well identify a connection I hadn't or couldn't.

"Waldemar." She touched the string that bound Adam to the woman. There were other strings, different colors for different connections.

"Fuck," Adam said. "I need to talk to her..."

"So do I."

She might as well have dropped a bomb in the middle of the room. Without a doubt, she was aware of it.

"Before you start lecturing me on all the reasons it's a bad idea, listen. At various points recently, Margareta Waldemar has been social with me and with Grandfather. She's been social with Milo—and she was apparently behind one of Em's kidnappings."

The look she gave Adam had him gritting his teeth.

"You've been working for her. She's King's enemy—as far as we can tell. So, the enemy of our enemy and all that would be reason enough. But I want to know where she stands in this game. I want your freedom too, Adam. I want freedom for all of you."

"Lainey..." His expression softened at the last comment.

How could it not? She was so fierce in her devotion and protectiveness.

"We should call Fletcher too."

"No," he answered almost immediately with a shake of his head.

Fletcher Reed. The man could be an exploding can of trouble, and had been in the past, but he had some skills.

"No," Adam repeated. "If we involve him..."

"You can call him," she said, flatly. "Or I can. This is too important. Fletcher wouldn't want us to protect him from this. Not when it involves Andrea."

Adam glared at her. To their credit, Ezra rolled his eyes and Milo just shook his head. The battle of wills had already been lost. Adam just hadn't figured that out yet.

He would.

Still... meeting with Margareta Waldemar—wild card, red herring, or bullseye?

Excellent question.

CHAPTER

FOURTEEN

LAINEY

T he first night we spent at Bodhi's place went well. I ended up sleeping between Bodhi and Pretty Boy —no complaints. Though I would never have to worry about being cold. I woke to Bodhi leaving the bed, and I followed him.

He headed for his gym, and I headed for the shower. Instead of leaving immediately, he lingered and "savored" the view. As tempting as it was to lure him into the shower, he seemed to be enjoying himself.

Wrapping a towel around me when I emerged, he pulled me to him and then gave me my first proper kiss of the day. I sighed beneath his mouth. The movement of his lips on mine was both playful and demanding, his kiss coaxing and claiming.

I could have kissed him all day, but he left my mouth to kiss the tip of my nose, then each eyelid before he pressed his lips to my forehead.

"You're really okay with all of us here?" I spread my

hand against his chest, the steadiness of his heartbeat grounding me. They all did. The insanity of the last few weeks, the ache of worry for Andrea, and the bruises on my heart and on the rest of me from the past couple of days.

"Yes." Simple, straightforward, and without an ounce of artifice. "I want you here. They need to be around you. They will also protect you, and I can keep an eye on them too."

Laughter bubbled up through me. "Thank you…"

He dipped his head and kissed me. "You never have to thank me."

"Maybe I want to," I reminded him.

"Very well, if the birthday girl wishes it."

Birthday girl.

Shock rolled through me. It was my birthday.

His eyes softened. "You forgot."

"I mean…in my defense, it's been a little crazy."

"You don't need a defense, Buttercup. Ever. You do need to decide what you want for your birthday."

A fist closed around my heart. "I want Andrea safe."

"You *will* get that." Could he really make that promise? "We will find her. We will disembowel anyone who has hurt her, and we will keep her safe forever after that."

It didn't soften the blow that there was a very real chance something bad *was* happening to her right now. The breath backed up in my lungs, but Bodhi curved his hand against my jaw.

"Don't tear yourself up, Lainey B. We will find her. We can save your birthday celebration until after we have her. Trust me?"

I met his gaze.

"Trust us," Pretty Boy said from the doorway. "None of us are giving up. I'm going to call Liam today too. We all have resources…"

That meant telling Em.

"She will want to help you," Bodhi insisted as if he'd read my thoughts.

"He's right," Pretty Boy agreed with him. "Ivy and you are too close, and she will want to help. I'm sure your friend Tally will too."

God. Tally.

I tilted my head back. I needed to call her.

"I trust you," I whispered, then blew out a shaky breath. "I need to check on my mother too."

"No leaving without one or more of us with you."

"I could call—"

"The bodyguard you despise?" The droll comment had my lips twitching. He wasn't wrong, I really didn't like Karagiani.

"Exactly," Bodhi said, then dropped a kiss on my lips. "I'll be in the gym."

"Thank you."

"Always."

Pretty Boy moved so Bodhi could leave, and then I crossed over to slide into the arms Pretty Boy held out to me. He pressed a kiss to the top of my head. "Happy Birthday, Mayhem."

Eyes closed, I held onto him. I had all four of them. Ezra was safe. Harper couldn't hurt my mother or Andrea again. We would get Andrea back.

As birthdays went—it was a day.

My phone started ringing in the other room. Milo's chest rumbled with laughter against me. "Go, the world doesn't stop for us."

No, it didn't.

Blowing out a breath, I drifted back into the bedroom. Like Bodhi's place in Virginia, this was a deeply masculine space. Oak furniture with a dark cherry finish. Massive king-sized bed. A couple of huge, oversized chairs that would be wonderful for reading and probably having sex in.

It smelled like him in here, the notes of amber and vetiver mixed with elements of something I couldn't quite identify but made me think of forests. So not only were we in his space, he'd opened all of it to us.

Opened it and made us welcome.

The name on the phone pulled me back to the present, and I sighed. The hospital was calling. It had to be about Mother.

"Elaine Benedict," I said as I answered.

"Miss Benedict, this is Doctor Enright..."

ALL FOUR, even Ezra, came with me on the trip to the hospital. When I would have insisted he stay behind and rest, he'd just shaken his head.

"If I stay, then Adam is either going to force more babysitters on me or stay himself." The man in question had given him a flat look. "He wants to be there for you and so do I. So—I'm going." It wasn't a bad piece of logic, and the fact Adam didn't even try to deny it supported his theory.

"You all just want points for being the best boyfriends on my birthday." It was a ridiculous notion, but the teasing helped buoy my own mood, and based on their smiles, I'd say it helped them too.

"You're not wrong," Bodhi said. "But I already won, so we're just looking at who gets second place."

Laughter burst out of me at the comment, even as Ezra said, "Hey!"

"You're in last place," Pretty Boy told him with a pat to his shoulder. "Just suck it up and hush. Adam and I will figure out the rest."

Adam's smirk was damn near adorable, as was Milo's. Ezra grumbled, but he settled when I threaded my arm through his. "That just means you might get to have more time to earn a better position."

The snorts from Adam and Milo were so perfectly aligned they actually blinked at each other. Bodhi just shook his head and held the door for us as I guided Ezra through it.

Despite his insistence that he was fine, he still seemed a little pale and shaky to me. The protectiveness that ran through all four of them meant he would be eager to leap into the way of trouble. Holding on to his arm meant he could lean on me, while Bodhi, Pretty Boy, and Adam watched our backs.

I could also watch all of theirs. Foolish men. Sometimes, looking after them meant letting them look after me. Thankfully, they also seemed to understand it.

Bodhi drove with Pretty Boy riding up front. I sat in the back of the stylish Land Rover Discovery. The deep green had to be a custom color, but I appreciated it nonetheless. Adam held my hand, and I had my head tucked against Ezra's shoulder while he rested a hand on my knee.

The dynamic would all take time to get used to, but I had no complaints. I rather suspected Em would give me no end of teasing. Still, she had to juggle seven of them—and I just couldn't imagine it.

These four were more than enough. It seemed impossible that it was working, yet they were making it work. When Pretty Boy glanced back at me, I summoned a smile for him.

I wished Em was here right now, and at the same time, I wanted to keep her far away from all this chaos. I wanted her safe on her tour—especially now that I knew she would be safe. Her boys wouldn't let anything happen to her.

A sigh escaped me when we got near the hospital. I didn't like visiting my mother on a good day and this— with everything that was happening—was not a good day.

We parked in the private lot, then headed inside. The hospital offered the kind of privacy and security our families generally desired. In a world where gossip was currency, it was better to keep things under wraps.

My heart thumped painfully as Bodhi took point. Adam moved up next to him to speak to the first nurse. The Reed name definitely carried currency. Eventually, we would need to deal with his father's death and a way to alert authorities so that the inheritance would kick in.

Not something I wanted to think about now. I was just glad the man was gone and had paid for at least *some* of his crimes.

"This way," a patient coordinator was saying as she guided us down the hall. Rather than a hospital room, she brought us into a conference room, and my stomach bottomed out. "Dr. Enright will be right with you."

"Breathe, Kotyonok," Ezra whispered, lifting my hand to press a kiss to it. I blew out a breath, but taking another one seemed even more difficult.

He pulled out a chair for me, and I nudged out the one next to me. He waited a beat for me to sit before he sat next to me. Adam took the chair on my other side, but Bodhi and Pretty Boy both remained standing.

The silence in the room was a smothering blanket. I had to force my hand to relax or I was going to leave divots in Ezra's skin.

The door opened and a vaguely familiar man strode inside. "Good morning, Miss Benedict. I apologize for the delay, I wanted to make sure I had the most recent test results."

Neatly trimmed snow white hair crowned his head. He was clean-shaven with generous laugh lines at the corners of his eyes. The lack of tan suggested that even if he spent a lot of time outside, he favored sunscreen. His dark rimmed glasses gave him a gentler appearance, and I accepted his handshake as he reached over the table.

"Thank you for making the time, Dr. Enright." I tilted my head. "Forgive me, but we have met previously, yes?"

His smile grew. "Yes, we have, but only briefly. You worked with my wife Alicia a couple of years ago on a library fundraiser. You stepped in for your grandmother I believe."

Alicia Enright. That was why I recognized him.

"I've been your mother's doctor for the past few days since she was admitted. A request came in from your grandfather for me to take over the case."

That fit.

"So he knows?" Of course, he knew.

The very polite, if sympathetic smile Dr. Enright wore as he pulled out a chair to sit warned me he knew more than I might care for having out there. Then again, the estrangement between my mother and the rest of the family was well-known.

"That she was admitted, I believe so. All of her medical files indicate that our first point of contact is her husband, Mr. Reed. But he has not been returning our calls. You are her daughter, therefore next of kin."

Harper wouldn't be returning anyone's calls again.

"I see," I said, then folded my hands in my lap and lifted my chin. "Can you brief me on her condition?"

The doctor's only hesitation was a glance at the guys, but he settled in a chair near us and set a chart on the table. "Let me begin by saying that no diagnosis is absolute, nor is any treatment…"

"I'll make this easier for you," I told him. "I accept that you are not a miracle worker and that you can offer me no guarantees. How is she?"

He nodded once. "Mrs. Reed is very sick. She's sustained significant damage to both of her kidneys and to her liver. We suspect poisoning, I lean toward heavy metal toxicity, but in order to find out, we have to test specifically. We have been—running every test we can."

Well, it made sense that Harper had used something challenging to diagnose. He wanted to be rid of her swiftly.

"We have been keeping her on dialysis to help her kidneys and to try and clean out the toxins. The problem is the liver enzymes in her system are rising, and that means the damage is continuing. I want to offer you a solution and treatment plan, but currently, we're fighting a battle against both time and information."

The doctor spent the next fifteen minutes walking us through the damage to her body. Cardiac muscle tissue was beginning to show possible signs, but they had to focus on her kidneys right now. They were the closest to failing.

Potentially, a transplant was an option *if* they could identify the toxin and eliminate it. In the meanwhile, the doctor was also concerned about the damage to other areas of her body.

Heavy metal toxicity could even lead to brain damage and cognitive dysfunction. She was in and out of consciousness. Dr. Enright offered the kindest version of *she's dying and we don't know how to prevent it* that I'd ever heard.

"Frankly, Miss Benedict, my greatest concern is that by the time we do identify the source—we may be battling organ failure. Shock has also proved to be a challenge. We're doing everything we can, I assure you…"

"But you don't have any guarantees that she will survive."

Wrapping my mind around that was proving even more challenging.

"I wish I could offer you more reassurance."

Did I wish that?

"Can I see her?"

"Absolutely. I will ask that we limit visitors and right now, I would like you to mask up while in there. Her system is already pushing it."

That made sense. Fifteen minutes later with my guardians standing like sentinels at the window, I followed the doctor into my mother's hospital room. As places went, it was pretty and well-kept, but there were so many machines and a lot of beeping.

Lying in the hospital bed, she looked—frail and almost insubstantial. Not the powerful, vivacious woman who thumbed her nose at everyone to do what she wanted with whom she wanted and to hell with the consequences.

"I'll give you a few minutes," the doctor said, and I closed the distance to study her. Her eyes were closed and her chest seemed to barely move with its slow, shallow breaths. There were a lot of tubes running in and out of her. A machine whirred to life then down again.

The beeping of a cardiac monitor gave evidence of a heart that she'd never really opened to me. When it increased in pace, I lifted my gaze to her eyes. They fluttered open.

"Harper..."

Pity filled me, and I covered her hand gently.

"He's on his way, Mother..."

She didn't need to know he tried to kill her. She didn't need to know he'd sold their child.

And she didn't need to know he was dead.

Not yet. If she survived...well, we could cross that bridge then.

"Elaine..."

"I'm here," I told her. "I'm right here."

CHAPTER
FIFTEEN

ADAM

The hours at the hospital trickled by with a kind of brutal finality. The doctors weren't saying it—at least not yet—but Melissa Benedict Reed was probably never leaving the facility. They hadn't been able to identify the toxin yet, and what treatments they'd done only seemed geared toward slowing down the inevitable.

Waiting outside of her room, as if by unspoken agreement, we didn't say anything. No discussions. No arguments. Nothing.

Staring at Lainey through the grid-marked glass, all I could think about was her grandmother and my mother. She'd already watched both those women slip away. Now she would have to watch it with her mother too.

Not that Melissa Benedict had ever been much of a mother. Her devotion to Harper had been all-consuming. Leopold Benedict hated Harper's guts. He hated all of us. I couldn't really fault him.

There were days I hated myself.

Knowing what I knew now, though, I had more questions than answers. Particularly about my mother. The way Melissa looked in that bed...

Had my father poisoned my mother? Had he been killing her by inches over the years? Leaving her weak and debilitated while he drank with his friends, showed off his mistress, and did whatever he wanted.

"If we could kill him twice," Bodhi said in a low voice. "I'd offer you the knife."

A snort escaped me, but I nodded regardless. "Thanks." It was the offer that counted. Eventually, Lainey left her mother's room and the exhaustion on her face and in her eyes tore at me.

It was her twenty-first birthday. We should be celebrating—*she* should be celebrating. Instead, she shouldered the weight of the world, and I couldn't even tell her she didn't have to.

Andrea missing.

Her mother dying.

My father—the bastard had her kidnapped then threatened to rape her until he knocked her up *after* telling her he killed her mother.

I really did wish we could kill him again.

"Let's get them home," I said, keeping every ounce of my temper leashed. I'd been stuffing my reactions down for years. I was well-practiced. What Lainey needed from us was cooperation and caring.

Yet, she resisted taking it when we all offered it so easily because her focus went to Ezra. He needed all of us too—in his own way. She would put him first, focusing on looking after him rather than feeling the turbulence swirling through her.

Guilty of much the same, I understood.

The drive back to Cavendish's place was filled with protracted silences, populated by all the things we weren't saying. At least I had her tucked next to me, even if she was holding Ezra's hand while she toyed with a necklace with her free hand.

"I should call Mrs. Waldemar when we're back."

"No," I told her without hesitation. One glance at her revealed the rebellion in her eyes. "She's not in the city on Wednesdays." It was a lie, but not tonight. She had already dealt with so much, even if she didn't think she needed a day—I did.

I also needed to deal with Ezra.

Not blinking, she studied me. The lie settled between us, and I didn't even know if it would survive a challenge. Instead of arguing, she sighed with a slow nod. "Of course she's not there," she murmured as if she expected it. "I won't be deterred for long. I can have the office reach out to her tomorrow."

Relief flooded me, easing the tension knotting the muscles of my shoulders and the back of my neck. Even if she didn't wholly believe me, she accepted the choice but warned me that she was only giving me the day.

I'd take it.

"Thank you," I told her, nuzzling a kiss to her cheek. She turned at the contact then pressed her lips to mine. There was no demand in the kiss, just a visceral request for comfort even as she offered her own.

I was the last person she needed to be comforting right now. When she settled her head on my shoulder, I caught Milo's glance from the front seat.

Yeah, he didn't believe me either. But he also didn't argue. Not today. Once we were back in Cavendish's building, a little more of the tightness threading through my back eased.

Bit by bit, I'd take it.

Flicking a look over her head, I caught Ezra's stare, but he jerked his gaze away as if he hadn't been watching me.

Right.

Time to deal with that.

"I'm going to shower," I said once we were back in the apartment. "And change. Why don't you guys decide on food or something? Or if you just want to get some rest." The last I directed at Lainey.

She wrinkled her nose, stubbornness settling on her like a crown. "I might go for a run—in the gym." She tacked on the last before any of us could protest. "Not sure my head is—" As though she didn't have the words for it, she just spread her hands.

Not being able to just fix this settled on me like a bad infection. If I could just take the pain for her...but I wasn't even allowed that much.

"Keep an eye on her?" I said in a low voice to Milo and Bodhi both. I didn't doubt that they would, but I also planned to draw Ezra out of here.

That started by ignoring him and just speaking to them. Stubborn as hell—Ezra and Lainey both. It was enough to give me a migraine.

"Yep," Milo said, then cut a look at Ezra before meeting my gaze again. I just shrugged but nodded once. Yes, I wanted to talk to him, but he fought every attempt to force it.

So, time to make him come to me.

I pressed a kiss to Lainey's cheek before striding out of the living area and up the stairs. All the way up to the room

I'd taken with Ezra, awareness of his gaze on my back settled like a heated brand.

Each of the bedrooms on this floor—all four of them—included en suite bathrooms. They were more than large enough to house all five of us, but Cavendish moved Lainey into his bedroom, and I could hardly fault him for that.

I didn't want Ezra on his own. His choices lately all involved some form of self-punishment or destruction. The violent chaos surrounding all of us was a threat even in this safe haven.

Once I was in the room, I stripped out of the suit I'd worn for the day. We were going to have to deal with Harper's death. I'd sent a message via his phone to the various contacts from lawyers to his secretaries that he was taking some time to be with Melissa.

She was very ill and he didn't want to be disturbed. It wouldn't last long, but I didn't need long. Then we'd sanitized the scene at the house and left directives for the staff.

Covering up his absence was designed to buy us time. I'd brought his laptop, phones, and other devices for searching. In the shower, I braced a hand on the wall and bowed my head to let the water beat down on me.

Near scalding, it heated my muscles even as it stung my face and my back. I craved the pain right now. The day Lainey had damn near twisted my nuts into a pretzel, I'd craved it then too.

When I fucked up, I deserved the pain.

He *sold* Andrea.

Sold.

I wanted to punch the tile until it broke or I did. But I couldn't. I couldn't break.

Lainey needed me.

Andrea needed me—goddammit where was she?

And...

"You going to parboil yourself?" The sarcastic edge to Ezra's voice pulled a reluctant, if real, smile to my lips.

"Maybe," I said, reaching for the soap. I went to work scrubbing every inch of me. Intellectually, I knew I wasn't in that much need of a shower, but I felt dirty. My DNA carried a lot of filth with it thanks to Harper. Awareness of Ezra's observation didn't hurry me along.

It was hardly the first time we showered in front of each other. When I finished, I shut off the water and shoved the door open. He leaned against the wall, the door mostly closed to the bedroom and his arms folded.

I stood there, dripping until he finally dragged his gaze up from my dick to my face. Apprehension rippled through his expression and I found a fresh new layer of disgust for myself.

"You gonna run?" I kept the question quiet even if I wanted to yell. A part of me said slam him against the wall and kiss him like I would Lainey. Kiss him until he had to respond to it and then we would know.

But that apprehension kept me in place. I never wanted him to be afraid of me. No matter how much he pissed me off, I would always have his back.

He didn't seem to *know* that, and before we took another step, I was going to have to find the words and he was going to have to listen to them.

Maybe vice versa.

"I don't want to run." That was a big admission from him.

"I don't want you to run," I told him and then I reached for a towel. The heat had definitely left my skin red and ruddy everywhere. "I want—I want to figure this out for both of us, but I can't do that without you."

"Maybe we wait—until you find Andrea. I know that's what you're worried about. Her and Lainey."

Yes, I was. "I'm also worried about you," I reminded him. "You tried to die on me."

That snapped his head up. "I did not *try* to die on you."

"Yeah, that's what it looked like in the hospital."

A scowl replaced the uncertainty in his expression, and I could have chortled. That was better. Ezra could be such an asshole, but right now, he wore defeat. I hated that for him more than anything else.

"Look, I didn't poison me. Either my father or Oksana's father decided to bitch out…"

"Maybe it was Oksana." The minute I made the suggestion, the hard reality of it slapped me.

Ezra frowned. "She wouldn't—" But he stopped too. Defending her should be easy; she was as much a pawn as he was. More so. But if the groom was eliminated, she was off the hook.

I was almost dead certain it was his dad, his father attempting to make a point, but right then? Ezra had been cooperating.

"I'll kill her," I said slowly. If she really had done this, I would throttle her without an ounce of guilt.

"You can't," Ezra said, putting a hand on my arm. I glanced down at that hand then up at him. "We don't know it was her."

"Uh huh." I met and held his gaze. "You can't even say that with a straight face."

"No," he admitted, and when he would have backed off, I put a hand on his chest. Stilling, he glanced down at the hand then back up at me. "I don't want it to be her. I've been trying to get her out of this for years—she has no reason to turn on me."

139

"Except she isn't us." Me. Lainey.

Hell—Milo and Bodhi too.

"We trust no one who isn't us."

"I trust Nicky," he argued, but then his shoulders dropped and his head went down. "Why the fuck do you put up with me?"

"I'd say you're good in bed, but that's never been the reason," I deadpanned.

A startled laugh exploded out of him. "Adam—are you serious? About—us?"

"Are you?" This time when I locked eyes with him, he didn't pull away or try to look somewhere else. "You've never said a word to me about your feelings changing."

"You're hopelessly hetero, man... you didn't want to hear that I'd dreamed about your dick or how many times I set us up with a girl so I could see you use it." He actually went a little red, then shrugged. "To be fair...I like dick just —most of the other dick I tried didn't seem great. I was more top than bottom."

I nodded. "That's what you want with me?" Cause I wasn't so sure I could handle bottom. Not an experience I'd been particularly curious about.

"I don't know," Ezra admitted. "Fuck, Adam, I never thought this was a possibility, and I didn't trust those guys."

"I've never fucked a guy."

He winced.

"I'm not telling you that to make you feel bad or what-ever the hell just went through your head." I blew out a breath. "I've never fucked a guy. Never thought about it."

"It's okay—"

I pinned him with a look and he mimed zipping his lips.

140

"Thank you." I pursed my lips. "I've been trying to have this conversation with you for a few weeks now. You kissed me."

"I did." No denials. No explanations.

Good.

"I didn't hate it."

He blinked. "You—"

"... didn't hate it," I repeated. "You kissed me, then you took off."

"I got scared." That admission cost him.

"It might get scarier before this is done—you might have to be patient with me."

"Man—you don't have to make yourself do anything you don't want to do. I know I put you on the spot, and maybe I shouldn't have. Sharing Lainey with you—it can be enough."

Could it?

Fuck it, I wrapped a hand around his throat and shoved him back to the wall. He wasn't Lainey. He wasn't smaller than me or slighter. I didn't tower over him. We were eye to eye, and when I narrowed the distance further, a half-dozen other differences struck me.

I was right there, his breath on my lips and I didn't close the gap. "Maybe it will have to be," I told him. "But I didn't hate it when you kissed me."

He swallowed, the jerk of motion rippling under my hand. My dick tightened and the flush of need went through me. His green eyes were filled with vulnerability. The shadows slipped away and left him bare.

Real fear populated his gaze.

But there was more to it—there was also hope.

"I'm going to kiss you," I whispered and he gave the barest of nods. It was all the consent I needed. Mouth on his, I braced myself for the taste of him. Before it had been a flicker of fire, musk from their sex, and a hint of Lainey.

Now? It was coffee and heat, something raspier. His lip had stubble on it. Did stubble have a taste? I teased my tongue along his upper lip, then his lower.

A gasp escaped him, and then his mouth was open and I thrust my tongue in to tangle with his. He sank his hands into my hair, and I flexed my hands around his throat.

My dick wasn't the only hard one. I could feel his erection through his jeans, and mine was definitely on display. I nudged his head to the side and tilted my own. He tangled his tongue with mine, pushing and then retreating.

Then the little shit bit my lower lip, and I jerked back a little. His eyelids were half-closed, and there was a smile on his mouth.

"You kissed me," he whispered, and I couldn't help it. I chuckled.

"Glad you noticed."

"Didn't hate it." He was giving me hell.

"Good," I said, then closed the distance. "Let's try it again. Once could be a fluke. Twice could be a coincidence..."

"Shu—"

I shut us both up and took my time to learn his mouth. Kissing him was not like kissing Lainey. Where she was soft, he was hard. Where she was small, he was so much bigger. Yet—there was something inescapably vulnerable in the moment, and I craved more.

I craved him.

SIXTEEN

LAINEY

The guys asked for the night. One night for me to rest, then we would call Mrs. Waldemar. Adam and Ezra talked. At least, I think they had. They seemed—in a better place. Or maybe we all had more things to worry about than the uncertainty around us.

I hadn't thought sleep would be possible, but Bodhi and Milo just wrapped around me, with my back against Milo's chest and my hand clasped in Bodhi's over his heart. The rumble of their voices lulled me to sleep.

Adam was in the kitchen when I came down. The weariness in his eyes sliced down to my soul. He'd been seated at the table with his coffee, shirt open at the collar and looking more than a little lost. Crawling into his lap, I just wrapped around him and held on.

The most unsettling part? He allowed me to comfort him. No turning it around or changing the subject. No pretending he wasn't disturbed or worried. When I sighed, he just rubbed his hand against my back.

The past few weeks had been a tumultuous time, yet the last twenty-four? Forty-eight? However long it had been since Ezra vanished on us and I walked into Harper's trap? Did it matter? It felt like an eternity.

"I'm here," I whispered, and Adam's arms banded tighter around me. I sank into the embrace and stayed there until the guys made their way down one by one, even Ezra who gave me the most soulful look.

No, he was giving my *coffee* the soulful look. Bodhi passed him my cup then handed me a hot, fresh-brewed one. There was a definite pause before all of us were laughing.

The tension bound all of us up in barbed wire, threatening to cut off both circulation and limbs. After breakfast, I made a call to Mrs. Waldemar and then went to find something to wear.

Bodhi had brought over a suitcase, but he'd apparently also had clothing delivered for me. From anyone else, it would seem almost too high-handed, too arrogant, but I understood what Phillip was doing—because he'd ordered clothes for everyone.

Eliminating issues we might have to make staying together work. I'd just stepped into a skirt and fastened it up when a knock announced Ezra's arrival. He poked his head in the door.

"I know we have an appointment...but can we talk for a moment? You and me, that is. I know I can talk to the guys, and I did talk to Adam—a little, but I want to talk to you."

I finished fastening the skirt then pulled out a silk blouse and slipped it on. Buttoning it up slowly, I pivoted to face him. "You can always talk to me. But—I'd rather this not be another apology followed by another promise that you don't intend to keep."

While I'd rather be in pants, I didn't think I had to worry about climbing down the side of a building. Mrs. Waldemar also read as old-fashioned. So I would meet her on her terms. Even if I was going to be accompanied by all of them.

Ezra dropped his chin, and he looked for all the world like a sulking boy who'd been scolded by his governess or his teacher. Those were the last roles I wanted in his life. "I suppose I deserve that."

"Yes," I told him easily as I tucked the shirt in and then pulled down a smart blazer that matched the skirt and slipped on a pair of sensible black heels. Bodhi had excellent taste, but the shoes could stand to be a little higher.

They would do for now.

Though, having them lining the one side of his closet, while his clothes occupied the other? It answered a hunger in me I hadn't even realized I possessed. Ezra stepped to the side to let me out of the closet as I headed over to the dresser.

I had on a simple pair of studs and a bracelet. I checked my cosmetics in the mirror. I'd gone for understated just like with the clothing. As I tested whether I wanted my hair up or down, I met Ezra's mournful gaze in the mirror. Someone felt terrifically guilty at the moment.

Damn, I wanted to make this better for him. I really did. But this wasn't the first time, nor even the second, that he'd bolted to do something stupidly martyred to protect the rest of us.

What made this time worse was he'd nearly died because of it. That—made my chest ache in the worst way. More because I hadn't known he was in that kind of danger and then because, while he was fighting for his life, I'd been locked up at Waltham Corners.

Closing the door, I reached for the brush to smooth out my hair. I could put it up, but down might also earn me a little sympathy. Make me seem a little younger, a little less capable. I wanted her comfortable but off guard. A challenging combination. I could do it.

"I'm listening," I said when Ezra continued to say nothing.

He dragged his gaze back up to mine in the mirror. "I want to protect you."

I knew that.

"I want—to protect him too."

Established.

"I drink too much. I party too hard. I try to forget about all the things I hate that I am trapped into dealing with." He let out a long sigh. "The only two things I've ever wanted... the two people...I think I can have you now and... it terrifies me, Kotyonok." The last four words trembled as he spoke.

Scrubbing hands over his face, he dropped to sit on the end of the made bed. Pausing, he studied his hands before he looked at me again.

"How angry with me are you?"

"I'm not angry," I told him, setting the brush aside and turning to face him. "I'm disappointed."

He looked so genuinely crestfallen, I wanted to comfort him. "I know, I'm hard to love but—"

"You're not hard to love at all." He never had been. "I've loved you for most of my life and been in love with you for years."

The shock and the surprise shouldn't hurt. It shouldn't, but it did. *Love him,* Bodhi had told me, *but make sure you see the flaws too.*

I got that advice.

See the flaws because they were there. In all of us.

"Loving you has *never* been the problem." Touching my tongue to my teeth, I ripped the Band-Aid off. "I have to be able to trust you. I have to know that when I turn my back, you won't just disappear."

He couldn't quite disguise his flinch. Not that I wanted him to hide anything.

"Ezra, being together—means we're *together*. We fight together. We have each other's backs. We protect each other. I know those three men downstairs aren't going to abandon me. That if I look up and need them, they will be there."

Curling his hands into fists, he couldn't dispel all the regret shrouding him.

After pushing away from the dresser, I crossed to him. With the lightest brush of my fingers against his chin, I lifted his gaze to me.

"Trust takes time. Time I want us to have. I love you." It was as simple as that. "If you run again, we're going to find you. I won't ask you to not run or to promise me you won't —I asked for that before and you did it anyway."

His exhale was harsh and then he closed his hand over mine. "I want to be better for you."

"I want you to be whole for yourself. I want you to heal. I want you to have that time. We'll all protect you, but it would be easier if you let us."

"I'm not so good at letting you do things for me, Kotyonok."

That made me chuckle. "Well, it's a good thing that I don't care what you *let* me do."

He frowned, the corners of his lips twitching. When I cupped his cheek, he wrapped his hand around my wrist. He studied me for a moment, then pressed his lips against my palm.

"Adam and I talked—some."

"Good."

"We need to talk more."

Yes, they did.

"I'd—I want you there when we talk? Would you be okay with that?"

Head tilted, I studied him. Asking had been a challenge enough for him. "Yes."

He blinked. "Just—yes?"

"Did you want me to make it conditional? Transactional?" I didn't need him to answer that for me. "I know the world you grew up in. That's not going to be us, Ezra. You need me, you ask. I'm there. Period. End of story."

"The same is true for you," he said, and it wasn't a hurry or an empty promise. I withdrew a step as he stood.

"Thank you." I meant it. "I like having you in my life."

With care, I pushed up and kissed him lightly.

"Now we have to go..."

He made a face. "I can't talk you out of confronting her? We—" The look on my face must have been answer enough. "Right, I'll get a jacket."

I had to bite back a smile as I followed him out of the room. Bodhi waited for me at the top of the stairs. He looked stunning and dangerous in the all black-on-black suit. He even sported a black silk tie. The tousled nature of his hair appeared deliberate.

Maybe it was.

Peeling back Phillip's layers and seeing the man he kept secure beneath would forever fascinate me.

"Everything good with Graham?" The low question brought me back to why we were here.

I gave a little shrug. "He's struggling."

He nodded, then flicked a look past me before meeting my gaze again. "You need me?"

"Always." When I stepped toward him, he wrapped an arm around my waist and dipped his head to kiss me. "But we'll look after Ezra. I can't make him trust us... just have to show him he can."

Undoing a lifetime of abuse wouldn't happen overnight. His talk with Adam was a good first start, but we had a lot more steps to cover.

"I'll keep an eye on him," Bodhi said before he nuzzled another kiss at the corner of my mouth. "If I asked you to get an embeddable tracker, would you?"

Em had one; we'd discussed it. I rather suspected that Milo had one as well. Was that where Bodhi got the idea?

"Would you get one with me?"

"Yes." Zero hesitation. "So will Reed, and we can persuade Graham."

"It would keep all of us safer." Not a difficult choice to make. "I'll get one, Trouble."

Warmth flooded his eyes, and he caressed my cheek. "You need a better jewelry selection. I'll pick your things up. We might also look into getting a larger penthouse at some point."

"At some point," I agreed. "I love your place."

"I love having you here."

We were still standing there when Ezra re-emerged, shrugging on his jacket. His hair was damp and his eyes a little brighter. He looked from me to Bodhi then back again. "Everything good?"

I smiled and then began my descent of the steps.

"That smile wasn't comforting," Ezra complained, and I chuckled. Milo and Adam were waiting for us downstairs.

"Then you got the right message," Bodhi informed him.

I caught the sound of him clapping Ezra on the shoulder and barely managed to swallow my laughter at the smirk on Adam's face.

"That was even creepier than her smile," Ezra complained.

"Are you calling Mayhem creepy?" Pretty Boy's tone was so mild that there wasn't even the suggestion of a threat in it.

"Nope," Ezra said. "Not even joking about it."

When I glanced at him over my shoulder, however, he made a face at me, mouthed "creepy," then smiled for real, and I grinned.

"Let's go before he starts a riot," Adam said. "This time, I'm driving."

They moved like a phalanx of guards, surrounding me as we stepped out of the apartment and headed for the elevator. It was both adorable and hilarious. I didn't complain, even if I wanted to tweak them a little.

No, I wouldn't complain. They'd gone to a lot of trouble to work together and to trust each other. I flicked a look at Ezra and then Adam. It was more challenging for some than for others.

Trust didn't always mean faith. I caught Milo watching me, and I winked at him. He shook his head, his smile affectionate.

Choosing to trust had its own costs. Bodhi moved up closer when we reached the parking garage, and he put his hand at my lower back.

Bodhi chose to trust them because I loved them. We still had a ways to go, but for once—the violence we were choosing was for the threats to us.

That was a violence I could live with.

SEVENTEEN

MILO

I was torn about meeting with Margareta Waldemar. Very torn. While Adam hadn't said much about his work for her, she was directly tied to the people who'd kidnapped Rome and Ivy several months ago. That put her in league with some ruthless, violent people. She had given Adam tasks not unlike King.

Yet, the woman I'd danced with at the event a few months earlier had an elegant kind of sophistication and sharp intelligence. While I hesitated to use the word *kindness*, it also seemed to apply.

The drive took us to Queens. While Ezra occupied the seat on the other side of Lainey, he didn't say much, though he held her hand like he needed the lifeline. Maybe he did. The guy had a knack for self-sabotage. It reminded me almost uncomfortably of Freddie.

The problem with that was no matter what we did, he had to want to save himself. For his sake, and Mayhem's, I hoped he figured it out.

The house was not what I expected either. While it was definitely older, it had a charm to it. The presence of guards reminded all of us that this was not just a social call. We were waved through, and Bodhi pulled up nearer the house.

Once we were idling, Adam glanced at Lainey. "Can I talk you out of this?"

"No," she answered, a smile tipping her lips. "But thank you for asking."

He flicked a look to me, and I could read the apprehension. Lifting my chin, I nodded. I got it. I really did. But Mayhem could handle this. She could handle just about anything. I'd never met a woman so self-possessed and sure of herself.

We were also with her. She wasn't walking in that house alone.

"Let's do this," Adam said. Then like we coordinated, all four doors opened. My side was the farthest from the front door, and Mayhem followed me out rather than Ezra. Good girl.

The twinkle in her eyes practically dared me. The wink though, the wink settled something in my gut. No, I didn't want her walking in there to challenge this woman. It didn't matter how kind or refined she seemed. She *was* a threat. The *threat* of her existed.

That said, I would have her back every step of the way. So would the others. Once we were all out, Mayhem smiled.

"Deep breaths, boys. This is a social call." The teasing remark generated a sour look from Adam and a worried one from Ezra. It was Bodhi who chuckled.

"Should we have stopped for flowers?"

"Hmm," she hummed as she slipped her purse strap over her shoulder. Between the smart business suit, heels, and the deep ruby color of the ensemble, she looked sexy as hell. "Maybe not this trip. I do like flowers though."

Bodhi nodded. "Noted."

I snorted, a half-laugh escaping, and she glanced over her shoulder at me still grinning. Bodhi's expression was relaxed, and I had perfected neutral in prison. Who knew it would be so helpful here?

The only two clearly unhappy were Ezra and Adam. Though, if I hadn't been watching them, I'd have missed the transformation entirely as Ezra's expression grew disinterested and bored, while Adam's discipline was far more focused.

We were all a little fucked up.

I flicked a look to Ezra. Some of us were more fucked up than others. Glancing away, I caught Bodhi's nod. We'd make this work. Mayhem was already ringing the bell.

The door opened to reveal Mrs. Waldemar, like she'd been waiting for us. Maybe she had. Adam said he would let her know we were on the way and that Lainey wanted to see her.

"Hello darlings," Mrs. Waldemar said as she swept her gaze over all of us. "Come in."

"Ma'am..." one of the guards who'd shadowed us said. "They haven't been searched."

"I'm sure they are all very armed, Mikhail. It would be rude to pat them down when they are here for a social call." Now she focused on Lainey, who met her gaze with equal grace.

"Absolutely a social call, Mrs. Waldemar. A long overdue one."

"I couldn't agree more. Well, come in, all of you. Jackets on the hooks then this way to the kitchen. I'm working on a new recipe, and I do love to chat while I'm making food."

Mayhem followed a half-step behind her, and I moved with her. Bodhi would wait for Adam and Ezra to clear the entrance before he followed. One of us would be on point with Lainey or pulling rearguard. Particularly with Ezra's penchant for running.

Mayhem hadn't worn a long coat, but she did unbutton her blazer as she followed. The kitchen was a bright, cheerful yellow. Fresh flowers sat in a vase on a table. While there were chairs, there was also bench seating.

The place reminded me a little of Ms. Stephanie's, and a pang went through me. Little touches of personality were everywhere. The only thing missing were framed photos of *people*. What photos were present reminded me of the kind that came with an image of a plant or a flower already in them when you bought them.

"Would you like some help, Mrs. Waldemar?" Mayhem asked as she set her purse down on the table.

"Do you cook?" The woman pivoted to look at her, curiosity plain in her eyes. "And please, call me Margareta or Reta."

"Not formally," Lainey said as she slipped out of the blazer and then unbuttoned her shirt at the wrists to begin rolling up the sleeves. "Most of what I learned, I learned in the kitchen with Marlene. She's an excellent teacher. Of course, if you'll call me Lainey."

Margareta studied her. "I would like that very much." She glanced past Mayhem to all of us. "Make yourselves comfortable, gentlemen. Coffee?"

"Please," Bodhi said in that laconic style of his. I stripped off my jacket and laid it over Mayhem's, then unbuttoned my shirt at the cuffs.

"I can chop," I offered. From the look of it, she was working on a stew.

Amusement curved Margareta's lips. "I knew I liked you —Milo."

"Thank you."

Within a few minutes, she had me chopping the carrots she'd peeled. Lainey worked on potatoes. Margareta prepared the coffee.

I could almost see the vein throbbing in Adam's forehead, but he kept his opinions to himself. Smart.

"How is your mother, dear?" Margareta asked, her focus on Lainey. "Or is that not a comfortable question. I know there was some issue between the two of you and your grandfather, so forgive me if I am treading into unwelcome territory."

"She's doing as well as can be expected," Lainey replied in this cool tone. "We don't see much of each other, no."

"I'm sorry."

Lainey gave a little shrug. "My grandparents are wonderful, and I wanted for nothing."

Lifting her cup to sip, Margareta nodded. She waited until Lainey transferred a half-dozen of the cubed potatoes before she continued. "Leopold is something of an austere man, fierce in business and in his collections. Also, very protective of his family."

"He is," Lainey said, wiping off her hands before she reached for the coffee that she'd been ignoring. "We're very close. He's taught me a lot—I'd say everything he knows, but I can't imagine passing on the wealth of his knowledge would be particularly easy."

"You are a wise girl. Our children don't always understand that our lives are well-lived before them. Too often— well—too often they think they know better than their elders." She flicked a glance at me.

I could have imagined it, but I didn't think so.

"You sound like you're speaking from experience." Lainey flashed her a smile. "I don't think I've met any of your family."

Margareta's smile dimmed, then she glanced away from all of us. Her attention was out the window toward the garden that seemed barren still, courtesy of winter.

"Unfortunately, my husband and I were only blessed with one child. We had a falling out years ago. My husband —" She turned to look at us, her gaze sweeping from Lainey to Bodhi to Adam and Ezra before coming to me. "He could be difficult. Everything had to be just so, and he did not care for disagreements or disobedience. Their last argument was..."

She let out a sigh, then shook her head as if trying to dispel the past.

"Jürgen left. We never saw him again, then he died." Disappointment filled her expression, and even I felt a twinge of sympathy. Lainey wiped off her hands before she held out one to her.

"I am sorry," Lainey said. "I didn't mean to dredge up bad memories."

Gripping her hand easily, Margareta summoned a smile. "Sometimes, I forget how stubborn Jürgen was. He and his father were too much alike; neither would bend. Now they are both gone."

The silence lingered like a dark cloud had filled the room, and Lainey didn't let go of Margareta's hand. The older woman seemed to be clinging desperately. Desperation was not a word I would associate with her.

"My sister's children survive, so I spend the time on them and on her grandchildren. It's almost like having my own." Then she gave herself a shake. "Now I have gone and made all of us maudlin."

"Apparently, difficult relations with family is something we have in common."

There was no missing the unspoken "all" in her sentence. I was guessing with Bodhi, but based on what I'd seen with Ezra and Adam, it wasn't hard to imagine his family relations were difficult.

Mine was a complete dick.

"But you have your grandparents," Margareta said, all of that focus lasered onto Lainey. It was hard to get a read on her. She went from deeply sad to wildly mercurial. Right now, I wasn't sure what to make of her expression. "Family is important, but it's also what we make it. Make the most of the people around you, young lady. Temper and intractability cost me precious time with my son and a future I could have had with him…"

"I understand. Some relationships though," Lainey told her as she returned to chopping the potatoes. "Some relationships are not so easily repaired."

"No, but the only regret you should have when you look back is that the attempt didn't work. Not that you didn't make the attempt." Suddenly, Margareta bustled into action again. She refilled the coffees and then swept all the vegetables together and added them to a huge roaster she had prepared with meat in the center.

It would be a few hours before it was ready.

"Now, I'm sure you didn't come all this way to listen to me muddle on about old family business. Adam indicated this was a matter of some importance. Though I am enjoying the fact you brought all of these fine young men with you. There has been quite the discussion over whom you'll end up selecting."

I didn't roll my eyes, but Lainey shook her head. "Definitely not here to gossip."

"Very well." The playful remark was almost too playful. "Do tell me in advance if you wouldn't mind. Sometimes there are bets during the auctions, and I'd love to have one over on the Adleys."

"You seem to enjoy having one over on everyone." There was direct, then there was the way Lainey studied Margareta and the way the woman in turn focused on her.

"I believe powerful women should support each other. I also believe that power is only useful if it can be secured, maintained, and used when appropriate."

"Like having someone kidnap a dancer and her boyfriend in order to get one over on another player in this —rather three-dimensional form of chess?"

Margareta didn't even flinch. "Sometimes, one must get one's hands dirty in order to achieve the goal. I believe the dancer is fine, as is her young man."

"You sound proud of the choice." Lainey did puzzled well.

"I was seeking an ally. The action brought me Adam. He's a dear boy and very stubborn. He reminds me of my Jürgen, but Jürgen never had the patience to do what Adam has done. So I appreciate that distinction."

Setting her coffee cup down, Lainey traced a nail around the edge of the mug. Was she weighing the next move? They'd been dancing verbally rather neatly.

Though I was suspicious of any answer we achieved that was too easy, I had to admit there was a kind of respect unfolding between them. Lainey wasn't pretending Margareta wasn't dangerous. For her part, Margareta wasn't pretending Mayhem was a fool.

Would her next move be a feint or...

"Speaking of Adam—and Milo—and everyone else, why do you want Julius King dead?"

Definitely not a feint, and I kept my gaze on Margareta as Bodhi shifted his weight. There was movement in the hall behind me.

It was Margareta's move.

EIGHTEEN

LAINEY

argareta Waldemar was an enigma. On the one hand, she was everything familiar about a matron of a wealthy family. Erudite and classy, she could more than hold her own on any number of topics. There was a genuine warmth to her, present as we worked together to chop and prepare vegetables.

The fondness that appeared in her eye when she glanced around the room at Adam or Milo wasn't lost on me. Nor was the fact that she spoke to her guards like they were family. Despite all of this, she wore power like an empress who did not need to defend her crown.

She knew exactly who she was, and she was extremely comfortable with it. Yet, her story about loss, about the falling out between her son and her husband—it resonated. For all the issues I had with my mother, she was still my mother. I didn't want her to die.

The cognitive dissonance of so many competing aspects

of this woman being true had me asking her about King. Clearly, she wanted him gone. But why?

Her methods involved leveraging Adam, kidnapping Em, and, for some reason, seeking out Milo whether in person or via Adam. The enemy of our enemy didn't mean she was our friend. Yet, she wanted to be, and that only made me more suspicious.

As fascinating as the whole interaction was, I stepped outside of the social dance to be direct. "Speaking of Adam —and Milo—and everyone else, why do you want Julius King dead?"

Silence flooded the room. The shifting sands of tension seemed almost loud against the tapestry of quiet. Margareta wiped her hands on a towel before she turned to fill a kettle with water.

Each action she took was measured and precise. Gathering the time she needed to decide her answer, perhaps? Or maybe self-soothing. I couldn't really tell.

My awareness of the guys seemed to climb higher. Milo was within arm's reach, and Bodhi had never sat down. While Adam and Ezra had, they were both in chairs that were easily abandoned.

"I applaud your directness," Margareta said as she faced me once more. "It's a rare quality these days, particularly in social settings."

"We're not exactly in a social setting," I reminded her. "Your kitchen. Your rules."

Amusement appeared in the form of a brief smile that vanished as she pressed her index finger to her lips as though shushing. "You have a point."

"Thank you."

Her gaze turned, assessing as she met mine, then she

looked at Milo. "As you are all present, may I presume we can all be as direct with each other?"

"Frankly, I prefer directness to all this fancy dancing around the damn topic." Milo met her stare evenly. "If you have questions, ask."

"That doesn't sound like you are saying you will answer all of them." The fact she tested Milo irritated me on a level I had to smother for the moment. It was movement, and we needed movement.

"As you've proven a fount of answers for all our questions," he retorted, "I see it as an equitable exchange."

"I do like him," Margareta said to me as though in confidence. "A kind of noble abrasiveness."

"Then answer him," Bodhi suggested. "Because if we're doing an exchange of questions, I'm calling dibs on going next."

The droll remark was perfectly delivered. Even Margareta laughed. "Very well, I will answer you shortly, Lainey. However," she continued, sobering. "I'd like to know more about your relationship to Julius King, Milo, and to your mother. You do work for him, currently, or has that ended?"

"His name isn't Julius King, or at least it wasn't. It was Jeff Hardigan. He was with my mother long enough to father a couple of kids, get her hooked on drugs, then abandon her when she kept using his product."

The recitation was delivered with a kind of banality that hurt my whole heart. He'd long accepted the abandonment. Long accepted that Jeff Hardigan hadn't loved him or Em.

"The day he decided to leave, he ordered me to go with him. I refused. It pissed him off. I wouldn't leave my mother or my sister. He walked, I stayed. My mother died of an overdose a few weeks later, and Ivy and I ended up in the system."

Milo lifted his shoulders in a kind of careless shrug of a man who'd *accepted* that he couldn't change what had already happened. Yet, he'd proven himself a man far better than his father at the age of seven, and he continued to prove it day after day.

"Flash forward a few years, I get word that someone is trying to take me down, take down the Vandals. It all tied back the Royals." He jerked a thumb toward Ezra and Adam. "They worked for King, ergo, he was the one who wanted me taken out. So when you ask me what is my relationship to him, I don't have one. I despise the man and everything he stands for, and the only reason I haven't killed him is I don't know what his endgame is and what could be triggered if I do."

"A child should never be put in the position of having to kill their parent." Margareta seemed deeply saddened.

"He was never a parent," Milo said. "Even now, everything he's done has been to put the screws to me, to keep me under his thumb. He *wants* a relationship with my sister."

"She won't because of how you have been treated." It was an accurate assessment, if missing a few other details. I didn't clarify, nor did Milo.

"More or less," he said. "So if the point of your question is, am I going to stand in the way of you killing him? No. I'm not."

"It was and it wasn't. You seemed like a good boy. An intelligent one. Julius King may have a monstrous side, but he is also cunning in a way few men are. He's skilled at manipulation and making others beholden to him. If he can blackmail, intimidate, bribe—or seduce—he will. It has proven successful for him over and over."

I grimaced when she glanced at me.

"You interest him, because you have a significant power base, one you need none of these young men to secure."

"I'm aware." Apparently, my inheritance brought all the insanity to the yard.

"No one will touch her," Bodhi said, his calm voice a reminder that he was still waiting his turn.

"Good," she said, then placed her hands on the kitchen counter. "This will get bloody, there is no avoiding it. Your families are all involved in one way or another."

I raised my eyebrows.

"Yours dear, because of who you are..."

"If you go anywhere near my grandfather..." I warned her.

A soft laugh escaped her. "No, you misunderstand, and do not worry about Leopold. That old goat is more than capable of defending himself and taking down others as well. There's a reason King has kept himself at a distance from him. Even the Reeds are wise to be wary of Leopold."

She flicked a look to Adam then Ezra before returning her focus to me. I had to resist following her gaze to them. They'd sat through this whole conversation without trying to take over. They'd *trusted* me to handle it, and they were still trusting me.

"It sounds like you know Lainey's grandfather well," Bodhi said.

"We have dined occasionally, and I am very observant. His fondness for her is impossible to miss. The games you've all been playing while you didn't know all the players—it's dangerous. Yet you've managed well."

"Who said we don't know all the players?" Bodhi's

question pulled all of her attention. "Only fools show their whole hand. It's why you're using emotion and tangled relationships to distract from Lainey's initial question."

I hadn't forgotten that I'd asked it, but the way Margareta compressed her lips suggested that he wasn't wrong.

"While you continue to play the deflect, deny, and distraction game, I'll take my turn to ask a question." He didn't shift from where he leaned against the wall. "You have a connection to one of them that has nothing to do with King."

I felt more than saw Adam stand. "Excuse me."

"I didn't hear a question, Mr. Cavendish," Margareta told him.

"I haven't asked it yet. You're a wealthy woman. You are connected overseas. Your connections in the city are tenuous, yet there is no door that is closed to you. You have a small army securing your compound, but they are the souls of discretion. Your people move like Bratva, or mafia, not standard soldiers."

Did they? The details sent a chill up my spine as Bodhi listed them out.

"Public details about you are harmless, banal, and rather incongruous when examined by anyone who met you. Your connection to the Reeds is unlikely. You wouldn't have taken Adam to work for you if you were connected. Yes, you wanted him to get at King, but you've resisted sending him. Why? I would imagine you've already grown fond of him. Does he remind you of your son in some way?"

Her expression drained of emotion the longer Bodhi spoke. The warmth disappeared behind chilly eyes that made me apprehensive.

"Milo was probably just a target, a way to get King

through his son until you met him. Then you found yourself intrigued. In all likelihood, another reminder of the son you lost. Your grief is visceral, and suffocating. Yet, you do not give into it. Instead of targeting Milo to use him as leverage, you sent Adam to befriend him. Again—it could be the enemy of my enemy. But I don't think so."

We were all listening to Bodhi as he laid it all out. The connections, tenuous as they might be, were there. She had expressed an interest in Milo since the night of the auction when I'd had to toss a drink in his face to give the appearance of a tiff.

"Definitely not Graham, though you have an interest there. He's too wild and out of control between his drinking and other bad habits. But he's useful, because unlike Adam or Milo, he could be malleable in the right hands. Maybe the hands of your sister's children? Is that what you call the Dovzhenkos?"

"What the hell?" Ezra was on his feet, and I held up a hand to stop his rush forward even as Adam gripped his shoulder.

"How did you put that together?" Margareta asked, her tone as cool as her eyes. "There are no public ties between us."

"You mentioned your sister's children and grandchildren." Bodhi shrugged. "Another tie to bind yet another Royal to you."

"If you're correct," Margareta said, seemingly regaining her equilibrium. "I do know the Dovzhenkos. They are—tied up with some very influential and powerful people in Eastern Europe. Unfortunately, those ties meant they had to relocate to New York."

"So you just, keep an eye on them?" Bodhi didn't believe her for a moment. To be fair, neither did I.

"I keep my eye on everyone, Mr. Cavendish. You, for example, are deeply unpredictable. You make it even harder to track your movements, much less your interests—until New Year's."

She flicked a look to me.

"I protect what's mine," Bodhi said flatly. "I will also protect what is hers."

Warmth spread out from my core because there was no mistaking his menace for anything other than what it was —a warning.

"I am no threat to Lainey," Margareta said, and I spared her a look. If she was tied to the Dovzhenkos, I would question that. Especially after what happened to Ezra.

"Are you sure about that?" I asked. "We're still not positive Oksana didn't poison Ezra."

That earned me arched brows. "How would she have poisoned him?"

"We're looking into that, and if she did do it..." I spread my hands. I let the implication hang there for a moment. "Like Bodhi said, I will also protect what is mine."

I didn't really care if they were connected, though I did experience some disappointment at the concept. The drift of Ezra brushing against my back had me holding out a hand to him.

He clasped it easily. Chin dipped, Margareta studied all five of us and then began to nod. "You just might be able to do what you say."

If she was only going to talk in riddles, however, we needed to leave.

"You asked me why I wanted King dead," she said, folding one hand over the other. The relaxation in her demeanor was absolutely feigned. This was another move in the game we'd been playing.

She was right about one thing. I had been trapped in a game where I didn't know all the players. That was changing.

"Julius King killed my son."

Just like that—the game changed.

Again.

CHAPTER

NINETEEN

EZRA

"*J*ulius King killed my son."

Of all the answers the old woman could have given, that was not even on my radar. Not even after she said her son had died. What did I know about Waldemar? Not enough, clearly. Not nearly as much as Bodhi seemed to know. Cavendish's intel was—*impressive*.

Didn't that sting to admit? Then there was the Oksana connection. Was she related? Was all of this part of some elaborate plot that had been unfolding for *years*? I wanted to go to my father and demand answers—go to Oksana and her family—and at the same time I never wanted to see any of them again.

My head whirled with all the new information and the implications it suggested. Margareta Waldemar had been quietly, effectively setting up a power base, inserting herself into all of our lives via the social circles. She courted allies while also setting us up.

Setting *us* up because of King. I couldn't wrap my brain

171

all the way around it. We'd been playing a game against far more opponents than any of us had been aware of. Worse, we'd been *played*.

I barely registered the rest of the conversation. A glance at Adam's stony expression reminded me that in the past couple of days, his whole life had been flipped—again.

His sister was missing. His father was dead—not that I felt an ounce of remorse about that. Harper Reed had been a bastard. Almost as bad as my own father. I wish Adam didn't have to suffer for any of it.

Then again, he'd kissed me. Really kissed me. We'd stood in that hot steamy bathroom while he only wore a towel. His skin had been burning under my fingers and his hair damp, then all I could think about was the way he'd dominated that kiss.

As terrified as it left me, I couldn't help but revel in the contact. We'd made out like teenagers. Despite the fact I'd ended up with the most painful erection and based on the tent in his towel, so had he—it hadn't gone any further.

Yet, he'd slept right next to me like it was the most normal thing in the world. Was all of this happening? My wildest dreams amongst some of my worst nightmares? The insanity of it all gripped me.

"We'll be a bit," Bodhi was saying. We were in his apartment. The realization sank into me belatedly. I'd been too preoccupied to pay much attention. Lainey had been holding my hand in the car, and I just followed her when she moved. "I want to verify some information. Particularly now that we have some idea of Waldemar's motives."

"You're going with him?" She turned her gaze to Milo. I leaned back against the sofa. Adam had vanished into the kitchen, but the other three weren't really paying attention to me.

"Yes," Milo said. "You need some time and none of us are running alone. Not while we have this many threats out there. Don't leave the apartment?"

"I won't," she said so easily I nearly gaped. Lainey didn't cooperate when we were protective. What prompted this? "Ezra really needs to rest and I'm—tired."

That admission did have me straightening.

"We can wait," Bodhi said, his attention intent on her. "If you need us here, we can wait."

"I will always need you," she said, and my heart fisted in my chest. "But you're right. I don't know what to do with Margareta's news. The fact that Oksana's family may be tied to her and that she blames King for her son's death. It's a lot. Harper was a lot. Andrea..."

"We'll find her," Milo said with a kind of certainty I wished I possessed. "Trust me on that one. None of us are giving up."

She nodded and I blew out a breath. "We need to warn Liam."

It had been niggling at the back of my mind. As much as Liam had distanced himself and King seemed to be leaving him alone—he was still considered a Royal. He still had ties to King. Waldemar had targeted him once already.

Now that she seemed to be reconsidering her options, she could easily send someone after him again.

"I'll call him," Milo said with a swift nod. "The Vandals will have his back. They'll have ours too. When we know who and where we're moving, I'll call them."

That was a concession for him. His protective streak towards Emersyn ran deeper and more firmly in some ways than ours had for Lainey. The Vandals were his family though, and they were a tough set of bastards.

"Good plan."

"Be safe," Lainey ordered, and she pushed up on her toes to kiss Milo. He wrapped her up, and I had to glance away from the intensity of the moment. The way he held her and she gripped him. It seemed so intensely private.

Then she was shifting to kiss Bodhi. That was still weird. The jealousy that normally clawed its way through me seemed—less somehow. I didn't stare, and I couldn't say I was a fan, but what had Adam said?

I didn't hate it.

"Stay inside, stay secure. Engage the alarm. It will alert me if anything happens," Bodhi ordered and she followed them to the door, then closed and locked it behind them. A moment later, there was a chime from the alarm as she engaged it.

Done, she pivoted to lean against the door before pulling off one heel and then the other. The shoes dangled from her fingers as she lifted her gaze to meet mine.

"Hi," I said. What a small, uninteresting word. "How are you doing?"

Pushing away from the door, she prowled toward me. It was definitely a prowl and not a stroll. "I should be asking you that."

"I'm tired, but I'll be fine." The ache in my chest had lessened. "I've had worse bruises." I was pretty sure the compressions and the cardio shock or whatever hadn't done me any favors—well besides saving my life.

She trailed her fingers down my chest to rest over my heart. A shadow drifted through those hazel eyes, darkening them. "I hate that you were hurt," she murmured. "I hate that you have had worse."

I covered her hand on my chest, then lifted it to kiss her palm. There were scrapes present there. They'd been circumspect about her "captivity" and subsequent rescue. I hadn't been oblivious to the bruises on her arms or her legs despite how skillfully she disguised everything.

"I hate that I wasn't there when you needed me and that—that my choice left you undefended." That guilt weighed on me. Not one of the guys had torn into me over it, but I felt it. In every single glance or considering stare, the knowledge that she'd been left alone to be taken had been due to my choices.

"It was my choice to go to my apartment. We thought it was Andrea." Pain flickered across her face, and I pressed my lips to her forehead. She spread her fingers over my chest, right over my heart, and I closed my eyes.

The contact steadied me in a way I didn't want to explore or explain. Instead, I reveled in it. Gripping her biceps gently, I tugged her forward and then wrapped my arms around her. She burrowed against my chest, and that bruise on my heart seemed to expand and contract with every beat.

My kotyonok was hurting. I was part of the reason. "I'm sorry," I whispered.

"I know," she said, accepting it so easily. But...

"No," I said, firming my voice and pulling back so I could meet her gaze again. "I'm truly sorry. I've put you through hell and I keep doing it. I have no idea why you put up with me."

"I love you," she told me as if it were all that simple. "I don't always care for your methods or your choices. To be honest, you do frustrate me. You frustrated me when you and Adam treated me like a child. You drove me crazy by always trying to keep me on a leash or in a cage you created... then you both changed the rules."

She dug her teeth into her perfect lower lip. That bruise in my chest deepened.

"I love you," she said again. "It's not the only answer. It might not even be the best answer. It is, however, the answer that tells me you're worth it. I will always fight for you."

"You know I'll always fight for you too." She had to know that. I needed her to know it, to be certain.

"Then you have to fight for *you* too," she whispered, fisting my shirt. "I know you heard me earlier...but I need you to hear me now. You *have* to *fight* for yourself. No more giving up on us or you. We'll face all of this together. If your father so much as looks at you again..."

"I'll kill him," Adam said from behind me in a cold tone that carried the sting of a whip on the last syllable. Still holding Lainey, I twisted so we could both see him. His blue-violet eyes seemed almost purple in how dark they'd gone. "I'm not kidding. He never touches you again. He doesn't get the opportunity to threaten or beat or harm you again. Period."

"I'll help," Lainey said in a voice that dared me to disbelieve her. "No one gets to hurt either of you again. Ever."

Rather than scoff, Adam dipped his gaze to her and his whole expression softened. It gentled for *her*. Of course it did, we both did. She was the one person we always agreed on. Even when we disagreed—that had more to do with jealousy than anything else.

"Have I ever mentioned how sexy you are when you get protective?"

Her laughter was low, but there was pleasure in her amusement. "Trying to tell me something?"

"If he isn't, I am," I said and tugged both of their attention to me. That...that attention was an embrace that I craved as it wrapped around me. "We've always protected you because *you* are the most precious person to us. But you aren't fragile. If anything—you remind me of an Amazon warrior, proud to stand up for herself and everyone around her."

"Well," she said with a little hum in her throat. "It's about time you two noticed."

Adoration, exasperation, and amusement filled Adam's expression. The combination was intoxicating. "I noticed a long time ago. Your heart and your daring—you were always taking risks, and if anything had happened to you…"

That killed some of my humor, and I tightened my grip around her. "What he said. It's why I nearly lost my mind when both of you went missing at the same time."

It wasn't until Adam gripped my shoulder that I realized I'd begun shaking.

"I know why, *now*," I assured them. "But I hated it. I hated being here and not wherever you two were—especially when I found out you weren't together. Liam—the bastard—left me tied up for two days while he figured shit out."

"To get you out of the way or to keep you out of trouble?" The guarded question from Adam made me laugh, and I met his gaze easily.

"Yes—to both. To be fair, he was right to do it. I wasn't thinking, I just reacted. They were trying to get Em out of Pinetree, and you were in Braxton Harbor." The last I directed at Lainey. "I didn't know that then, but…yeah."

Lainey wrapped around me tighter, then Adam wrapped his arms around me from the back. They were holding onto each other, but they were also cradling me. Closing my eyes, I drank in their nearness.

Both of them.

This—this was what I'd been missing. Even that first night we'd finally shared her, we hadn't had this. Lainey lifted her head, and I met her gaze. I had no idea which of us moved first, but I closed my mouth over hers. Her lips parted, and I tasted her sweetness.

The squeeze of my heart redoubled as I glided my hand down to her ass. When she scraped her teeth over my lower lip, I laughed. The sound startled me as it broke free. My kotyonok had sharp teeth.

Then Adam shifted and swooped in to kiss her. We were all hooked together. He had an arm around my shoulders and one around hers. She had arms around both of our waists, and I found myself stroking his hair as the two of them blurred together.

A sigh escaped me, and then they were breaking apart. Her lips glistened and so did his. The last thing I expected was Adam to kiss me, but then he did, and I tasted them both on my tongue.

The world spun, and I swore it was like falling on a roller coaster and surging back up again. Impossible delight poured into my veins with every hammer of my pulse.

Lainey groaned, and that had me pulling back, and we both stared at her as she licked her lips. "Don't stop on my account," she whispered. "That was... amazing and hot."

Genuine pleasure shimmered in her eyes, and I kissed her again, then Adam ran a hand up my back before he fisted my hair. When he dragged me backward, I found him staring at me.

"We have time," he said. "Right now. All three of us."

A shudder went through me.

"You in?" The question pinged through me like a pinball, and it struck against one of the bells over and over again, almost jamming there as if as undecided as I was.

"Please," Lainey whispered, and I didn't miss the way

Adam smiled for the hint of wonder under the word. Fuck, I couldn't help but be delighted by it.

"I want you," I told Adam. "But you don't have to do anything you don't want to do. I meant it when I said I could be satisfied with just sharing Lainey."

My dick thickened in my pants, the pulse of heat in my spine seeming to flood my balls. The idea of being with them both either to share Lainey or to genuinely share Adam as well? Yeah, I wanted that.

But I wanted Adam happy more than anything. I needed them both to be happy.

"I want to know," Adam said. "I told you we'd figure this out...and we're going to."

Holy shit. Shock held me captive. My gaze locked on his and I forgot how to breathe.

For real? He wanted—*me*?

The answer burned in his gaze.

He wanted me. He wanted her.

He wanted us.

I was dizzy from the admission.

Then Lainey was pulling away, and it cracked through the moment. She unbuttoned her jacket and began sauntering to the stairs.

"Come along, boys—the first one naked in that room is getting a blow job and the second one..." She tossed a wicked look over her shoulder. "He gets my pussy—for round one."

Round one.

Neither of us moved until she hit the second step, and then we were running and a kind of wild laughter exploded out of me. It was a freedom I hadn't ever felt.

A freedom to be me and to enjoy them.

I didn't even care that Adam made it in there first. We were all going to win.

TWENTY

LAINEY

It was like a wildness spilled into me. Grief and worry had a chokehold on my heart. Grief for Ezra's suffering, worry for Andrea, and yes—even for my mother. More worry for my grandfather and what this would all do to him.

Still more again for Adam. Sooner or later the grief for his father would hit him. No matter how much he hated him or how invested in his death he'd been. Harper Reed had still been his father. After Margareta's confessions, my brain was a wild morass of confusion.

Our problems seemed to keep mounting. We could handle it. I knew we could, because Bodhi had been armed with the most powerful tool of all—information. Now he was out gathering more. Need to take care of something had me on edge, then I'd had that front row seat to Adam and Ezra's kiss.

The heat burning in their connection had dampness

soaking my panties and desire twining through me. They...
were beautiful together. I'd never seen how they looked
when they kissed, not like this. Not the way the muscles in
their jaws flexed or how their stances shifted to brace each
other.

They never let go of me as they soaked in each other's
touch, and I wanted more. More for me. More for them. We
had a few hours and...then I threw that dare out there and
headed up the stairs.

I diverted into the room they'd been sharing, my shirt
was off, and I'd shimmied out of my skirt. Adam made it
through the door a split second before Ezra did, and I got to
enjoy the visual of them stripping. Adam's cock sprang free
a half-a-heartbeat before Ezra's did, and I ran my tongue
over my lower lip as I crawled onto the bed.

With a curl of my finger, I beckoned Adam to me. There
was no hesitation, no preparation, just the heat of his cock
stroking my lips. Droplets of pre-cum were like a salty
mixture to gloss my mouth before I opened to take him all
the way to my throat.

"Fuck," Ezra whispered as he watched me, and I opened
my eyes to meet his wild green eyes. The naked desire in
them detonated fresh need in my belly. Adam fisted my hair
and thrust deep.

Yes, that was what I wanted. I wanted to feel them both
so deep that it left marks on my soul. Ezra stroked my cheek
then slid his hand to my throat. On Adam's next thrust, he
squeezed gently.

Black spots danced before my eyes, and I groaned. I
wasn't alone in the sound, because Adam let out a moan so
dirty and hedonistic, I swore my pussy clenched, desperate
for something to fill it.

"Thick man, filling her throat like that." Ezra glanced

from me up to Adam. "You like the feel of her choking on you..." He flexed his fingers lightly on the next thrust, and I dug my fingers into the duvet.

The wickedest little laugh escaped Ezra, but he didn't stay there, because Adam held onto my hair while he also gripped Ezra's. Then, continuing to thrust, he pulled Ezra up to him and they were kissing again.

Tears spilled out of my eyes at the force of the thrusts and the absolute beauty in their kiss. Chest to chest, they touched and devoured each other in equal measure. Then Adam slid his hand down from Ezra's hair.

Only the fact he stilled, with the heavy weight of his cock on my tongue, allowed me the perfect view of the next moment. Adam wrapped his hand around Ezra's straining cock. The beautiful pierced length of it seemed to flex at the touch.

A shocked gasp came out of Ezra's throat as Adam stroked him from balls to tip, and again. The raw bliss on Ezra's face captivated me, then I tracked my gaze to Adam's. Naked want blazed there, but beyond that were questions.

And most vulnerable of all—uncertainty.

The man who wanted to control everything wanted to do this, but he wasn't sure how. When I raised my eyebrows, I asked him if he needed me to take this. To let me command.

His head tipped back, and I swiped my tongue over his slit. He let out a hiss of breath even as he kept stroking Ezra. They were trapped again in a cocoon of hunger and pining.

With another thrust, Adam pushed into my throat and then dropped his gaze to look at me. The blue-violet of his eyes seemed to be clashing between what color was predominant.

Then he mouthed the word "please."

I swallowed around his cock, teased my tongue along the underside of it, and he gave a little buck before I pulled off of him. Covering his hand on Ezra's dick, I grinned. Ezra jerked his pleasure-drunk gaze toward me.

"Kotyonok?" So much meaning punched up the endearment. I walked my hand up Adam's chest as I helped stroke Ezra. Yeah, his pupils were so dilated, we could barely see the color of them anymore.

"Let me?" I whispered. It was the same question I'd asked Adam. *Let me be in control. Give it to me.* How many times had he been raw, dominant, and demanding? He'd fucked me until I couldn't walk before and owned every moment of it.

"Yes," he said it almost reverently. "Anything you want."

Anything? "Do you want to taste Adam?" I leaned forward and swiped my tongue against the tip of Adam's dick, collecting the pre-cum. He hissed out a breath at the teasing touch.

Then I turned to kiss Ezra. He plunged his tongue against mine, seeking the taste with a kind of desperation I understood. How long had the three of us wanted? That first time with Ezra had been a total loss of control. With Adam, it had been like a fever.

Even when Ezra joined us though, he'd fought for control. Pulling back, I licked my lips. I could taste Adam, and Ezra still looked dazed.

Teasing my fingers over his piercing, I dipped down again to lap at Ezra's pre-cum. I didn't even get a chance to ask. Adam fisted my hair and pulled me up. He kissed me like a man on a mission. A part of me wanted to tease him, to keep those drops to myself.

They were both breathing raggedly when Adam lifted his head. Who was I kidding? We were all panting. I wanted them both, any way I could have them. They looked at each other and at me—torn.

"I've learned something over the last year," I whispered to them, barely recognizing my own voice. "Surrender is a beautiful thing."

Adam's eyes narrowed and Ezra bumped his hips forward because I had slowed my strokes.

"Trust me," I said. Maybe they were still struggling with trust in their shifting relationship. Fine, I could be the bridge to help them get there.

"Yes," Ezra said a half-a-breath behind Adam. Warmth bloomed like a hot summer breeze blew right through me. I eyed all of us and where we were.

"Adam, on the bed, stand up over the pillows." There was a place for him to grab the headboard if he needed it.

Surprise appeared on both of their faces, but Adam moved then I twisted and scooted until I was between his legs and looking up at that beautiful cock.

"Ezra, take my panties off." I hadn't had a chance to yet.

"Yes, Kotyonok," Ezra said, wasting no time in hooking his fingers in the side of my panties and peeling them down. He paused to lick me from entrance to clit and then back again before swirling his tongue around. "You're soaked for us..."

A laugh escaped me as I arched my hips. "Yes, I am." I met Adam's gaze as he stared down at me. I worked the bra free and then tossed it away. "I want you to fuck me, Ezra— fill—fuck."

I forgot how to think because he buried himself to the hilt. No hesitation, no preparation. The stretch burned in all the right ways. The play of his piercings were a reminder of how good they felt.

"I like this," Ezra said with the most delightful grin as he glanced down at me then at Adam's dick. "Oh..."

"Yes," I said, careful to push the word out. "Adam's going to fuck your throat, and you're going to fuck me. And a little later, we can trade."

I gripped Adam's calves, a reminder that I was there. I swore his dick flexed at my description. Ezra looked back at me, dazed, and then up again.

"Do you want to swallow my cock?" Adam asked him. The heat of his skin seemed to redouble, and his voice was harsh and breathless.

With a bump of his hips, Ezra pulled back and then thrust deeply. "Fuck yes...I can have both of you at the same time?"

I licked my lips as Ezra traced his tongue along the underside of Adam's dick. It was like he had to test the waters; he had to know. Adam let out a long breath and then a very heated, "Fuck!"

"Yeah." Ezra exhaled. "My thoughts exactly." Then he wrapped his mouth around Adam's cock and swallowed against it. I braced Adam's legs as he took hold of Ezra's hair.

The muscles along his neck went a little rigid, standing out as he gritted his teeth.

"He's got an incredible mouth," I whispered and Adam let out a short laugh.

"But he's forgetting to fuck you," he said it in the most aggrieved tone. While he was still buried inside of me, I didn't mind the lack of action. "Bad Ezra."

Ezra tried to thrust but even as he did, his head slowed on his sucking and swallowing.

"Poor thing," I said with a gasping laugh. "His mouth is full so he can't get himself in trouble."

"Hmmm," Adam said and there was something dark and delicious in his tone. "May I amend your plans?"

Ezra had one hand around the base of Adam's cock and he reached for my breast with the other. The pinch of his twisting grasp stung the nipple, but it just spiked the pleasure.

"Anything you want..."

"Anything?" Adam checked and Ezra went completely still. That question hadn't been directed at me. I waited, holding my breath.

Ezra made a low sound in his throat. It sounded like a yes. He also tried to nod, but Adam kept his head in place and pushed his cock deeper into Ezra's throat.

A couple of experimental thrusts and Adam let out a little grunt. "That's a good boy, ease up and relax that jaw. Let me do the work. You're going to take every inch of me."

A shudder rippled through Ezra, and his hips bumped mine. I clenched around him, and he groaned. The sound vibrated through his chest, and Adam hummed.

"That's it... keep taking me." His whole cock vanished into Ezra's mouth, and then he backed off again.

My mouth watered and so did my eyes in sympathy. Drool gathered at the side of Ezra's mouth but vanished when Adam thrust again.

"There we go, just like that," Adam said through gritted teeth. "Now, you fuck her. I'm fucking you, and I'm not coming until you get her off, and you can't come until I do."

The whine of protest that escaped Ezra was so mournful and at the same time, he rocked into me hard enough to push me up on the bed. Oh, hell yes.

"Good, Lainey?"

"Oh yes, please," I whispered. "I want to see you both come."

"You first." Then he began to rock his hips in a matching rhythm to Ezra's, and I shuddered as I watched his slick cock appear and disappear. Ezra dropped both of his hands to my breasts as he gave up all control to Adam, and I wrapped my legs around his hips.

It shifted the angle, and fuck yes, his piercings stroked all the right places. Every push seemed to let his groin tease my clit, then he'd rock me right up to the edge, and a pinch of his fingers to my nipples sent pain feathering through the pleasure.

The edging was unmistakable. Then Adam let out a harsh grunt and a snarl. "Stop playing with her and make her come."

Ezra's laughter revealed the game to me. He was tormenting us both and loving every moment of it. My heart swelled at the thought, and then he stroked my clit as he picked up the pace. Thought collided with feeling, and then I was clamping down on him as I came.

"Thank fuck," Adam roared a sound, and Ezra made a choking sound before Adam pulled back. His cum splashed against Ezra's face, then his chest, and more sprayed onto me.

Instead of slowing down, Ezra pumped his hips harder, chasing his own release. The rush of him filling me had me shuddering all over again. I was lost to the feeling of him and the look of ecstasy on his face.

Adam dropped to the side of me as Ezra collapsed against my chest. He buried his face against my throat, and I lifted my gaze to Adam's. With gentle fingers, he stroked my hair.

"Thank you," he mouthed and then dipped his head to

kiss Ezra's shoulder once before he kissed me. When he wrapped himself against my side, Ezra shuddered all over again. But Adam was pressed up to him too.

He was shaking, and we hugged him between us. Everything had shifted. What bound us together had changed. The change was a welcome one. Eventually, Ezra passed out, spent, and I didn't care about how sticky we all would get. We could clean up later.

Stroking Ezra's hair, Adam looked over at me. The genuine fear in his eyes had me stretching my hand out. He gripped it tightly.

"We'll protect him," I promised. "We'll make this work. One day. One step. One fuck at a time if we have to."

He pressed my hand to his lips and kissed it. "I never knew," he whispered again.

"I know," I told him.

"I damn near lost both of you." That admission cost him. "Now...you have Bodhi and Milo."

"And I have both of you," I reminded him. "We have each other. We'll figure this out..."

He nodded, but I wasn't sure if it was to the first statement or the last. It didn't matter. I wasn't letting go.

"Lainey...?" he said, after a while. I thought he'd gone to sleep.

"Hmm?"

"How do you feel about pegging?"

I opened my mouth, then closed it again. "Never tried it," I admitted finally.

"Me neither," Adam hummed. "Want to?"

"I'm in," Ezra mumbled. "After I come back from the dead."

Even as laughter escaped us, I grinned until my cheeks ached. We had a lot of possibilities to explore. We still had a lot of obstacles too, but I wanted to treasure these moments.

I would treasure them.

We were going to have a hell of a lot more of them too.

I didn't care what I had to do.

TWENTY-ONE

BODHI

Missing kids. The connecting thread tying all these disparate events together. It was right there the whole time. I couldn't see it because I was focused on a small part of the picture.

Milo sat silently in the passenger seat. As with the day before, he hadn't wanted to leave Lainey any more than I had. Those three, however, had issues to work out that required privacy.

In the meanwhile, I wanted to put more resources on the Dovzhenkos. Verifying their ties to Waldemar was the next step. She'd been quite forthcoming. Maybe *too* forthcoming. By the time we returned home the previous night, Lainey and the pair had been absent, tucked away in Adam and Ezra's room.

She came down at breakfast to see us prior to our departure. The weariness around her eyes didn't belong there. It wasn't about the other two. More calls about her mother. There was a real chance she would have to go back to the hospital. So far, there'd been no mention of Harper Reed's "absence."

We'd make arrangements to deal with that soon. Though I had heard that Hamilton was back in town. My contacts kept me well-informed.

What I needed to do next was verify and investigate. Collin expected us at the office, and I would introduce Milo to Cavendish. I should probably arrange security clearances for him so he could come and go as needed.

I added it to my mental to do list. "She needs to see PPG."

Milo shot me a look, then just shook his head. "Yeah, I know. She doesn't want Ivy in the middle of all of this."

"She would want to help."

"You trying to pick a fight with me?" The question seemed to come from nowhere, but I understood the implication.

It was one of the things I liked about Milo. He didn't assume, he asked. Out of respect for his directness, I responded in kind. "No, when I want to fight you, I'll just hit you."

"Reasonable." The droll remark amused me, then he chuckled. "I agree that she needs to see Ivy. I know Ivy would want to be here. But Mayhem would never forgive herself if Ivy got hurt while this battle wages on."

I found no fault with that logic. PPG had been through enough. So had Lainey B. They were both fighters, and the relief of time spent with a best friend? "Then we make it safe for them to see each other."

"What are you thinking?"

"Still working on the plan. Give me a few hours, we're meeting with my cousin Collin about the various research angles." I turned into the underground garage of the

Cavendish building then made a sharp right into the executive lot. "I want to add your potential sibling to the list and anything you know about PPG's adoption."

I let that sit for a moment then slipped out of the car. Milo followed more slowly, his expression guarded. While he was aware that I had a sibling I searched for, he wasn't fully apprised of all the details.

Whatever mental wrestling he needed to do, he finished with a long exhale. "I don't know how much I know, how much we put together, and how much we assumed."

"Fair. There is a nest of connections between all our families. Your biological father is tied up in it as deeply as my own, as Reed was, and as Graham most likely is. The only one I see with clean hands is Leopold."

We were alone in the lot, but I didn't miss the way Milo scanned the area. A wise choice. "I like that old man," Milo admitted.

"So do I." I shrugged. "I think he's clean, or as clean as a person can be and still maintain the wealth and power he's accrued."

"I don't live in a fantasy world. Most of the time, the truth is shit. But I really don't want him to be involved in any of this."

I didn't say anything. I didn't have to. If he were involved, then it would hurt Lainey B. Neither of us wanted that to happen.

Collin waited for us in his office. After introducing them, I took a seat and leaned back in the chair. "Brief us on what you have, and we'll add some more details to try and flesh it out."

~

TWO HOURS LATER, we left Collin with more research. The Sharpes' involvement might be more difficult to trace, but they had staff and employees. Information left a trail *somewhere.*

A message from Lainey detoured us from getting Milo the security access. We'd take care of it later. Instead, we were on our way back to collect her, Adam, and Ezra for a different type of meet and greet.

"You're armed?" I verified with her when she climbed into the back of the SUV. I swapped vehicles since we had to go farther and I wanted her comfortable.

The swift smile she wore needed no definition. She *liked* that I always verified. "Yes," she said. "Three weapons and the taser you left for me."

I nodded.

"You didn't leave me a taser," Ezra grumbled with the faintest spark of humor.

"Stick close to Lainey B; she'll protect you." The dry remark made him laugh, and Milo shook his head. It was Adam who rolled his eyes though.

"At some point," he announced. "I am going to do the driving."

"You can do it right now, except you'd be on your own and we're not running alone." I pinned him with a look, but it was Lainey's gentle hand on him that shut him up.

Good. I didn't mind the fight usually. I wouldn't even mind it now, but we didn't need the delays.

"Look," Milo said over his shoulder. "We're happy to let you play chauffeur at some point. We'll even get you one of those fancy stretch limos so you can be all the way up front. Mayhem would probably enjoy the role play."

The dry comment, delivered without an ounce of humor, crackled in the silence. I snorted, but it was Ezra's snicker that actually splintered the impasse. Lainey's barely suppressed laughter filled the air with a warmth that had been missing.

Eventually, Adam chuckled. "You're an ass, Hardigan."

"You know, I've heard that before," he said without apology. That set Lainey off into a fit of real laughter, bleeding away more of the tension in the vehicle.

Our appointment was in New Jersey. Instead of an address, we had GPS coordinates. I was familiar with the area. A series of old one- and two-story office buildings, sparsely occupied, but still maintained.

It was the perfect place to arrange private meetings where few if no witnesses were the goal. It also meant work could be completed uninterrupted. I appreciated the dedication.

The coordinates took us through the warren of various office buildings to a street that ended in a cul-de-sac in front of a lot populated by huge, oversized trees with grassy spots overtaking the cracked sidewalk.

The exterior of the two-story building boasted the bare minimum of care. Paint peeled from the door and window frames. Chipped brick faces and faded defacement suggested that it had been the victim of tagging at some point.

Still, the fat trees offered shade and disguised the thicker glass panes, security stripping, and the code boxes on the doors. Just because it looked vulnerable and unkempt didn't mean it was.

Lainey's phone buzzed as I parked under one of the larger trees as directed. "Door code," she said.

"You sure about this?" Milo checked with her, then me. I waited on her nod before I added my own. The quiet outside was unnerving. In the distance, the rumble of vehicles passing was just a barely there hum. No voices drifted on the breeze. The wind itself seemed to take on its own level of vibration, whistling and sweeping across the empty lots and around the buildings.

We formed up around Lainey, but Milo dropped back to wrap an arm around her. The cold slice of the breeze threatened a chill. I took point. I'd rather be the first through the door.

She recited the code, and I entered it. The door buzzed, then the series of locks betrayed the rest of the security. For some reason, *that* reveal settled some of my concerns. I pulled the door open, and Milo braced it as I went first. Lainey B was right behind me.

The interior looked more like an interior grotto at some shopping center or cultivated landscaping in a higher end establishment. The warmer, humid air carried the fresh scent of flowers. Running water drifted over rocks and then down a series of splashing steps as though mimicking a waterfall. Thick foliage added a touch of rough nature to the elegant layout.

"What the fuck?" Ezra muttered, and I appreciated the effort.

A flicker of motion had me snapping my attention to the man striding alongside the paradise-like grotto straight toward us. Long dark hair framed a longer face with sharp blue eyes and barely suppressed smile. His beard was neatly clipped, and he sported new tattoos.

Or new since the last time I'd seen him. Fletcher Reed and I went back a long time, though we hadn't been in the same location in more than a decade. He looked good for a man who'd been spiraling then.

"There's my favorite cousin," Fletcher said without giving me a second glance. Lainey surged forward, leaving all of us behind as she half-skipped forward, and then she wrapped her arms around Fletcher's neck and he picked her up.

"Ass," Adam grumbled, but even he wore a hint of a smile as Fletcher spun Lainey around. She allowed it so I didn't comment. Instead I scanned the three others who were following.

The woman—Vienna Drew—I knew very well. More by reputation than anything else, but we'd had the occasion to meet once or twice. Worked together once. If you could call it that.

I tracked past her to the two men following. While she wore an almost indulgent smile as she watched Fletcher with Lainey. The two men with her were new. One was a beast of a man, big and built. There was an ease to his movements, but he studied all of us with the same kind of assessment I used.

The other man though—

"FBI," I warned Milo in a quiet tone and felt more than saw Ezra draw back a step. Didn't know why law enforcement was with them, but I didn't want to take any chances with Lainey.

Fletcher set Lainey down but kept her tucked under his arm as he gripped Adam's hand with a smirk. "She's always going to be the favorite. Besides, she's way prettier *and* nicer than you are."

"All true," Adam commented. "You look good. You look —*real* good."

I agreed. Fletcher looked a hell of a lot healthier. Didn't make me like the presence of law enforcement any better though.

"Don't worry about Cash," Fletcher said, meeting my gaze. "He's our dick though. And not even the biggest."

"Thanks," the man in question said.

"Look, I can't help it if you walk and talk like a cop, man. We've been *trying* to help make you cooler." Fletcher rolled his eyes.

"Retired," Cash said. His posture didn't agree, and he was armed. Not that he made any attempt to hide it. He locked his gaze on me, and I kept my expression neutral. He'd studied every single one of us and then fixed on me.

Threat assessment?

"Really," Fletcher said. "Take the stick out of your ass for a minute, can't possibly be comfortable to sit with it up there."

Lainey chuckled. "Fletcher..."

"Yes, cousin?"

"I'd say behave, but this is entertaining. Still—maybe we should do introductions?"

"Absolutely." He pivoted with her still under his arm. "Drew darling, this is my favorite cousin, Lainey. She's fantastic. Adam's the other cousin. He's a bit of a dick, but I still like him. Actually, outside of Lainey, he's probably my other favorite cousin."

Adam sighed with a hint of a exasperation, and behind us, Ezra actually chuckled. "Fletcher can always tweak him."

I could see that.

"That's Phillip Cavendish, the elegant and dangerous. Don't look at him too mean like there, Cash. Phil's a good guy to have on your side and a terrible enemy. That's Milo Hardigan, he's with the Vandals, so we know him though we haven't worked with him. He and Kellan are good friends, and his sister is the aerialist we saw a few weeks back. That's Ezra Graham hiding back there trying to stay out of trouble."

Lainey elbowed Fletcher, and he mimed an oof before raising his hands in surrender.

"Sorry, you know I have to give him shit."

"Later," Adam suggested. "After we talk."

"Deal," Fletcher said, then swept his arm toward his group. "Lainey, Adam, and company, this is the love of my life Vienna Drew. She's perfection. The guy on her right is Rick. He's the best chef ever and can bench press a car, especially if you don't clean up after yourself."

The monster of a man just snorted with amusement. Clearly used to Fletcher. Made sense.

"The other dick here is Cash Morgan, *former* law enforcement, but all-around enforcer and pain in the ass. He looks a lot scarier than he is."

Right.

Lainey took a step forward toward Vienna and offered her hand. "It's nice to meet you."

"And you," Vienna said easily. "Fletcher told us what happened. That's why we're here—to help."

"Yeah, speaking of which—let's go." Fletcher motioned us forward. "I'll fill you in on everything we've found so far."

CHAPTER

TWENTY-TWO

LAINEY

F letcher hadn't changed one bit, except—he seemed happier. His smile came more swiftly, but his humor was no less biting.

"As fun as hanging out and picking on your taste in friends—Phillip Cavendish?" Fletcher gave me side-eye as we walked.

"We can walk and you can pick on me as we move?" I teased. Vienna had moved up to walk with us on his other side.

"I always did like to multitask."

The guys followed behind us, the tension rising and falling as they eyed each other. Fletcher wouldn't have invited us here for anything nefarious, so I just had to trust the guys could all handle it.

The door Fletcher opened to wave Vienna and me through let out the most delicious scent of fresh-warmed pastries and rich brewed coffee. My stomach growled in appreciation, and I cleared my throat as Vienna actually gave me an amused look.

"Sorry, I didn't realize I was hungry." I hadn't really had much of an appetite for food.

"Don't apologize," Vienna told me. "Rick makes the most wonderful foods, and he spent the morning preparing for us to have company."

She threw a grin toward the man in question. He was huge, fierce, and then he wore the most adorable smile.

"Then I will look forward to trying it."

"Great, let's get everyone coffee and food," Fletcher said as he stripped off his hoodie and directed me toward a computer set up that filled an entire corner of another room. The place had an open office layout, but it seemed cozier.

I'd have to ask later.

Pretty Boy tugged a chair in from the other room for me. I brushed my fingers down his arm in thanks before perching on the chair while Fletcher slid into his seat.

Rick appeared with a small rolling table. There was coffee, and croissants, and something that looked like cheese danishes—maybe. It smelled so good.

It took a moment to sort everyone out. Vienna had her coffee, I had mine, and Fletcher had a big tumbler sitting on his desk. I took one of the croissants to nibble, but I was having a hard time looking away from the multiple screens Fletcher had up.

I'd always known he was talented, but I'd never seen him work before. Adam had taken a position next to me and behind Fletcher. Ezra leaned against the wall between Milo and Bodhi. Bodhi and Cash were both bracketing the entrance to the room while Rick moved over to Vienna.

"I've been tracing Harper's incoming and outgoing calls

for the past two weeks using his main cell, his backup cell, his office phone, the phone in his office at the house, and the secretary VOIP line he started using after he married your mother." The last carried a note of apology.

While I appreciated his attempt to soften it, I didn't need the explanation. It never occurred to me that Harper would be faithful. I rather doubted he'd been "faithful" when my mother had been his mistress and Adam's mother had still been alive.

"These three," Fletcher continued, isolating three numbers and bringing them up larger on the screen nearest me, "are the ones I find the most interesting. The first is located somewhere in the Lake Balaton region. A little more difficult to pinpoint, because it is a mobile phone. But I'm already working on a better program to track it."

Lake Balaton appeared on the screen.

"It's roughly one hundred and thirty-five kilometers southwest of Budapest. The second number is in Rózsadomb, that's in Budapest itself. Very wealthy district. I've got that one down to a couple of streets in the Buda Hills. That leaves this third number…"

Hungary.

Had Harper sold her to someone in Eastern Europe? The croissant, no matter how flakey and buttery, turned to ash on my tongue. How long had she already been there?

Adam gripped my shoulder, and Pretty Boy settled his hand on the other. Their strength grounded me, even as they kept me upright. I didn't want to imagine what was happening to Andrea right now. We needed to move faster.

"This one is harder. It's actually a German number, but typically it has been used in Belarus. But at the moment…" Fletcher typed in two things and a map popped up. "Its last call was taken in Szolnok—east of Budapest. The number has been off for the last twenty-four hours, but I have sniffers that will tell me the moment it pings a tower somewhere."

"Do we know who owns the phones?"

"Aliases. Unknowns. False fronts." Real disgust curled in his tone. "The reason they are the most interesting is because I can pinpoint the others down to a home address. These three—could be anyone. Three needles in an infinite haystack."

Closing my eyes, I took a deeper breath. "But she could be with one of those people."

"Or they could just be the courier." Cash's flat delivery did little to bolster my confidence.

"Still a lead," Bodhi countered. "All we need is one thread to pull to get us to another, Lainey B." The confidence helped.

But Hungary was a long way from New York. The fact there was a German number in the mix didn't mean anything. Our phone numbers went with us no matter where we lived. Just that the person had been in Germany when they got that particular phone.

"The Network has some contacts in Eastern Europe, primarily in Prague and Gdansk, but we have some at least in bordering states and a very wealthy family that owes me a personal favor for previous assistance," Vienna said, and I twisted to meet her gaze. "We can at least begin the tracking, I have reached out to one of our operatives already. He's a little unpredictable, but he lives for the hunt."

We knew more.

But not enough...

"Why the hell are you helping us?" Adam asked abruptly. "The Network is closed to most newcomers, and you don't usually do any favors for free."

It was my turn to put a hand on Adam.

"Hey, asshole," Fletcher said abruptly, surging out of his chair. "Don't be a dick to Drew. She's offering to help, because I'm offering to help."

"Because your sister," Vienna continued without an ounce of rancor or irritation, "is Fletcher's family. That makes her *our* family. We will always protect our family."

"Even when they are raging dickheads," Fletcher said, cuffing Adam upside the head even as he glared at him.

"Adam..."

He glanced down at me. The torment in his eyes shredded me. He was so used to being in control of everything, and that control was being tested on every front.

"You're right," he said, squeezing my hand before looking at Vienna. "My apologies, Miss Drew."

"None needed. Words and tone can hardly hurt me. Now—Fletcher has given me enough information to get hunters on the way. But I doubt any of us want to leave it at that."

"We can't go to Eastern Europe," Cash said abruptly. "No matter how much we might want to." He wasn't looking at us, but at Vienna.

"I'm not going to take that as an insult to my ability to create impeccable credentials, Cashy-poo. I'm really not."

"Good, cause it's about what we're needed for here. Not that we don't want to help. I have other contacts that fall on the more legal side of things," Cash said, not rising to Fletcher's bait. "We can involve them when you're ready."

"Until then," Vienna said, her calm voice was almost soothing against the rising tide of testosterone in the room. "We can help you at least leave the country undetected, if *you* want to go there."

Eastern Europe? I knew plenty of people there, but—

Tally would know more. She had one grandmother from Morocco, but the other was from Prague. I needed to call Tally anyway.

Margareta Waldemar had contacts in Eastern Europe.

Oksana's name flashed through my mind. I almost bit my tongue keeping the thought to myself. The conversation continued around me. Ideas. Suggestions. Dismissals. More

Fletcher put a hand on my knee and pulled my attention to him where he crouched in front of me. "We're gonna find her, Lainey. I don't care if I have to hack government spy satellites, we're gonna find her. That's the one thing you gotta hold onto, okay?"

I summoned a smile because I did believe him. Just like I believed Pretty Boy, Adam, Ezra, and Bodhi. We would find her. "I just need her to be in one piece when we do—"

"If she's anything like you, she's a survivor. But we're not slowing down and we're not giving up." He gave me a firm look. "You're not allowed to either."

I took a deep breath. As much as I might not like it, I did need to hear it.

We lingered for another hour, tossing out ideas and shooting down some on either side. Eventually, we needed to go. The hospital was calling. Fletcher would put together a series of credentials if we needed to leave quietly.

In the meanwhile, he would keep hunting. He and Adam exchanged a brief hug and spoke in quiet tones. I left them to it. There was Reed business to discuss eventually, especially with Harper dead.

Milo wrapped an arm around my middle and pulled me back against him as we stepped outside. The colder air was a shock after the warm humidity inside.

"Doc knows some people too," he murmured against my hair. "I'll reach out to him."

Everyone was doing something. "Thank you."

He didn't say anything. He didn't have to. Eventually, we were back in the car again, and I was tucked between Milo and Adam this time.

"You know, normally, I like shotgun," Ezra complained, but he was reaching a hand back to hold mine.

"Let me guess," Bodhi deadpanned. "It's because I'm not a cuddler."

Ezra gawped at him.

Milo, on the other hand, chuckled. "You cuddle with Lainey just fine."

"He is not Lainey," Bodhi responded as he pulled out.

"Point," Milo said. "Maybe if he tried to look like Lainey?"

I couldn't help it, a snort of a giggle escaped as Bodhi appeared to consider it.

"Still too tall. She fits right under my arm."

Adam cracked a smile at that, and Ezra twisted to look at me.

"I get no respect," he muttered.

"I'll cuddle with you anytime." I squeezed his hand.

"Ha," Ezra said, before he stuck his tongue out at Bodhi.

"Still not respect." The bland delivery shut Ezra up, but only briefly.

"Lainey is better than anything else. So I still win." He sounded practically triumphant.

"Can't argue with that," Bodhi said as Milo pressed his cheek to the top of my head, still chuckling.

"I need to call Tally," I said after a moment as the silence wrapped us up. The laughter, spiky as it was, had been very needed. It helped to alleviate *some* of the tension.

"She have family there?" Bodhi asked, flicking a look at me via the rearview mirror.

"She did. At least enough to know who might be the bigger players. I've never really paid attention to foreign society that much. There was always so much here..."

"Different city. Different rules." Ezra squeezed my hand. "We have contacts in Russia. I can see what they might know. It's not Budapest, but—everything over there is a lot closer than it is here."

That was true.

"Except Russia," Adam said. "Be careful with who you call there. We still don't have a bead on the Dovzhenkos or their play."

Another thread we needed to pull. "Could he have sold her to them?"

The question crackled through the interior of the car. It wasn't something I wanted to think about, but... I refused to stick my head in the sand.

"We already have questions for them," Bodhi said, his tone cooling rapidly. "We'll put that one at the top of the list."

Despite the distractions, the drive seemed to speed past, and we were at the hospital. I didn't ask if we were going to divide and conquer. The guys weren't leaving me with only one or two of them, especially when we were all worried about Ezra too.

He'd grown a little paler over the past hour. I needed to talk to the doctors, then get him home. He was still recovering too.

One glance at the doctor on their way to speak to me and my heart sank. I just wanted one piece of good news.

One.

I wasn't going to be getting it from him.

TWENTY-THREE

ADAM

The need to protect Lainey, Ezra, and Andrea cut into me, looping around me like razor wire encasing the prison keeping me trapped between who I'd been born to become and who I was—the person I *wanted* to be.

Did I even know who that was anymore?

"Going to Reed is a risk," Bodhi said before taking a sip of coffee.

"We're going to have to take some," I informed him. "It's been nearly a week since Harper disappeared." I didn't bother with the air quotes. "If I don't move now, I won't be able to consolidate before Hamilton tries to swipe power."

"How much of a threat is he?"

I had to give Bodhi credit. For the past three nights, Lainey had slept between me and Ezra. While sex was on the table, it had been more about comfort. I relaxed when she was there. Ezra relaxed. It was less about addressing all the tension and just being there.

Clearly, I would be fine with her sleeping with me every night, but she had relationships with Bodhi and Milo. They wanted time with her too. Time I needed to make allowances for...

"He's more of a nuisance currently," I said. "That said, in my father's absence, Hamilton will see advantage. He will move to take that advantage. As the eldest, my father controlled everything and he never trusted Hamilton with anything too deep into the company."

"But he trusted him with just enough to make him dangerous." Bodhi understood. Of course he did; his family tree probably had a few snakes in it too, alongside the nuts and spoiled fruit. "I still don't think you should go alone."

"With everything else going on, I don't want Lainey there." Particularly after my father's plans for her. "No offense, your company and mine—not always on friendly terms."

Bodhi shrugged, but Ezra leaned on the doorframe to the kitchen where we were having coffee. "Then I'll go with you. I know the players and the game. We ran around together enough, my being there won't set off alarm bells like if you took Milo."

I dipped my chin as I studied Ezra. The past three nights of real sleep had done him good. The shadows beneath his eyes had lessened, but he was still pale and a little jerky. I'd caught him getting a drink the night before, but he argued that one drink wasn't a bad thing.

It wasn't. Except with Ezra, it rarely stopped with one drink. "When are you scheduled to do your follow up?" I should know the date, except I didn't.

He didn't quite roll his eyes, but he did fold his arms. "Next week, unless I have any episodes or issues. I've had none."

"Toxicology reports came back," Bodhi said. "They called you two days ago."

Now it was my turn to glare.

"Way to throw a guy under the bus," Ezra said, scowling at him, but Bodhi was unmoved.

"I gave you two days to tell him, apparently you didn't. We already knew about the beta blockers. What was the final analysis?"

He shrugged. "I'm going to need to do some studies. Cardiologist shit. It can wait."

"No," I told him. "It can't. We can't defend or protect against what we don't know about."

"We're going to be heading to Eastern Europe. We all know that. I'm not staying here hooked up to some machines while all of you take off across the ocean. Not happening."

I pinched the bridge of my nose, frustration mounting.

"So take steps," Bodhi said. "Be in charge of your own care, but don't make anyone chase you down for it. Schedule the appointments. We'll make sure someone is with you..."

He sounded so damn reasonable.

"Ezra," I said and then blew out a breath. "Please just reach out and start the process. I don't want to think about any actual damage that may have happened either. But I also don't want you having a heart attack at thirty thousand feet."

Silence pooled into the kitchen.

"I'll make some calls today, while I'm at the office with you. Kill two birds. Maybe three if your uncle is there." He sounded almost hopeful, and I wasn't sure if it was for just one or all of the above.

"Stay with Lainey?" I focused the request on Bodhi.

"She mentioned talking to her grandfather about a care facility for her mother."

Even dead, my father was still inflicting damage.

"I'll keep her safe," Bodhi said without an ounce of rancor. Why he was so damn relaxed with the whole situation made no sense to me. I would cheerfully jettison him and Milo both if I thought Lainey would let me.

But would you really?

That niggling inner voice poked a hole in that theory. "Let us know.."

"Yes," Bodhi said as he pulled out his phone and began to skim the contents. "I'll keep you apprised of our location. I've scheduled time with my physician for her tracker. She wants both of you to get one as well."

Both of us. I slanted a look at Ezra who looked already to rebel until he met my gaze. "I'm fine with it. It will give her peace of mind."

And Ezra was right, we were going to Eastern Europe, sooner or later. Like Lainey, I wanted Andrea back. Not just leaving and tearing up town after town to find her seemed anathema. But we needed more than just those locations.

If we wasted time on false leads...

I cut off that line of thought. We'd find Andrea.

There was no other acceptable outcome.

THE DRIVE to Reed Enterprises steadied my nerves. I liked being in control, and riding around with Bodhi doing all the driving with Milo calling the secondary shots had grated. Still, it had put me in a position to be right next to Lainey and to comfort her.

So I guess it didn't have all the downsides.

"Thanks," Ezra said abruptly as I pulled into the executive lot in the parking garage. He'd been painfully quiet all the way in. Like me, he'd changed into a suit. His looked good. The deep brown suited his coloring as did the caramel shirt and gold striped tie. A little flashy, but in an understated way.

Considering nothing else about him was understated, I appreciated the effort.

"For?" I said after I backed into my spot, then did a sweep of the area. Granted, I could have brought more security, but that wouldn't be the show of power I needed to put on. If I came in with bodyguards, it would suggest I had something to be afraid of.

Not the message I wanted to send.

"Letting me back you up," Ezra mumbled before he pushed open his door and climbed out. Something in his tone was off.

Or maybe it was me. Fuck, I needed to stop second guessing everything, yet I felt like I had to. Had to dig deeper, to understand more.

It—frustrated me on so many levels.

I climbed out, scanning the area as well before focusing on him. "You've always backed me up."

He snapped his gaze to me. "I used to think so, but It doesn't always feel like that anymore."

"I know," I said slowly, not looking away. "I broke that trust."

For a moment, his gaze dipped and he swallowed hard. "So did I."

"We're working on fixing that, right? And maybe making it better?" The other night, his mouth on my cock? I hadn't forgotten any of that or how intense it had all been. But this was about so much more than sex.

He blew out a breath. "I hope so," he said. "I just keep thinking...I'm gonna fuck this up. Or—you guys are going to decide I'm not worth it. I already almost got her killed when they tried to grab her before and...if I hadn't taken off, maybe you guys would have been there when your dad's people..."

"I'm not gonna be the guy who says you didn't fuck up. You did. Maybe you fucked up because you were sacrificing yourself for us..." I still kind of wanted to punch him for that, but it wasn't what he needed from me right now. "Or maybe we fucked up because we didn't leave at least one of us with her."

"But she can protect herself," Ezra countered in a wry tone, and I spread my hands.

"Yes, she can. As fragile as we've treated her, myself in particular, she's a lot tougher than she looks. She broke herself out using chairs to break through the shutters and the glass. Then she climbed down the wall." I shook my head. "Here's the thing, we still want her safe."

"Yes," he said with a firm nod. "We do."

"She and I want *you* safe too. Considering Bodhi's reaction this morning, you're going to have him and Milo watching your ass now."

He grimaced. "Probably not the time to add a little wiggle to my step, huh?"

A wry chuckle tumbled free, and I shook my head. "You're just asking for trouble now."

"Maybe." He sobered and then met my gaze. "I'm scared. And—I'm not telling you 'cause I want you to fix it or to make me feel better. Not really sure you can. But right now...even with everything shitty going on, I actually have the two people I've ever wanted. I don't—"

His struggle was killing me.

Bracing a hand on his shoulder, I locked my gaze on his. "I get it." Because I did. Having Lainey and Ezra in my life was everything. "I do—I didn't predict you, but maybe I should have because you've always been a part of any plan I ever had."

"Yeah?" The hope in his eyes clawed at me.

"Yeah," I said. "The Milo and Bodhi parts? I could skip it but... they make her happy. You make her happy."

"So do you," he argued as if I needed the backup. Maybe I did.

"Ezra, wherever we end up—lovers now and then, lovers in total, or just lovers when we're with her—the rest of our relationship is solid. You're still my best friend. You want to get rid of me, you're going to have to work a hell of a lot harder."

He smirked. "I can be a handful."

"No. Shit." The deadpan delivery actually yanked a real smile out of him and he cast a quick look about before he gripped me in a fast hug.

"Thank you," he whispered. "I think I needed to hear that."

I rubbed his back and held him a beat longer before letting him pull away. "This touchy-feely stuff still takes a minute," I admitted with a grimace.

"Fuck my life," Ezra said with a groan as he raked a hand through his hair. "Right?"

I shook my head. "I thought this would be easier now..."

"Because we almost fucked?" The directness was appreciated. "Well, correction, I sucked your dick and you cuddled me later. But you only actually fucked Lainey the next morning after I fucked her."

Then again, maybe it was too much directness. "I—"

"Wait," Ezra said, closing the distance between us. "I'm

215

picking a fight I don't want." The admission seemed almost as broken as he was. "You trusted me...that's huge. Do I want more? Yes. Am I happy with what we have? Also yes."

"You deserve more," I admitted. "I keep thinking all of this will be easier, with you—with Lainey. In the moment, it is."

"So, what I hear you saying is throw you down and just go for it? We'll figure it out?" The strained notes of teasing amidst the suggestion pulled a reluctant chuckle out of me.

"Maybe," I told him. "Maybe not. None of this is working out how I imagined." Then because I didn't want him to misunderstand, I put a hand on his face. The stubble where he hadn't shaved scraped against my palm. "Let me be clear, just because this isn't *how* I imagined anything, doesn't mean I hate it."

He closed his eyes and leaned into the contact. I took that moment to drink in the sight of him. The rawness in his expression had always been there—the need.

"Thank you," I said, and he snapped his eyes open, a frown tightening his brow.

"For what?"

"For having my back. For being there. For wanting to be there even when I didn't see what you were asking me for." Those words he'd thrown at me, how I'd never seen him. He was right, I hadn't. But now?

Now I couldn't look away.

"I got mad at you for not seeing me when I worked really hard to hide it," he said. "Dad—hated the idea of me with another man. Couldn't really tell him it was you, just let him think I was bi. Which is only marginally better than gay in his world."

"Fuck him," I snarled. I could throttle Wallace Graham. Before this was all over, I planned on it.

"No thank you," Ezra deadpanned without missing a beat. "He's not my type. Not to mention it's gross..."

I groaned, chin dropping as I shook my head. "I don't know what the hell I'm going to do with you."

"Anything you want," he promised, throwing an arm around my shoulders. "But first, let's go make your uncle's life miserable and start taking over the world. Then later, we can discuss whether you like to suck cock or not."

I'd never really thought about it.

"Got that in your head now," he said as he guided me forward, a shit-eating grin on his face.

"Yes," I said, turning the idea over. I'd seen his cock. It wasn't bad looking at all. He'd always had a little length on me. The piercings though—and now I was thinking about them. "Dammit."

He laughed and hit the button to summon the elevator. "You're welcome." Then he winked at me. "We got time to figure it all out..."

We better damn well have time. Still, imagining him nude as we took the elevator up forty some odd floors left me with a most uncomfortable erection.

The little shit knew it too based on the way his grin grew.

Ass.

TWENTY-FOUR

LAINEY

"No," I said as I paced the length of the landing that formed a perimeter to the room below. "Grandfather, I know how you feel, and I know why you made the choices you did. I'm not asking you to go and see her."

The library shelves would normally be enough to keep me here for hours. Bodhi's collection wasn't just for show. Based on the mixture of modern and classic titles, the lack of dust, and how well-thumbed some of the books were, he read a lot.

On the other end of the line, my grandfather sighed. "But you would like it if I did?" It was as much a question as a statement. In his own ways, Grandfather meant well. For all his bluster, I was very aware of how much my mother's choices had hurt him.

If it had only been him, I thought he might have forgiven her a long time ago. Maybe not taken her in, but at least, forgiven her. No, she hurt my grandmother. That was an unforgivable sin. I'd say she hurt me too, but I'd never known a life where she was a regular part of it.

So, no, it was for my nana that he was so fierce. But Nana wouldn't know anything about it now. I worried about *him*.

"I don't know if it's about like," I admitted. "The doctors are clear, even if she makes it out the other side, there's going to be serious cognitive diminishment. She has damage to several of her organs. Her life is never going to be what it was."

The heavy metal toxicity was bad enough, but they'd also found signs of other issues—underlying ones that were now far more severe. I sighed as I leaned against the railing and gazed up at the books.

"I saw her this morning," I told him. Milo and Bodhi had taken me to the hospital. I'd met with her doctors and her attorney. In Harper's continued absence, I was the next of kin and thus in charge of her care.

I wish I'd gotten to help kill Harper now. I'd been present. I got to watch them take him apart while I looked after Adam.

Eyes closed, I blew out a breath. "They indicated she will need longer term care. I won't send her back to Waltham Corners. I know you don't want to bring her to Der Sonne."

The squeak of Grandfather's chair carried over the line, and I could picture him sitting at his old oak desk. He probably had a fire lit and a stack of papers to review. He still read hard copies of all contracts and meeting minutes. He just liked the paper.

I could even smell the burning tip of his favorite cigars, an indulgence that he didn't need to wait until cocktails for... The tension in his sigh reminded me that I hadn't told him about Andrea. I wrestled with that news.

Did I tell him and risk the stress of getting him involved? Or did I let him sit this out for now until I had more data? If it were me, I'd want to know.

"I don't know what I can do for her, sweet girl," he admitted after a long moment. "Melissa made her choices a long time ago, and I've had to make my peace with them. But you want her somewhere Harper can't get to her."

It wasn't a question.

"Yes," I told him. "I don't want anyone to bother her. I don't know if she'll make it, and maybe she doesn't deserve it—but I'd like it if she can at least be comfortable."

"Let me make some calls," he said. "I'll get her somewhere secure for you. I know you're not saying too much, but I'm not a fool. Something is wrong. After I take care of this, you will come see me and tell me what's going on."

"I will," I promised him. "I love you."

"My life is better for it every single day, sweet girl. I love you too." Then the call ended and I squeezed my eyes shut. I wanted to scream. I wanted to break things. I wanted to sob.

I couldn't do any of those things. Not yet. I needed to maintain my composure. I needed—

"Buttercup." The softness in Bodhi's voice rolled over me and wiped away the tears I refused to shed. Twisting, I burrowed against him as he wrapped his arms around me.

The earthy scent of him tickled my nostrils, and I fisted his shirt as I took a deep breath. The vague notes of cedar, patchouli, and rosewood steadied me. The warmth of his arms was a barricade.

"I don't want to cry," I admitted. Crying felt like defeat,

and I didn't want to surrender. Never again. Not after everything...

"Then don't," Bodhi said, then he swept an arm under my legs and picked me up. "Don't do a damn thing you don't want to do."

A traitorous sniffle escaped me. "I still need to call Tally."

"But you don't want to," he said aloud the rebel thought I'd been swallowing.

Talking to my grandfather had taken everything. "I hate lying to him."

"You're not lying to him directly," Bodhi said as he strode along the landing then down the stairs. He moved with a kind of effortless grace, like I was no burden at all.

Once we were in the living room, he turned toward the main stairs and climbed them two at a time. "It doesn't feel that way."

At the door to his bedroom, he pushed it open, then shoved it closed with his foot. Only then did he stop and turned that fierce gaze on me. My argument faded under the intensity in his eyes.

"Do you know exactly what happened to Andrea yet?"

"No..."

"Your mother's condition, while deteriorating, is not your fault. Now that you have the full scope of it, you brought him up to date immediately."

I swallowed. "Yes."

"When you know about Andrea—you will tell him then." None of these were questions. "You are not keeping secrets to harm him or to keep your own intentions from him. You are simply not involving him yet because there is nothing for him to do..."

Except...

"There isn't, Lainey B." Bodhi set me on the bed with utter care, then he reached for the soft Uggs I'd been wearing. Like the oversized sweater I had on and the buttery soft leggings. I craved the comfort. "Telling your grandfather now would mean excavating a lot of speculation alongside the facts. These would all muddy the waters."

There was truth in that.

He set my boots behind him then nudged my sweater upward. "It would also require that you dance around the secrets you carry for all of us—the secrets you would never betray—and *that* would require you to lie to him. Something you do not want to do even if you could merely tell him it is not your story to share."

I frowned at the description, and then my sweater was off and I was there in a soft blouse that he unzipped on the side and nudged up. The apartment was more than comfortable, but the chilly air beaded my nipples tight.

"You feel bad about not reaching out to Tally because something about your friend worries you."

The objection to that died before I could even give it voice.

"You aren't sure, but something she has said or done has given you a reason for concern. Whether the concern is related to all of this, I don't know—I don't think you do." He ghosted his fingers over my abdomen, pausing at one of the pair of bruises I still had from the abduction.

It was faded from a dark bluish-purple to an ugly yellow-green. In a few more days it would be gone entirely. He traced his thumb in a circle around it.

"I need to call her...I mean I should. She knows people over there."

223

"You can call her when you're ready. We all know people. Fletcher is working on it. Collin is also doing some digging. I sent word to Hugo. We'll find Andrea..."

Each time he said her name, his tone firmed. It was as though he offered a promise.

With a curl of his fingers, he hooked the waistband of my leggings and swept them, and my panties as well, down. I fell backward on the bed as he stripped me bare.

"You're getting me naked," I murmured.

He walked his hands along the bed on either side of me to lean over me before he unhooked my bra from the little catch in the front. More shivers raced over my skin, leaving goosebumps in their wake.

"Oh, you noticed," he said, the barest hint of teasing in his voice. "I thought I was going to have to..." He bit one nipple lightly. It was more a scraping of his teeth over the sensitive peak.

The gentleness in his touch turned rougher as he locked his lips and sucked the nipple tighter. My pussy clenched in anticipation. The deep inhale had to sustain me 'cause I didn't want to break the moment.

Tighter and tighter, he drew on the nipple until I swore he was going to leave a bruise. There was slickness on my thighs as I flexed my ass against the bed cover. It hurt and felt so damn good at the same time.

All I could feel was the heat of his mouth, the lash of his tongue, and the sting of his teeth. A sound escaped me as I threaded my fingers into his hair. I wasn't sure if I wanted to pull him away or push him tighter to me.

Then he released my nipple, and the abrupt ceasing of suction sent my blood flowing to it. Then he blew and I bucked as a spasm of pleasure rocketed through me. What the hell...

He lifted his gaze to meet my eyes, and I wanted to drown in him. My breath came in fast little pants, and I could practically feel the dampness sliding down to my crack. Had I ever been this wet before?

It was embarrassing except—

"Bodhi..." I whispered his name, and he nodded.

"Good girl. I'm the only one you think about right now. The only one you feel." He swooped down, his lips millimeters from mine. "The only one you taste." Then he kissed me. It was a brand, a staking of his claim, and I arched up to meet him.

When his tongue swept against my lips, I opened my mouth to him. The hints of coffee and caramel were on his lips and his tongue. I wanted to drown in the taste of him. With every lash of his tongue, he coaxed mine to dance with his, and then he was dancing his fingers down my side.

The harsh twist of my neglected nipple, had me sucking in another breath. Pain, sharp and piquant splintered through the pleasure, flooding me with heat. A keening noise escaped me, and he devoured the sound.

I swore my nipple peaked to ice before he let go, and then he abandoned my lips to lave his tongue over the nipple. The stimulation overwhelmed my thoughts, crashing through them and leaving sparks in its path. The massage of his lips removed the sting, and then he blew a breath over the damp tip and I was writhing against the sheets.

What was he doing to me?

"Where are you?" He murmured, kissing a path to my other nipple as he alternated between them. One he teased and laved and loved upon; the other he tortured and twisted. I couldn't focus on one before the other crashed through me.

I kept grinding my ass against the bed in an effort to push up to meet him, but his weight over my hips kept me pinned.

Then he bit the breast he showered in loving sensation. "Where are you, Buttercup?"

The demand to answer was there. "With you," I whispered. "With Bodhi."

"Good girl," he repeated, then he traded again. I'd just get a feel for his rhythm and he'd change it. Tears slipped down the corners of my eyes and splashed against my cheeks, but Bodhi gave me no mercy.

I was pushing and pulling against his hair when he left my breasts and began to lick, nip, and kiss his way down my abdomen, then he lifted so he could stare down at me.

"Spread your legs, Buttercup...yes, just like that...wider. Oh." He exhaled that last word like a caress. "Look how wet you are for me."

Heat flashed through me like a fire, and his soft chuckle delighted and comforted.

"So gloriously wet." He slid a finger along my slit as if to prove it, and I clenched everything. He was so close to my clit. It was like the whole world narrowed to right there. "Do you want to come, Buttercup? Do you want me to make you come?"

"Please..." I didn't quite whine the word, but I was pleading. "Please make me come." I was right there. My nipples ached in the most sensual way, and I couldn't sit still.

I twisted to look down at him, and the cloud of desire in his eyes just added to the fire inside of me.

"Yes, you've been good. I'll give you this orgasm, then we can work on the next."

The n— I couldn't even finish the thought as he pressed two fingers against my clit. The pressure was blinding and perfect. Pleasure spliced through every part of me, and I was pretty sure I soaked his hand. I held his eyes until my own closed and my body arched upward.

The blossom of pleasure was too much. I couldn't catch my breath, and I bucked against his hand. The moment I ground against him, he increased the pressure, and I split right down the middle.

I drifted on that sea of pleasure, floating on it as he eased his hand away.

"Rest for a moment, Buttercup," The dark delicious note in his chuckle made me smile as he lapped up the wetness from my pussy. "So good." The strokes of his tongue steadied me. "But we are far from done."

I was still floating when he rolled me onto my stomach and then there was a drizzle of lube along my ass. The temperature couldn't match the heat in my skin. It wasn't long before he was teasing my ass with his finger, and I groaned.

"Is that a yes or a no?" The inquiry came as he teased cool metal against my skin. Pushing up on my elbows, half-drowsy with release, I looked over my shoulder to find him studying me.

"Is that a plug?"

He held it up to show me and the glittering gem that highlighted the flared base. "With a real emerald."

Surprise fountained inside of me. Surprise and a very real hunger of my own...

"Yes, Bodhi," I told him. "For you it's always yes."

"You will tell me no when it is too much." The order resonated with me, but he overwhelmed me in the best ways.

"Yes, Bodhi," I whispered and he grinned before he went back to teasing my asshole.

"Now relax... Like I said, we are far from done."

TWENTY-FIVE

LAINEY

The hum of pleasure under my skin had me stretching like a cat. At the same time, Bodhi smoothed his hand over one of my ass cheeks then gave it a firm squeeze.

"Be still."

Folding my arms, I pillowed my head against them as he drizzled more lube along my ass. He teased the hole, working his finger against it and alternating with the plug. A soft laugh escaped me.

"Something amusing?" The simple pleasure in his voice just added to my smile.

"You got me a butt plug." It was... sweet.

"I did," he said. "I've never bought one before. Took a while to find one that would be perfect for you... still not sure about this one."

"It's adorable." I sucked in a breath as he worked the plug in past that first ring of muscle.

"Relax," he ordered, rubbing his hand along my ass

cheek to my thigh and back up again. Closing my eyes, I slowed my breathing and focused on doing exactly what he said. I *relaxed.*

"It's funny," I murmured, breathing as he added more lube. It was warm, and it kind of tickled. Even if the stretch had turned into a burn—I didn't mind. "Normally, I get stubborn when people give me orders."

"I'm not people," he said, almost absently, then dropped a kiss against my shoulder. "You're doing beautifully. It's almost all the way in and this is going to look wonderful."

I smiled. "No, you are definitely not just people."

"I will also accept your no with no questions," he said, his voice as patient as ever. "A little more here, push back to take it."

I obeyed and the stretch had me gasping, but it was in. The burn was both intense and at the same time relieving. Exhaling a long breath, I clenched around the plug. It was alien, large, and definitely filling me. Not like Adam had, but it—

A vibration went off and it shivered through my whole body. I lifted my head to look over my shoulder. Bodhi watched me with the most sinful smile. "That's a one."

"A one?" I checked.

"Want to feel two?" He held up the remote.

"You bought me a vibrating butt plug."

"With an emerald." He looked so very pleased with himself. "What do you think?"

The vibration was a low, shuddering sensation, and maybe I was too languid from my earlier orgasm but it was just there. "Let's try two?"

"For science," he said, then nodded before he nudged

the device. The intensity increased, and a shiver raced up my spine. I couldn't help it, I giggled. "You like?"

Licking my lips, I rolled over and spread my legs, because he was watching me with so much eagerness. The desire to know seemed to radiate off of him.

"Oh yeah," I admitted. The two was teasing all of me, and I swore my pussy clenched in time with my ass. "How high does it go?"

He leaned forward, then took a long inhale along the inside of my thigh before he bit down right where my thigh met my torso. The intimate caress had my back arching and then he ramped up the vibration and a little cry broke out of me.

It was a laughing sob. It wasn't quite too much, but it was edging me in the most wonderful way. He traced his tongue over the spot he bit then moved to bite my thigh on the other side.

The scrape of his teeth scraped through me, demanding all of my focus, and then the vibration jumped again and my hips pushed upward. He gripped my hip as he raised his head, pinning me in place.

I flexed my hands, the languor was gone, and it felt like I was on the edge. My nipples were tight and aching, my pussy clenched at nothingness, and my ass shimmied so hard, I swore my clit pulsed in time with it.

"Four is good," he whispered, before running his tongue over his lower lip.

"It is..." I practically panted the words. It was so wild to go from utterly replete to bordering on mad. Then the whisper of clothing falling hit me and I dragged my eyes open. When had I closed them? I pinched my own nipple with my left hand and teased the other with my right.

Bodhi gazed down at me, his cock standing out so hard

and proud. There was dampness on the tip. His face flushed and his lips were wet, then I realized he was licking them over and over.

"Not going to be gentle," he whispered. "Keep playing with yourself, Buttercup. I want you ready to come…"

"Oh, I am," I promised, then pushed my feet flat to the bed and lifted my hips. "Come," I told him. "I want you inside of me…. I need—"

I didn't finish the thought before he moved, gripping my hip with one hand and his cock with the other. He didn't hesitate to sink into me, and all the veins on his neck seemed to stand out in stark relief.

"*Fuck*!" He elongated the word as the vibrations from the butt plug seemed to hit him. I barely held onto reason as the pressure of him pushing into me shoved me over the edge. I shook with the first wave of the orgasm hitting me.

He let out another oath as he drew back and then thrust again. The shaking translated from me to him. When I reached up for him, he grasped my hands in his. A wildness kindled in his smile as he began to drive into me with a relentless force. It was wild and exactly what I needed.

I don't know which of us held on tighter to the other. With every push of his cock into me, every stroke that hit that spot inside, I came apart. A scream swelled up inside of me and then ripped out.

The vibration in my ass ceased abruptly, but Bodhi thrust a few more times before he came in a hot rush. He arched, holding my hands fast as he filled me. Despite the cessation of the plug's action, I still shook as though it continued.

Bit by bit, Bodhi slowed, easing the rocking of his still semi-hard cock inside of me as he dipped his head to my hands.

He kissed my knuckles before loosening his grip and dropping down to nuzzle kisses along the corner of my mouth. "I want to take you to the Underground and fuck you on a stage while the others watch."

The words rippled through me, igniting a lazy fuse that wandered through my system. My over-sensitized and still trembling system. The languor of earlier had redoubled. I was a puddle of pleasure.

It took concentration to trace my fingers over his face. "You do?" Oh, look. I found my words.

He chuckled. "You were interested when we were there... some of the rooms appealed to you."

"Not sure about strangers watching me." I clenched around him. I was so full. His cock. The plug. My heart.

"No strangers—just Milo, Adam, and Ezra—if he behaves."

A giggle escaped me at the chiding remark at the end. "He would sulk if we made him sit in a timeout."

"Then he will learn to behave and not worry you so much." Bodhi kissed a path along my jaw to my ear. "I love having you like this."

"It's my pleasure," I promised him. It really was. "I am still...so entertained that you got me a butt plug."

"A vibrating one." Yes, he was very pleased with himself. If that didn't warm me on a really primitive level.

"With an emerald," I added as he had earlier, and he grinned. It was just so damn open.

"I want you to have everything," he said.

"I do," I whispered. I had all of them. "When we find my sister, and your sibling...we'll have it all."

He kissed me again, slow and teasing. The roll of his hips had his cock moving again. His cock, which had begun to stiffen in the time we lay there. Oh, I ached in all the best ways.

"Again?"

"Hmm," he said. "I have an idea."

"Oh God," I whispered, half-delight and half in playful fear. "I'm still recovering from your last idea."

"Trust me." Then he was pulling out and I whimpered at the sudden absence. He pressed a kiss to his fingers then to my lips.

I shuddered, even as I tried to push myself up on my elbows. He retreated to the door and pulled it open. "Hey, Milo... can you come up here?"

My eyes widened. Or at least they felt like they'd turned into saucers. Bodhi flashed me a wicked grin, then winked as he picked up the controller.

He blew me a kiss and retreated toward the bathroom at the sound of the footsteps approaching.

"What's up?" Milo said from the other side of the door.

"Our girl is still feeling a little frisky... think you can give her a hand?" With that, he closed the door to the bathroom and I looked from it to the bedroom door as Milo pushed it inward.

The heat in his eyes was scorching. He drifted his gaze over me from head to toe and when he eyed my pussy, I resisted the urge to close my legs. I was soaked and Bodhi had just come.

This wasn't like with Adam and Ezra.

"You're a mess, Mayhem," he whispered in a voice that was a downright growl.

"A little," I said, then rocked my hips, squirming. I hadn't forgotten the plug or the fact that Bodhi had taken the remote into the bathroom with him.

There was no shower water on. He was sitting in there and listening.

Milo glanced from me to the bathroom then back. "You want me to take care of that?" He leaned a shoulder against the doorframe, like he could take all the time in the world.

"I think...Bodhi wants to share me with you, and I adore that he does. But I don't want you to do anything you're not comfortable with."

It was one thing to know I was with the others. It was something else to see me with them. To see me like this.

"You're not losing me," Pretty Boy said as he tugged his shirt off and pushed the door closed. "But if you're sore or don't..."

"I always want you." My voice dipped to a whisper. "I always will... I love the idea of being with both of you."

"Or being traded back and forth?" That idea kindled another wave of heat through my system. Adam and Ezra had done that and yes—I did enjoy it.

"Yes," I answered, keeping it simple and straightforward. "Are you okay with that...?"

He unzipped his pants, and his cock was already straining before he finished shedding them. "Is Bodhi staying in the bathroom for this or does he want to watch?"

The door opened. "I want to watch her," Bodhi answered. "But I'm fine to give you privacy."

Milo shot him an amused look. "That's what sitting in there listening felt like... privacy."

Bodhi shrugged. "It's all an illusion, but isn't she beautiful?"

I squirmed under the heat of that compliment, and when Milo focused on me, the hum under my skin grew visceral. I didn't think Bodhi had turned on the plug, but I was already shivering from the force of it.

"She's always gorgeous," Milo said, dropping one hand down to the bed before kissing me. I wrapped my arms around his neck. He tasted of fresh coffee and a little whiskey. Had he added it to his drink? There was some suggestion of salt too, and then it was all him.

Instead of draping over me though, he lifted me and moved to sit on the bed with me in his lap. I blinked at him, the cum sliding down my thighs soaking him and leaving me even more aware of Bodhi's watchful gaze.

Bodhi...

"You put me on top, so he can see..." A sigh escaped me. "That's very thoughtful."

"I'm a thoughtful guy...now are you as frisky as Bodhi said?"

Was I... "Yes," I promised him. It didn't matter that I'd just had three or four orgasms at least. I wanted Milo and I wanted him now.

When he fisted his cock, I braced my hands on his shoulders then sank down on him.

"Better than lube," Milo said through clenched teeth and for some reason, the fact he was stretching me out so easily just added to the heady experience. "Fuck, you're tight."

Hands gliding down my back to my ass, I knew the moment his fingers grazed the plug.

"It's a toy," Bodhi explained. "Well lubed and she can take it for another fifteen minutes or so..."

A shudder went through me as Milo tested it. I was so damn sensitive everywhere.

"It has a surprise," I told Milo and his eyebrows climbed. "Want to feel it?"

Hedonistic? Absolutely. But the spark in Milo's eyes coupled with his breathy, "Oh hell," was everything I never realized I wanted to hear. Bodhi had introduced me to something amazing, and now we were gonna share it with Milo.

"Oh heaven, Pretty Boy," I promised as I began to rock on him. He slid his hands to my hips to control the rhythm, and as braced as I was, I still shook when Bodhi amped up the vibration from one to two, then to three in rapid succession.

I had no idea who came first, but I was *crying*.

TWENTY-SIX

MILO

The drive across town to King's place gave me time to consider his cryptic message. Again.

Come to breakfast. I can help with the hunt for Andrea Reed.

The problem with the message was how direct it was. King *always* seemed to have an agenda. His actions affected so many people. After meeting with Waldemar, I had to recalculate the range of people he impacted.

It...was insane.

Leaning against the back wall, arms folded, I stared at the numbers as they ticked away our climb. We weren't meeting at his house but at a building in the city. Fine. I didn't want to go back to that place anyway.

The number of boltholes King had to slip away in would impress me if it weren't so damn frustrating. Always have an exit.

Always.

"Relax," Adam said from where he stood by the buttons.

When the elevator doors opened, he would be out of sight. Not that they couldn't be watching us on the cameras.

I flicked a look to him. When the message had come in, Mayhem had been *incensed*. The absolute fury in her hazel eyes threatened to spark real fire. She'd thrust my phone back at me and stalked into the kitchen.

Rather than go to see him, I called. But, of course, King didn't answer. The bait had been laid out to make his offer attractive, and the door opened. He was offering no alternatives.

If I blew him off, I risked losing whatever information —*if* he really possessed any—he held. That was an option. Lainey wouldn't blame me in the slightest. It was a trap. We all saw it. The problem was, King had to know I wouldn't decline.

I *couldn't* decline.

Even a minuscule piece of information that might lead us to Andrea was worth the chance. Whatever happened to me—it happened. As prepared as I was for Mayhem to insist on going with me, she surprised me when she looked at Adam and said he had to back me up.

What shocked me more was how readily he agreed. Adam and King had their own differences, their own relationship stretching back more than a decade and a half. The man had robbed Adam of a childhood.

King was *really* good at that.

"This is relaxed," I said as the elevator dinged and the doors opened. A pair of guards waited, armed and standing at what looked like parade rest. I strode forward and cut left to head to his office.

If they tried to search me, it wouldn't end well for them. Neither made a move until Adam left the elevator. I sensed more than saw them take a step.

"Don't," I told them, not pausing or glancing back. "He's with me."

Something kinetic and altogether violent shifted under my skin. I'd never been the one who *wanted* the fight. I'd never shied away from one. Never had a problem immersing myself in the danger, but I wasn't the one who wanted or needed it.

I waded in to protect my friends. My family. Occasionally my sanity and my life. Prison had honed my restraint *and* my violence to a razor's edge. Others watched Bodhi like he was the dangerous one. They were right to be wary of him.

He was.

Then again, so was I.

The man nearest me reached for Adam's arm and I pivoted, curved my arm through the guard's to wrench it back behind him, and removed his gun.

A grunt of pain escaped the man because of where I had his arm, I could break it just by applying a little more pressure. Gun pointed at the second guard, I said, "Two fingers, left hand, remove the gun and hand it to Adam."

I didn't leave room for misunderstanding or debate. But the other man wasn't moving fast enough for me.

"*Now.*"

At the single syllable, he opened his jacket, pulled out the gun with two fingers and passed it to Adam. He freed the bullet from the chamber and then dropped the magazine from it. He pocketed both before he cold-cocked the second guard and knocked his ass out with the gun.

"Nice move," I said, ignoring my guard's hiss of pain as I gave his arm a little more pressure.

"Thank you," Adam said, almost graciously. "Want me to take care of that for you?"

241

"Please."

"My pleasure." He took the gun and repeated his earlier move to unload it as well. I didn't have time for anything more elegant, so I twisted and then rammed the guard into the closed elevator doors.

The impact made me grimace at the jolt it pushed through me. But when this guy woke up, he was gonna have a lump—and a headache.

I pulled out some zip ties from my pocket and secured him while Adam kept watch, then his guard before I dragged them both over to the other wall and just left them there.

Dusting my hands off, I caught Adam's speculative look.

"What?"

"You have hidden layers, Hardigan."

I smirked. "I'm like an onion."

The corners of his lips twitched. "Noted."

We continued through the doors into the private offices. No more guards presented themselves, so he'd offered those up as a tacit sacrifice, or he had something else planned.

It could be all of the above.

Like so many of his other setups, this was a generic set of offices, with empty cubicles that offered up a lonely desolate setting for this meeting. How many of these did he really have? And did he actually own them, or was he taking advantage of their locations?

Empty real estate in New York would be at a premium. It was in most cities. Still, it gave me another thread to pull for later.

The office angled toward a set of closed doors on the far side. They had the appearance of a much larger office space.

I didn't bother to knock, I just opened the doors and pushed them inward.

Baiting the bear?

Probably.

King stood next to his desk, cup of coffee in hand with a stack of files waiting on a table in the sitting area. The scent of coffee filled the room. There was also a platter of danishes and more.

"Come in boys, I've been waiting for you." He didn't display even an ounce of surprise at Adam's presence. Then again, maybe he wasn't. "I take it Carter and Nathan are merely incapacitated and not dead?"

"You don't need to ask questions for something you already know the answer to." He would have been watching us on the cameras. There were three large screens on the wall. All of them were dark, but I'd bet they hadn't been a moment before we opened that door.

"Have some coffee," King said, ignoring the verbal jab. "I appreciate you digging the time out of your day." He paused on his way to the sitting area though neither Adam nor I made a move. "Then again, with Andrea missing, you're probably both desperate to find her. How is Miss Benedict?"

I ground my teeth in an effort to wrestle my temper back into the bottle. Yes, he wanted to provoke me. Unfortunately for him, I wasn't driven by my passions. I refused to start now.

"What do you have?" Adam asked rather than me. "If you've taken her..."

Yes, that was the one tactic we had discussed in the car. Put him on the back heel. Why else would he tell me he could "help" unless it was yet another move in this game he'd been playing for most of my life?

"I wouldn't kidnap a child." He actually managed to sound insulted. "I made a deal with you." The last he said to me. "As I stated earlier, I honor my deals, even when the people I make them with don't honor theirs."

Trying to weed out the bullshit from the facts was nearly impossible with him. I had a feeling he knew it too.

"Don't try to sound so offended," Adam informed him. "You have no problem blackmailing, intimidating, or killing to get your way. Kidnapping a teenage girl really doesn't seem like a stretch."

A ding of the elevators in the distance had me tilting my head.

"Ah," King said. "The last of our guests have arrived." He was pouring coffee for us, and I frowned. Then the doors burst open behind us, and I scowled.

"I'm here," Ivy announced as she stalked into the room. Even her voice sounded stronger. For all that she'd been a slight thing, she'd put on muscle in the last few months. The hollows in her face had filled in, and the shadows in her eyes were fewer.

The confidence she possessed? It had always been fierce, but it practically radiated from her.

"What the hell are you doing here?" I cut my gaze from her to King. "You son of a bitch, you couldn't help yourself."

"I thought she'd want to know," he said with a faint smile as if we weren't all on the edge of violence. "As I recall, Miss Benedict is her very dear friend and young Mr. Reed actually proposed at one point."

The last carried just a note of warning.

"Then you tried to have him killed," Ivy snapped. She was all fire. Thankfully, she slowed her advance when she got to me. She was dressed in a heavy coat, boots, and a little knit cap. It was almost adorable, except for the pissed off look on her face. "I canceled my next three shows to be here. What happened to Andrea?"

"I'll brief you when we're out of here," I told her before I advanced on King. Surprise flickered across his face because I was done playing with him and with this.

I got ahold of his shirt and fisted it as I marched him backward and slammed him into the wall. We were similar in height, but I had fifty pounds of muscle on him, easy. He might work out, but it was about maintaining a trim physique, not strength.

"Think about your next actions very carefully, Milo," King warned me.

I smirked. "I've been thinking about ripping your head off and shitting down the hole since I was seven years old. I know exactly what I'm doing. You took your first opportunity to yank Ivy back here because I wouldn't call her for you. This is not about Andrea... it's about her and me—and *you*."

"Are you so certain of that?" He dared me, but he wasn't fighting me.

"If he is, then so am I," Ivy said. Bless her for not coming any closer. Adam had shifted his stance when I moved. He would protect Ivy. He'd proven that over and over again. "The only reason I came is you said *they* were going to be here too."

They. She thought Mayhem would be here.

"You should have called," I said over my shoulder.

"Don't start with me," she snapped back. "I'm here now and that's what matters. I hardly came alone."

Of course, she didn't.

"They outside?"

"Yes," she said. "Waiting for us."

Refocusing on King, I said, "Do you really know something?"

"I know a lot of things," he said, head tilted. The arrogance of this man. Nothing touched his confidence. "You are not as smart as you think you are, son. You trust the wrong people and you never listen."

"Right, you abandon your family. Blackmail children into doing your dirty work. Sell off your kids to suit your purposes." The last was a calculated dig. His nostrils flared and his lips compressed. "I think I'll worry about your opinion of me, never."

"He doesn't know shit," Adam said. "Or he'd have already dangled it. He used us to get Emersyn here."

He wasn't any happier about it than I was.

"I know the name of the man who brokered the deal for Harper." It was King who smirked. "Come have coffee with me, Emersyn dear, and I'll tell you."

"Wow," she said slowly. "You really are a piece of shit."

The insult resonated, and he snapped his gaze from me toward her. There was something so unfriendly in his expression that I jerked him to me and slammed him back against the wall.

"Ivy—do you mind giving us a minute?"

"I don't," she said softly. "But I don't want to leave you alone with him."

"I'll be fine," I told her. "Go on. You don't need to be here."

"Want me to walk her out?" The offer from Adam was a kind one. He'd stay. He'd help me take King apart if I wanted him too. Waldemar wanted him dead after all, so offing King would do us all a favor.

"Please." I didn't look away from King. His expression grew more remote and foreboding the longer we stared at each other. This close, the masks fell away. Maybe he could play gentility with everyone else.

But I knew him.

I knew Jeff Hardigan.

The drug dealer.

The deadbeat dad.

The desperate...

He was desperate. It oozed out of him.

The door closed behind them but we weren't alone.

"Mickey J," King said through clenched teeth. "The man who thinks he's good enough for my daughter."

"Shut up, Jeff," Doc said as he came to stand next to me. "You killing him or questioning him?"

"I haven't decided."

Of course Doc was here. Mickey. The guy who'd found me and Ivy after our mother died. He'd only been a teen himself. He'd been a runner for Jeff Hardigan. He saved me. He saved Ivy. Over the years, he'd looked out for both of us.

Now he was with Ivy just like the rest of the Vandals. I didn't have to understand it to appreciate it. I'd gotten over my hang-ups where they were concerned a long time ago. He might be almost twice her age, but he worshiped the ground she walked on.

He'd kill for her.

They all would.

It was more than enough for me.

"Tell you what, Jeff, you answer the questions and stop the bullshit games—maybe you live to walk out of here. You keep pushing him, they won't even find evidence that you used to exist." It was cold, it was precise, and it was delivered in an emotionless voice that didn't betray Doc's level of hatred for my father.

His beef with Jeff was far different, but no less passionate. Maybe he knew even more about him than I did. I could accept that. What he knew, he didn't like and he didn't want anywhere near Ivy.

On that, we were in firm agreement.

"Fine, I'll give you the name of the broker. It's all I have, and I know it because he handles most sales on the East Coast."

Most sales.

"Human trafficking. What the fuck is wrong with you?" I demanded. I suspected. I was almost certain that he was involved in all this depraved shit, but hearing him admit it...

"Trafficking happens whether I'm involved or not. I know the players. I know the game. You're a fool if you think you can stop it. It's too deep. Cut off one part, someone else sweeps in to fill the space. Do you want the name—or not?"

TWENTY-SEVEN

LAINEY

I was already descending the stairs when the door opened to let Adam and Milo in with Emersyn and a host of others. The Vandals were not all here, but I didn't count who was missing as Em broke away from the group to come straight to me.

We crashed together in a hug. "You shouldn't be here," I scolded her.

"Of course, I should." She tightened her arms. "You should have called me when it got this bad—especially if King is involved."

That struck another match to my temper. Of all the people to involve her, of course it was the man Milo had been trying to keep away from her. Pulling back, I grinned at the ferocious look in her eyes.

"I've missed you," I admitted.

"Me too."

Another long hug, then she pulled back to thread her arm through mine.

"We need drinks, and food, and a place for you and me to talk. Sorry boys, you're not invited."

"Not even me, PPG?" Bodhi said in a dry voice that had her grinning.

"Sorry, Bodhi. Double X chromosomes only." Then she shot an enigmatic look at Milo. "Besides, I'm sure you boys have all kinds of planning for violence to do."

"Brat," Milo said to her, but his smile held so much affection. For her part, Em just stuck her tongue out at him.

"Behave, Little Bit," Doc said to her before he dropped a kiss on her forehead. "Lainey."

Em just laughed and gripped my hand. "Come on," I said. "Coffee in the kitchen, then we'll..." If we were in my apartment, I'd take her to the library. I glanced at Bodhi.

"Solarium is on the second floor at the end of the hall. It opens to the outside, but I'd prefer you stay inside. The glass is bulletproof. Well, bullet reinforced anyway."

Good to know. "Full of surprises." Like gem-encrusted butt plugs that vibrated. The man definitely knew how to leave an impression.

The guys settled around the room, passing out drinks and seeming like they were waiting for us to absent ourselves. I got our coffees made, then dropped a kiss on Ezra, then Adam, and Milo before pausing next to Bodhi.

Em made her way around the room, with a touch here, and a kiss there. Rome and Liam were both present, so were Freddie, Doc, and Vaughn. The only two missing were Jasper and Kellan.

"You boys be good," I said, giving Bodhi an amused look, "especially if you're going to talk as men do."

His amused smile tickled me, and then Em and I were off and up the stairs. Sure enough, there was a solarium at the end of the hall and it was... wow.

I did a slow turn inside of it.

"It's like a gilded cage," Em said slowly. "Only—not."

She wasn't wrong. The design was elegant, and it had a dome at the top and the arching struts between the wide glass gleamed a golden sheen. The wintry sun seemed so much warmer in here.

There were some loungers and a table. The floor was tiled, and the pattern made me think of a map. When I tilted my head back and looked up again, I could see the symbols and designs etched into the fixtures.

It had to be related to his mother. Maybe one of their adventures...

"This is..." She paused mid-turn to look at me and my face heated. I didn't usually embarrass easily, yet, Bodhi had sent us out here for privacy without even the appearance of hesitation. "This is amazing," Em said. "He really loves you."

The heat swept me from head to toe. "I—"

Her eyes softened and so did her smile. When she gripped my hand and offered support, I squeezed it.

"It's a lot," I admitted. "They're all... working together and finding a balance that I didn't even imagine would be possible."

The five of us were finding it, and the guys were working so hard together... even Adam, and I could never have pictured it. Not once in all these years. Then...

"I'm really happy for you," Em said, tugging me over to one of the loungers. "But I'm also worried about you."

I sighed. "I really hate that he told you." Admitting it aloud let me take some of the power back. "Milo doesn't want you near him, and I can't say that King has given me any reasons to trust him or his motivations."

"As much as I dislike and do not trust that man," Em

told me firmly as she sat cross-legged, facing me and I leaned back against the lounger. "I'm glad I know. When I needed you... you were there. No hesitations. Let me be here for you now."

Locking gazes with her, I had to bite the inside of my lip as a wave of terrible sadness and fear slammed through me. Everything I'd been fighting to contain, to keep it from clouding my choices. I needed to be able to think. To be rational. To...

"He sold her, Em," I whispered. "That's what he said. That son of a bitch sold her." The tears clogging the back of my throat hurt so damn much. "I don't know where she is or who he sold her to. He wouldn't say. It didn't matter how much they tore him apart—he held onto that last bit like a giant fuck you."

That was the part that haunted me. We'd killed him. While I had no doubts that he needed to die, I worried... I worried we'd killed the only lead to her.

"The guys—Bodhi, Pretty Boy... they don't think he actually knew where she was at that point. That he handed her off. That once she was out of his hands, he really didn't know." Pain stabbed through my heart. "Because he didn't care."

I was digging my fingers into her hand, but she didn't let go.

"He poisoned my mother. He probably killed Adam's mother, Emily. He—sold my sister. He planned to keep me as his prize and to be a broodmare." Disgust leaked out around the bleakness. Yet, the emotion that burned me more than the despair was the anger. "He just—treated all of us as disposable. I never liked Harper Reed. I always thought he was a disgusting man, but I had no idea how much of a monster he was."

Maybe if I'd known or if I had paid closer attention...

"Ezra's engaged," I said. It was like now that I'd opened the door, it all came spilling out. The floodgates wouldn't be closed. "To some girl named Oksana...his parents arranged it. Apparently, they arranged it years ago and he's been trying to get out of it forever. But now, they are blackmailing him by threatening me and Adam. Worse, someone tried to kill him when he threw himself on the chopping block."

The tears burning in my eyes fell out and splashed to my cheeks. I tried to swipe them away, then took a sip of the coffee.

"Adam's struggling because his father betrayed him again. Pretty Boy gave himself up to save Andrea from King and now she's missing and at least he's back, but King's right there. Driving him mad with whatever game he is playing."

And Bodhi... Bodhi had his own hunt and secrets, all of which he'd seemed to put on hold to help me.

"Everyone has secrets and there are so many lies. Tally is lying to me. Avoiding me. I don't know why." Or maybe I did. Maybe Bodhi was right. Tally's secret was some man she shouldn't be involved with, and it was likely someone we all knew.

I swallowed the hard lump in my throat then lifted my coffee. A couple of drinks helped, but nothing could stifle the pain threatening to smother me.

"This is why I didn't want you to come," I admitted as the tears fell.

"You know I'll never tell," she whispered and then she wrapped her arms around me and held me tight as I cried. Giving in to the sorrow meant accepting that all these horrible things may not have a good resolution.

"I can't lose Andrea," I whispered. "If Mother dies—I'll hate it, but she chose that life. But Andrea didn't."

"We will find her," Em said. It was an oath, a prayer, and a promise all in one. "No matter what happens, we'll be there for her. She has the best sister on the planet. I know you will do everything to help her, and so will I. We have a lot of practice at this, and you—Lainey you're the best. You really are. So cry if you need to. I'm not going to melt."

I'd told her something similar when she'd broken down after Pinetree and admitted her uncle's abuse. I gripped her tighter. We were holding onto each other now just like we had then.

"I've missed you," I whispered.

"Missed you too—next time, you call me, dammit."

I could practically taste the tears in her admonishment. Still, a warbling, sobbing laugh broke free. Eventually, the tears eased and I was able to pull back. My face hurt, my nose was snotty, and my throat was sore. Em wasn't much better.

"We're terrible cryers," I reminded her, and she lifted her shoulders.

"Depends on how you look at it. When you're the strongest person I know, sometimes, you need to kick down the doors to let it out."

I almost snorted. "Right back at you." Because Em really was the strongest... I sighed and tried to ease my sore throat with more coffee. Since Em was doing the same thing, it was kind of gratifying.

"Now," Emersyn said, lifting her chin. "The other reason I'm here. I know a lot of people in Eastern Europe."

"You do?" Shock ripped away the grief. "How?"

"Two world tours," she reminded me. "When I was 'loaned' out, I would work with touring companies there. I

254

know a few people in a few cities. I've already sent emails to a dozen that I could think of. Kellan is keeping an eye on my emails right—"

I hugged her all over again.

"You're not so mad that I'm here now, huh?" The tease landed and I laughed.

"I wasn't mad before." It wasn't a lie. "I just—it never occurred to me. But you did, you were over there for a while."

"Not that I can make any promises. But Milo said you got information from Fletcher, locations and stuff, I thought between that and the people I know..."

"We could narrow some things down. How likely is law enforcement over there to help us?" Even as I asked the question, I saw the skepticism on her face. "Right."

The afternoon drifted toward evening as we sat out there. Eventually, the door opened and Bodhi glanced at us. Thankfully, our tears were dry now, and while my eyes were still sore, I didn't think I looked like I was crying.

I hoped anyway.

"We have some news," he said. "Doc said the results came in."

"The results?" I frowned and Em sighed. "What results? Are *you* okay?" Worry plunged through me, but she gripped my hand fast.

"I'm fine, but we decided to do a little test on our way back." She stood. "C'mon..."

"What test?" I glanced between her and Bodhi.

"A DNA test. The working theory about King is that he is related to one of the families. He's not cooperative. No one wants me to talk to him for any length of time, and I don't know that I could trust him anyway. We all had some form of bloodwork done after Uncle Fuckbucket."

I did not laugh at that name, but I loved that she could say it without the shadows swarming her. Bodhi held the door wider for us as we approached.

"You tested you and Milo against—all of us?"

She glanced at me. "Yep. Milo talked to Mickey about something a week or so ago. So he ran those tests. We were waiting on the results. Now we get to find out who we're related to, if we are."

All these balls in the air.

"Can you give me and Lainey B a moment, PPG?" Bodhi said, his gaze firm on me.

"Always. Take all the time you need." She held out her hand for my coffee cup, and I surrendered it. Then she disappeared inside and Bodhi closed the door.

"You've been crying," he said, studying me.

"Yeah," I admitted. "I needed that. I needed her."

He nodded slowly.

Then I narrowed my eyes. "You knew that though."

With a shrug, he wrapped an arm around me and I curled into him. Eyes closed, I burrowed into his embrace and leaned on him. Letting him hold me there.

"You are strong, Buttercup," he murmured. "You are good at being strong for everyone."

"Thank you," I whispered. "For letting me."

"It's not about letting you," he said, leaning back to look down at me. "It's about supporting you. I will never take away from your strength or your right to choose how you respond. I reserve the right, however, to intercept with support when you need it."

"I love you, Trouble," I whispered. The words glided off my tongue so easily. "I am grateful for you too."

"As I've said, my world is better for it." He smiled, then pressed his lips across mine. "I love you, Lainey B."

Eyes closed, I drank in his nearness and then gathered together my composure. When I was ready, I nodded and Bodhi opened the door.

"By the way," I told him as I trailed my fingers down his arm. "I love the solarium."

"Yes?" He glanced back at it. "It was always missing something before."

"What?"

He winked. "You."

The compliment warmed me and made me laugh, probably exactly as he intended. When we rejoined everyone downstairs, I drifted over to where Milo stood and threaded my fingers with his.

Ezra and Adam were focused on something Liam was saying. Em was perched on Rome's lap, her attention on Freddie, but she was also holding Vaughn's hand. Bodhi came to stand with Pretty Boy and I, and for a moment, I drank in the normalcy of all of us being here.

Well, all of us minus a couple. But close.

Still, it was Doc who cleared his throat and the conversations broke off one by one until we were all looking at him. "Now that we're all here..." He looked at Milo, then at Em. "You ready to find out?"

"I think we all are," Milo said. "So let's put an end to one mystery. Are we related to anyone here?"

CHAPTER

TWENTY-EIGHT

EZRA

I checked my watch as I—we—waited for the Dovzhenkos to arrive. The night before had run long, particularly after Doc revealed the DNA test results. It was enough to wrap around my mind that I was related to Milo and Emersyn.

They were—cousins, most likely. First or second, as far as the test results had revealed. I liked Em. A lot. Kind of made me wish I could have helped her more. Smoothing down my tie, I tried not to fidget. Not that I was having a lot of luck with that.

"Relax," Adam said from where he leaned against the wall. Hands in his pockets, suit coat open and the shirt stretching tightly over his physique made him look like he was about to bust out of it.

Or maybe I just wanted the distraction.

"Not sure that's totally possible." I wasn't pacing yet. The itch between my shoulder blades increased.

"Pretty Boy and Bodhi are right outside," Lainey said,

looking cool as a cucumber in the mint green suit she'd worn today. From the tops of her matching green pumps to the pale cream blouse she wore under the jacket, she looked like something right out of a spring catalog.

The contrast to the cold, dreary weather outside made me smile. Her hair was free and flowing. It added to the ethereal lightness of her. Nothing restrained, even if she was buttoned down.

"Whatever you're thinking right now," she said, her tone dry as the desert. "I'm not giving you a blowjob while we wait."

Laughter escaped on a snort. That—well that hadn't been on my mind, but now that she'd mentioned it. "Later?" I added just a bit of hope to the syllables.

"Maybe," she said, but her smile warmed. Her distraction worked.

Well-played, Kotyonok. Though I kept that to myself for now.

My phone beeped and Adam slanted his gaze toward the door. "They're here."

Yeah, I'd guessed that. They wouldn't come in without Milo and Bodhi searching them. It would be Oksana and her father only, unless her mother or brother came with them. Guards would remain outside.

Lainey moved to stand closer to me, while putting me between her and Adam. The ferocious protective side of her was sexier than I ever imagined. Once we got through all of this though, I'd make a point of never putting her in this position again.

Ever.

The doors opened, letting Oksana and her father inside. I caught Milo's gaze past their shoulders. He nodded— once. My cousin was good at reading people.

My cousin.

That was definitely going to take some getting used to —especially since I sent one cousin to help another. Not that *they* were related.

"Ezra Graham," Dovzhenko said in a firm tone before he looked from me to Adam then Lainey.

"Fyodor Dovzhenko," I said, extending my hand. "Thank you for meeting with us."

He eyed my hand briefly, then me, before he clasped it. There was no mistaking the tattoos on his hand at this distance. They weren't as illustrated as some prison-based tats were for Bratva that I'd seen, but the Cyrillic was there.

"Oksana," I said, greeting her second, and that seemed to please Dovzhenko. Just because I flouted protocol and found it boring as fuck didn't mean I didn't understand it. "I hope you're well."

She pouted. "I'm fine. Papa and I have been speaking more."

Dovzhenko eyed her and then shrugged. "My daughter has a good head on her shoulders. I thought she was more like her mother... turns out she is more like me." Pride glimmered in the man's eyes.

Right. Sharp. Conniving. More than capable of making a deal. Oksana would be just fine.

"I don't know if you've ever been formally introduced— Elaine Benedict and, of course, Adam Reed." He'd been there the first time Adam met both of them.

"Of course," Dovzhenko said, eyeing Lainey first. "Miss Benedict. I have heard much about you. Wallace is not what you could call—a fan."

She smiled and offered up the most delicate of shrugs. "I can't say he terribly impresses me either."

Dovzhenko let out a sharp laugh and a nod before he focused on Adam. Then his expression sobered.

"Let's just get right down to business. I'm prepared to offer you five million dollars to just sever the marriage contract right now. No strings attached on either side. We walk away with Ezra, you walk away with your daughter and the money."

"Profitable," Dovzhenko said. "The marriage contract from Wallace, however, included stock and futures in other business projects. Construction primarily, and it would help establish a better foothold for us here."

"Then we'll make it twelve million," Lainey said. "That will compensate you for possible losses in future business. But you're also no longer bound by Graham and their projects. That means you'll be available if Reed or Benedict has work in the future. Expansion is always on the horizon, after all, and I expect there will be more than enough projects to keep multiple companies employed."

Oksana looked puzzled though Dovzhenko seemed thoughtful. "That's a very specific number," she said and for the first time I could recall in one of these conversations, her father didn't shush her or give her a silencing look. "Why not raise it only by one or two million, why go directly to seven?"

"Because your father doesn't really want to have all of his prospects tied up in Graham. While the guarantee of work is attractive, it's not lucrative. Graham wouldn't have to pay top dollar in a competitive market."

Adam hadn't removed his hands from his pockets as he added, "Twelve million, however, is more than enough to set up a couple of offices, equipment, and licensing in addition to what you already possess. It makes competing on a grander playing field more accessible."

It was so damn hot how they volleyed and served to each other. They seemed in near perfect sync. Dovzhenko, on the other hand, seemed more intrigued by the offer than turned on by it.

Well, and why should he be? Lainey and Adam were mine. Not his. If he were turned on that would be gross. I shook off the distracting thought.

"Make it seventeen," Dovzhenko said. "Then we will consider it a closed matter and a contract fulfilled rather than broken. No strings, of course."

"Of course," I murmured with a slight shake of my head.

"For seventeen," Lainey countered. "I want something else added to the deal."

Oksana focused on her. "What would that be?"

"An answer." She made it sound so simple. I didn't really think we needed to pursue this, but Lainey refused to accept that option. Adam didn't seem to be in a hurry to stop her either.

"An answer?" Oksana frowned, then glanced at her father before looking back at us. "An answer to what?"

"To why you tried to kill Ezra on the day you two negotiated the last marriage contract." Adam delivered the bomb in the most even of tones. It was almost bored. If I didn't know him so well, it might even hurt my feelings.

Dovzhenko jerked, surprise rippling through his expression before he could quite contain it. Oksana, however, looked neither surprised nor moved.

That... that disappointed me.

I had done everything to try and make this work for her and she tried to kill me.

"We have no idea what you're talking about." Her father sounded so certain. But really, how could he be? Except, he would now protect his daughter. He had been in the negotiations.

"Maybe you don't," I said, accepting the truth of that. "I just wish Oksana didn't."

He snapped a look from me to her, and as if on cue tears filtered into her eyes and she looked at her father. In rapid Russian, she denied having anything to do with it. She had no idea what they were talking about.

The lie was right there.

And I wasn't the only one who saw it.

He took a step back from her, then his scowl deepened before he looked at us again. "She is my daughter."

"I know," I told him. "I really do. I even like her most of the time. Did my best for her..."

"Why did you try to kill him?" Lainey asked and she'd moved, strolling forward until she invaded Oksana's space. The girl glanced to her father, but he didn't move, and then she was forced to retreat as Lainey moved ever closer. "If you didn't do anything, you wouldn't be so afraid right now. Especially because killing Ezra was an impulse, not a plan."

She swallowed. "I didn't want to get married. I thought...if he was sick—then it would be called off. A weak heart. Papa would never force me to marry a weak man. After he disappeared, I had hope, then he came again."

Finally, Oksana looked at me.

"I wasn't trying to kill you. I promise—it's Papa's medicine. I know a little will help. I just... my hand slipped. I didn't think it would be so much."

Dovzhenko put a hand over his mouth as he stared at his daughter.

"I'm sorry," she whispered, then looked at Lainey.

"I believe you," Lainey said, and I agreed with her. Then

Lainey punched her so hard, I actually flinched. The crack of sound echoed through the room and Oksana went down, clutching her face. "That's for making the mistake of touching him. Don't ever do it again."

For a moment, Dovzhenko stared at Lainey with something like hunger and any trace of a smile I might have had went away. Adam straightened and strode forward. Yeah, I wasn't the only one who saw it.

"Seventeen million and you keep your daughter away from him and us. We'll consider it done. But if anything happens to him—if he gets so much as a papercut, *she's* the first one we're coming for."

Lainey left them both and moved over to me. She threaded her arm through mine and then stared at Oksana's father. Oksana was still on the floor, holding her face. I thought she might have been crying, but all the empathy I'd had for her had long since evaporated.

It died on the way to the hospital and was buried with the heart damage I'd received.

"Done," Dovzhenko said and offered his hand to Adam. "I don't want a war with any of you. I just want my business and to make it grow."

Adam shook his hand. "Why negotiate a marriage with Graham anyway?"

"Julius King advised it. He said Graham could open doors. Then over time, I suspected that it was falling through, but King called a few months back. Said it was long past time Ezra toed the line and reminded me and Graham both of the deal we'd made with him."

That was the last puzzle piece.

King.

"What the hell did he get out of this deal?" I had to know.

265

"Originally, money and power." Dovzhenko shrugged. "It's what all men want. But over time, his interests have grown more personal. The marriage was as much for business as it was for settling personal scores." He flicked a look toward Lainey.

What. An. Asshole. All the anger that had dried out for them threatened to drown me now. King and my father. They were likely brothers. Did they know?

I suspected they did.

But King used it as leverage. Used it to get my father to do what he wanted. I defied King. Milo defied King. Force my hand. Make me marry and hurt Lainey to hurt Milo.

Sick, sadistic bastards.

"Just power?" Adam said. "Don't you think he'll be put out with you taking our deal?"

Dovzhenko reached a hand down to Oksana, and she let him pull her up. He pulled a handkerchief out of his pocket and passed it to her before he looked at us. "I am a man of my word. I made all the arrangements. Their failure to deliver is not a reflection on me. You have offered me a better deal, and they are now outbid. I don't really care what he decides."

Oksana touched the handkerchief to her bloodied and swollen lip. The mark on the side of her face was growing ruddier by the moment.

"Good luck," I said, and the teary-eyed girl looked at me. "I hope things work out for you, and no offense, but I'm very happy we're not getting married."

She tried to smile then grimaced. "Me too," she finally said, then with a wary look toward Lainey, she moved closer to her father. "Are we done?"

"Yes," he said. "I'll expect the wire."

"You'll get it," Adam told him before he guided them to

the door. Opening it, he ushered them out, leaving Lainey and me alone.

I lifted her hand to examine it. The knuckles were definitely very red, but the skin wasn't broken. "That was hot," I told her and she chuckled.

"Me punching another woman was hot?" She practically dared me with her sexy smile and heated hazel eyes.

"Extremely," I told her, gripping her chin gently before I kissed her. "I can't tell you how protected and wanted I feel."

"Hmm," she hummed.

I lifted my head. "What?"

"Hitting her doesn't feel like enough. But you didn't die and Bodhi was right. A measured response is better in the long run."

A slow grin tipped the corners of my lips. "You'd kill for me?"

"Yes," she told me without an ounce of hesitation, and I wrapped an arm around her neck and dragged her back to me for a kiss.

"I'd burn the world down for you," I promised her.

"I just need you to live," she answered as my lips brushed hers. "Live and be safe."

I would work on that. Laving my tongue over her lower lip, I sighed as she welcomed me with sweeps of her own tongue. When she threaded her arms around my neck, I groaned and picked her up. I didn't want to rumple her cool suit, but I did want to heat us both up.

The sound of the door opening behind me had me grunting. She stroked her nails along my nape and bit my lip lightly before I lifted my head.

"They're gone?"

"Yep," Milo said. "Bodhi and Adam are following them out making sure they are well and truly gone."

I glanced over my shoulder at him. "You were right," I said.

He sighed. "So far, everything that has happened had his fingers in it."

I set Lainey down. She threaded her fingers with mine and leaned against me, but her attention was on Milo.

"We're also going to have to deal with my father," I admitted. Getting rid of Oksana and her father was just a patch. My father would lose his shit when he realized we'd circumvented him.

"We will," Milo said, but Lainey's phone vibrated and she pulled away to get it out of her purse. "One step at a time. King is proving more and more that his goals are not ours."

They never had been, but I didn't have to point that out.

"We have another problem," Lainey said, showing us the screen on her phone.

"Mrs. Waldemar wants another meeting. This time just with me."

TWENTY-NINE

LAINEY

"No," Adam said even as Ezra added, "Absolutely not."

"Can we talk this through?" Milo asked rather than just order. That was something. Ezra pivoted to glare at him, but Adam just pinched the bridge of his nose. The only one curiously nonverbal was Bodhi.

"Yes," I said. "We can. Margareta Waldemar wants something from me. Clearly, I'd have to be blind, deaf, and dumb to not notice it when we were there, and I'm none of those things."

"Agreed," Bodhi said. "Tea?"

"No," I said, though a smile pulled at my lips. "Coffee would be great, though."

We were back at Bodhi's apartment. I was actually hungry, but Mrs. Waldemar asked me to come to her place for tea, and that would be in roughly—I checked my watch—two and a half hours give or take.

"I go with a driver. So one of you can play the role of Wood."

"Can one of us pretend to be Karagiani and go inside with you?" Ezra said, his scowl firmly in place.

"No," I told him. "I have no problems if you're just down the street. But I wouldn't let Karagiani sit in on a private conversation either. Besides, she made it clear she wants to talk to *me*."

"That is a concern," Bodhi said as he carried the carafe of coffee out with a series of mugs. He set the mugs down and poured me one before facing me again. The guys were apparently welcome to get their own.

"I appreciate that." I absolutely did. "However, I am capable of having a conversation with a woman who is rapidly approaching her seventieth birthday."

"You realize this is the same woman who sent people to kidnap Emersyn and Liam, right?" Adam said, his blue-violet eyes darkening with every syllable. "I've met her, far more times than you have, and yes, she might be an older woman with a great deal of style and class—but she is perfectly capable of ordering a murder."

"I know," I said, meeting his gaze. "Adam, I haven't forgotten anything. But, for the sake of argument, let's say we all go. How does that end any differently than our last visit? Except now, she knows she can't trust me to honor a request."

His sigh held a deep eloquence all its own. Milo frowned then glanced at Bodhi. "You have to have something that will let us listen."

"I do?" He met Milo's gaze with a bemused smile.

"Yes," Pretty Boy said firmly. "Because you're no more willing than we are to send her in somewhere alone without a modicum of knowing what is going on."

"True," Bodhi said with a nod.

"Do you have something or not?" Ezra half-exploded, his exasperation was mildly amusing. But only mildly. I put my coffee aside and went over to him.

"I'll be fine," I reminded him. "I'm never unarmed these days. You will all be right there. Even if something happens, I can hold my own long enough for you to get to me." Not that I really thought she was going to do anything physical. "But I truly believe this isn't about intimidation or anything inherently dangerous to my life."

"It's a game," Bodhi said. "One of strategy. Only, we're playing at a disadvantage. I don't care for that."

Neither did I. "I'll wear a wire, if you have something that isn't screamingly obvious and that I can at least color coordinate." The last comment earned a smile as well as a snort from Pretty Boy.

"Never change, Mayhem," he said as he closed the distance, then cupped my face. "Never change."

I didn't plan on it. Bodhi scratched at his jaw as he studied me. "You really want to do this?"

I considered the whole of the question, not just the part that applied to this meeting. "Margareta Waldemar has more contacts in Eastern Europe."

"Right." Bodhi stood. "I'll be right back."

I leaned against Milo even as Ezra squeezed my hand. Adam met my gaze and then nodded his head. "I don't like it."

"I know," I said. "But I will use any and all resources we can exhaust."

A couple of hours later, Bodhi drove through the gates to drop me off. "I'll be listening," he said. "So will they. You won't be able to hear us."

That was the one caution. They could hear me, but I couldn't hear them.

"We'll make it work. Thank you."

"Stay safe, Lainey B. That's the deal. Take it or leave it."

"I'll take it." Then I touched his shoulder, a ghost of a touch as one of the guards opened the door for me. "I'll call when I'm ready to go." The last I said easily, dismissing my driver.

While I'd half-expected a pat down, the guard merely nodded me toward the house as he directed Bodhi to turn the car around and out. Milo, Adam, and Ezra were less than a block away. I'd changed, choosing something more casual yet smart for the afternoon tea meeting.

All at once, I wished I was free of all of this and on the back of one of the horses or at the range or the gym. The restlessness came when my control had been threatened. I preferred to manage my own schedule and choices.

I acted.

It was one of the lessons Grandfather instilled in me. The past few weeks, all I'd been able to do was react. That needed to change.

The door opened to a behemoth of a man with relatively no neck and he reminded me of Andre the Giant, except not quite as tall, but definitely huge.

He backed up a step and nodded to me. Then he pointed toward the kitchen.

"Thank you."

Rather than reply, he just waited for me to pass him, then he closed the door. I wanted to glance back but resisted the impulse. Instead, I made my way into the sunny kitchen.

The smell of baking filled the air, and there was a gentle whistle from the kettle. The woman who was preparing little sandwiches when I walked in cast me a smile.

"Prompt," she murmured. "I appreciate that. Feel free to hang your coat there by the door and have a seat. I thought about taking this into the library or one of the other rooms, but I'm still renovating."

She paused for a moment, then glanced around the kitchen before she focused on me again. "The kitchen is the heart of the home. It's where you nurture and care for your family. So yes, I think we'll have our tea in here."

That seemed nice. So I took off my coat and glanced around the cozy kitchen. She'd added more plants, and there were new photographs near the table. Some were older, black and white, and the details indicated sometime in the 1940s or earlier.

One of the older women reminded me of Mrs. Waldemar. There were photos of children, and places. Another from a wedding. Was that hers?

"Family," Mrs. Waldemar said as she carried a three tiered serving platter with various cakes, and pastries, as well as the little tea sandwiches she'd been making. "Several generations. I have an older photo of my grandparents. One of the first taken in our family, but I keep it in a secure box that's fire retardant. Some things can't be replaced."

"That's true," I said. "Can I help at all?"

"No, no. I love this ritual of tea and preparing all the bits for it. It soothes me. Now do you most likely take your tea as western European? Sugar and milk?"

"Yes, thank you. Occasionally, depending on the tea, I like it with honey and lemon. My grandmother used to brew tea every summer and served it to me over ice. She said it was sacrilege, but I just didn't like hot tea when I was little."

Mrs. Waldemar chuckled. She brought over another three-tiered platter. I hope some of her guards got to eat after we were done. When she finally settled at the table with me, she'd brought our tea pots filled with the freshly boiled water, and she offered me a selection to brew my own tea.

"This is lovely, dear," Mrs. Waldemar said as she began the process of making her own tea. "Thank you for indulging me. I wasn't sure you'd be able to make it so directly."

"Considering where we were when you sent the invitation, I rather doubt that." I let the tea steep and selected two small triangles from the sandwiches and one pastry.

"Hmm...how is your hand?"

It was a little sore. "Oksana's face took the worst of that."

"So I heard," she said with a soft sigh and a shake of her head. "Her father is quite vexed with her. But she's always been a headstrong girl. He should have figured out she wouldn't be married off no matter the arrangements."

"You knew," I said, not bothering to dance around the subject.

"I did." She added a spoon of jam to her tea and began to stir it slowly. "I wasn't aware of your close ties at the time. Though you were much younger when the proposal was first made."

"You do business with King." It was speculation at best. But if her family was...

"I do not," she corrected. "My nephew has done business, but that is to study the man. To get a feel for him. To see what he finds valuable. You can learn a lot about a person by how they do business."

"My grandfather taught me something similar."

"Leopold is a cagey man and a dangerous one. I like him very much. I do wish I'd had more time of late to get to know him, but I rather suspect he does not trust easily, and I had other commitments."

It was my turn to smile and I lifted the tea to sip. It was excellent. Even as hungry as I'd been before coming, I didn't find much appetite for the food no matter how appealing. "He can be stubborn, but he's also an excellent judge of character." Most of the time.

Then again, Harper Reed lived down to every awful thing Grandfather had ever said about him. Mother... My humor fled.

"My apologies, dear girl, I didn't mean to bring up a topic that bothers you."

"Everyone has some issues with their family."

"Leopold is well, isn't he?" Now genuine concern seemed to inhabit her blue eyes.

"Very healthy. Very spry." Much to his own chagrin.

"Your grandmother," she said softly. "I did talk to Leopold about her condition one afternoon."

"He misses her," I said. "So if you fancy my grandfather, I must urge you to not pursue it or him."

"No, I can see that. He's very much a one woman man. I admire that about him and have too much respect to overstep."

"Thank you." Back and forth we went. As much as this felt like a dance, it also felt like a game of tennis. The serves had been soft so far, but they didn't promise to stay that way.

"Of course, though, I must venture closer perhaps to a more sensitive topic."

I raised my eyebrows, letting her take the lead as I took another sip of the tea. Then made myself take a bite of one of the sandwiches. Oh, it was a perfect cream cheese and cucumber. The crunch was right there and the rest of the sandwich soft.

"I'm aware that you have a strained, or should I say estranged, relationship with your mother. I could pretend I haven't done my research, but clearly I have and you are too intelligent for me to act differently."

"It's hardly a trade secret. Mother has her life and I have mine."

"Yes, she chose to be the mistress of a married man and then married him when his wife passed. Now he keeps other mistresses. Unsavory business, yet it is also the way of the powerful it seems. They are never happy. They never have enough."

I couldn't disagree with her so I merely lifted my shoulders. "As you say, it's the way of things."

"What has me curious is what do you know about your own father?"

"My father?" I didn't have to feign surprise now. "Very little, I'm afraid. He's a non-entity in my life. Most likely a passing affair that my mother had and didn't want to share with anyone. To my knowledge—she's never told anyone who he was." To that end, he didn't matter.

"I find you too cunning a young woman to leave yourself open by way of ignorance. What if someone were to appear and tell you that you were related? How would you know whether you could believe them or not?"

I finished the sandwich then washed it down with some tea before using the napkin to dab at the corners of my mouth. "I wouldn't believe them at all. Without any kind of concrete proof or verifiable facts—I would have no reason to believe them."

Mrs. Waldemar looked pensive for a moment. "That is a

fair assessment. You have a good head on your shoulders. Honestly, you impress me more and more. Your sister is missing, Harper Reed assaulted you, you're involved in a war on two different fronts, and you just paid my nephew seventeen million dollars to go away." She gave me the barest of smiles. "I think he got the better end of that bargain, but then you wouldn't have offered if you didn't think that young man worth it."

"Why are you bringing up my sister?" I cut away from the rest of it to focus on Andrea.

"Because, she was put on a plane to Germany roughly two weeks ago according to my contacts with a chaperone who would see her to Frankfurt. From there, they would take a train to Hungary."

My stomach bottomed out. "You know where she is?"

"No, I know where she was, and I am more than willing to give you that information. You are a good sister, and I think you deserve to know. Where she is precisely, I can't say. However, my cooperation does have a cost, and I know you will pay it."

Of course it did. I could practically hear Adam's barely restrained growl. He was likely furious.

"I thought we weren't playing games."

"We're not," Mrs. Waldemar said. "What I want—five minutes with your mother, Melissa Benedict Reed and the head of Julius King on a pike, but considering the difficulty of that in the States, I'll accept delivery in a box."

"You keep going back and forth on whether you want to kill him immediately or later." She'd told Adam she wanted him dead a few times, then she withdrew it. Now again. I knew why she wanted him dead, but why now? "What's changed?"

"The only thing that matters is will you do it?"

277

"I won't do anything without a better reason than you may be able to give me more information on my sister's current whereabouts." I leaned back in my seat. "What do you know about the person or people my sister was sold to?"

For a moment, Mrs. Waldemar just stared at me. No expression shifted across her face or in her eyes. Then slowly she began to nod. "Good girl. Take control of the negotiation."

"That's not an answer."

"No," she said with the faintest of smiles. "It's not. I've made my offer, I'll hear yours now."

"Here's my offer," I said as I stood, calmly folding the napkin and setting it on the table. "I'll find my sister. I'll take care of my family. I'll make sure my people are safe. You can keep working on your house and your connections. We don't have to do business at all."

"Except that Adam works for me and owes me a debt."

"No, he doesn't. That debt was to get more on King. You've already used him for that. Now you keep him on a string because you were looking for more—apparently, you wanted to talk to me and you were going about it in a circuitous route. Fine, we're talking. Mrs. Waldemar, with all due respect, I will not be your errand girl. If you want King dead—do it yourself." With that, I collected my coat. "Thank you very much for the tea."

"You're quite welcome and do call me Margareta."

I slid the coat on and studied her. "Why would I do that?"

"Because you've earned it." She rose. "Otto..."

The man from the door reappeared.

"Do walk Miss Benedict out. I'm sure she'll need to wait

for her car. Give her the envelope please. Then come help me finish all these sandwiches."

The man nodded and turned to head to the door, leaving me to study her.

"You're an interesting opponent, Margareta," I said. "Do you play chess?"

She smiled. "I prefer cards or checkers. But I can handle a game or two of chess."

I nodded slowly. All of this had been an opening gambit to what... an alliance with me?

"Thank you for the tea, it was delicious."

"Have a good afternoon, dear, and do tell those young men of yours that I am sorry I couldn't invite them this time. Maybe next time."

That almost made me laugh. Almost.

I headed toward the front door where Otto waited. He handed me a large manila envelope then opened the door. The cold air washed in. I probably had a couple of minutes before Bodhi would get here.

I opened the envelope and stared at the photos.

Andrea.

More information on her flight. Snaps of her looking happy, and laughing as she spoke to the woman. She seemed familiar but I didn't know her. But Andrea seemed to be very comfortable with her. A teacher maybe? A tutor?

There were more pictures at an airport in Germany. Then at a train station. Andrea was buying postcards. Did she think she was going on a vacation?

Who was more willing than a captive who didn't know they were one?

THIRTY

BODHI

The meeting with Waldemar netted more information, but the pieces didn't all fit together. Not specifically. The fact she'd actually tried to direct Lainey B to kill King for her had been mildly irritating. Was this some kind of bizarre initiation trial she put all of her people through?

Adam and Milo had looked equally annoyed, but of all of them, it was Ezra who laughed. Under the stink eye from the other two, he'd shrugged.

"Our girl is not known for her obedience to being told what to do."

His explanation made me smile. Milo smirked, but it was Adam who snorted. "This is true." A moment later, Lainey turned her down in a polite, elegant manner that seemed to amuse Mrs. Waldemar. Then she'd given Lainey the information anyway.

Everything she'd done had been a challenge and a test for Lainey. It was why I'd left early this morning to visit my step-great-grandmother. I wanted to bring Lainey with me, but she had more reading to do and they wanted to speak to PPG and her boys as well as Fletcher.

It wasn't until I was in my car in the garage that Lainey's message came through on my phone.

You're going out alone, but unbruised and in excellent health. I expect you to return in the same condition.

My marching orders had arrived.

Yes, ma'am. I will present myself for inspection as soon as I get back.

Her laughing emoji made me smile. We'd enforced backup with Lainey and Ezra everywhere. Milo and I hadn't been as strict with ourselves. Then again, no one had tried to take us.

I would love for them to try. A shiver of anticipation slid through me. Oh, how I would love for someone to try and take me. That would be an excellent exercise in purging aggression.

With that in mind though, I headed to the Upper East Side. Sophia kept a lovely pied-à-terre in the city. Otherwise, she'd moved to Vermont on one of my great-grandfather's older estates. She'd spent the last twenty-five years renovating it and restoring the farm to its eighteenth century glory days.

She preferred to live there, away from the backstabbing and corporate maneuvering. It also meant when she came to town, everyone leapt to accommodate her schedule. I'd asked her once if it was her intention to throw everyone into chaos randomly.

Her smile said she wasn't disappointed by the effect, but no, she just liked living away from all the "right" people. She liked the quiet of the country. Still, she enjoyed theater trips to the city.

Collin or I had accompanied her many times. As had Eliza. Occasionally, she squired around some potential beau who wanted to impress her. The savvy older men in their suits and ties with old world manners were rather sweet.

My guards made sure no one misbehaved. I enjoyed Sophia, her sense of humor, her intelligence, and her charity. I also liked that she didn't let the gilded glamor and glitz of our world ever change her.

My great-grandfather had impeccable taste in his wives. His first wife had been known as one of the kindest in the city. She took in all types and never shunned a single person for their choices. Her death had been a blow, but then he'd met Sophia.

I'd only known him briefly when I was very young. Yet, my mother had been very fond of him and she relayed many of his stories—including the idea that you could have more than one soulmate. Loving both in no way, diminished the love you had for each.

Or in Lainey's case, the love she had for all four of us. Soulmates was a vague concept. An intellectual exercise, I supposed. It didn't happen for me immediately. Then, I'd known Lainey since she was a child.

It wouldn't have been appropriate then, nor was she the woman she'd become. I'd been rougher then, less capable of being the kind of man she needed. So, yes, I found my soulmate. We just both had to grow up.

Sophia Carsters-Cavendish waited for me, curled up in a high-backed chair next to the electric fireplace in her apartment, a cup of coffee in hand and a warm smile on her face.

"Good morning," I said as I leaned down to kiss her cheek. Her staff had let me in after I called up from the garage. No one came up on the direct elevator without clearing it through security. "You look lovely today." She'd had her hair done since the last time I'd seen her. The cut was neat and touched her shoulders.

"You charmer," she said with a laugh. "Do sit down, darling. I had them pour your coffee when you called up to say you were here."

"Always looking after me," I teased as I unbuttoned my suit jacket before taking the seat opposite her. She was still in her dressing gown, but then she'd only been up for an hour.

"I always shall," she said. "Now, have a seat. Eliza was up far too late and is sleeping in today or I'd have messaged her to come up."

Eliza also had an apartment in the building. Despite their vastly different schedules, the women made time to spend together at least twice a year.

"I understand, and it was an impulse that brought me here this morning."

"Then I'm glad I'm in the city, though it's been a while since you came up to Vermont. You should come see the changes we made."

"I'll put it on my list, I promise."

"Good, you'll bring the lovely young Miss Benedict to see me?" While playful, her coy tone was an affectation.

"Someone has been gossiping," I murmured, not at all displeased. If Lainey were linked to me, then her potential antagonists would have no one but themselves to blame when I dealt with them as I had Harper Reed.

No one would harm her.

Ever.

"Well now, you sweep out with the heir to the Benedict fortune on the heels of a wedding announcement at a New

Year's Eve party, yes, darling, everyone talks. I must have received no less than a half-dozen calls, well-wishes, and even more invitations over the next three days."

I snorted. "You never gossip about family."

"No," she murmured. "That is true. But I do so enjoy when everyone tries to court me into doing so. You get to learn the most delicious things."

The glow in her eyes was quite real. She may not enjoy all the trials and tribulations of dealing with high society regularly. Who could blame her, truly? "Well, they should provide you with a great deal of entertainment soon. There have been some shifting tides and power dynamics."

"Oh." She straightened. "Those are even more fun because they frustrate your father."

Chuckling, I raised my coffee cup to her. "Always a perk. But—as much as we will enjoy some of that potential fallout, I didn't come here to discuss those particular details."

"But you did come to talk to me about *some* details?" Hope lived in her voice. It made me wish I had some particularly juicy piece to give her. She would love it, but for now…

"Questions, more than details. I think you might know some pieces to the stories that we're missing. You have known all the players for so much longer. Their quirks, and flaws, are not surprises to you."

"Hardly," she agreed. "What do you need to know?"

"Julius King—Eliza and I discussed him before. She mentioned there had been rumors for some time that he'd been born on the wrong side of the sheets?"

We'd gotten DNA confirmation, but I wanted to know how much others knew and possibly when.

"Oh, yes, I suppose. I've only met the man once. Very unpleasant."

My eyes narrowed at the description. "What did he do?"

"No, nothing like that. You don't have to worry that he was rude or misbehaved. More—a feeling you get when dealing with him. There's an air of pretentiousness about him. Like, he expects to be treated poorly, while he in turn, offers you the best of manners and refinement." Sophia frowned and shook her head a little. "It's like trying too hard to fit in, when it should just come naturally. Only people with something to prove work so hard to prove they don't belong."

Resting my elbows on the arms of the chair, I studied her. "I've seen that before."

"Of course you have, we all have. It happens when new money mixes with old. I don't mean to sound arrogant or unwelcoming, it's just a matter of course. If someone were kinder to him or he had more friends, perhaps they would smooth the way."

"But he doesn't. How much do you really know about him?"

"I know he made some politically unsound moves for a time, but that was to gradually absorb the Royals. Your great-grandfather was a Royal, one of the first from our family. Though his father was more than wealthy enough to have been considered, he didn't like to be handed anything."

Her eyes took on a distance.

"Initially, the Royals were an open secret amongst the founding families in the old Bay Ridge area. Bit by bit, the families expanded. Some intermarried. Some brought in new blood. Founding families slipped away, new branches were brought in—but the legacy was always present."

I nodded.

"It evolved into something of a gentleman's club, but

the ladies weren't fully excluded, just—bored of the games. It shifted again after World War II, more corporate and less woo-woo stuff."

I didn't laugh at the woo-woo description.

"But twenty-five or six years ago now—I feel like it was yesterday; you were still very young and your mother was still very much with us—there was a falling out between a couple of the families. Rather than choose sides, everyone kind of took a step back... then one day Julius King was there and he'd begun to take over. I honestly couldn't tell you precisely how he did it, but he had to have had support. He was always closest to the Grahams."

That fit. It would fit more if Wallace Graham was aware of him.

"Where criminal mischief might have been something of a lark before, it took a darker turn." She sighed, then paused as the maid came in with the fresh coffee. She refilled our mugs, then gave Sophia a firm look.

"I will bring a tray with your breakfast and your medication. Is Mr. Phillip joining you for breakfast?"

"No," I said, when Sophia glanced at me. "Thank you for the offer. But I'd be happy to sit here with you while you eat."

"Thank you, Darla."

"Of course, ma'am. Mr. Phillip." Then she swept out again leaving us alone.

"As I've said, a lot of people don't think I pay attention, but I do. I knew Wallace's father. Thoroughly unpleasant man. He was a womanizer, kept multiple mistresses. Most of the time, he paid to have their unwanted pregnancies taken care of, but Julius' mother refused. That was the rumor, and you do know how some ladies like to gossip." She winked at me.

"Was he born Julius King?" 'Cause where did that name come from? So far, no one had been able to track that down.

"Oh, darling, that I don't know. I rather doubt it. The mother was—a dark Irish lass who worked in his offices. I never met her, only heard about her."

That made sense. I paused while her breakfast was delivered. "Go on," she told me. "Ask me more questions, this is fun."

I chuckled. "You are hoping for a morsel, aren't you?"

"Absolutely. I like knowing things that others do not."

I could respect that. "Elaine Benedict."

"Wonderful girl. I have met her," she told me. "If I'd known that was what kept you single all these years, I might have been less pushy about making you take me to the theater so often so I could parade some possibilities in front of you."

"That would have been a shame," I assured her. "I loved going to the theater with you."

Her laughter and smile belied the tsk she sent my way. "Elaine Benedict," she prompted me.

"Do you know who her father is?"

"Oh ho, one of the greatest scandals of the season just twenty some odd years ago." Sophia took a bite of the single slice of bacon on her plate. She nibbled it thoughtfully. "Leopold was incensed, and I think if not for Allegra, they would have disowned Melissa then and there."

"Children out of wedlock isn't quite the scarlet letter anymore." I hated the idea of anyone looking at Lainey as less because of circumstances she was hardly in charge of.

"Oh, no, I know it's not. But it doesn't change the matter that Melissa was the wildest, most inappropriate of children. She *loved* to thumb her nose at convention and expectations. On the night of her first coming out ball, she danced nude in one of the fountains at Tammerly, where the Adleys were hosting. It was the source of enormous gossip for months. It never seemed to touch her. Scandalized everyone, embarrassed her mother, incensed her father and Melissa? She loved it."

"Very different from her daughter," I murmured.

"Oh incredibly different. Everything I've seen of Elaine Benedict is well-spoken, intelligent, and clever young lady more than capable of handling herself in all situations. Leopold raised her well."

"But no one knows who her father is?" I found that so hard to believe.

"Well, there were rumors. There are always rumors. Melissa's involvement with Harper Reed was probably the worst kept secret of the time. She wasn't even done with school and he was stepping out on Emily with her. When she turned up pregnant, everyone presumed—even Emily."

That wasn't the whole story.

"Her father isn't Harper Reed though."

"No, shockingly enough, but I think there might still be a Reed involved. Eliza told me once that Jason kept a lot of secrets for the Reeds. He is the one of course who took care of the school and those families after that awful tragedy that happened with his son."

The school shooting. I remembered that. I'd been old enough to understand the cover-up when it happened.

"Jason has never been close to his brothers, but he's always taken care of their messes and their indiscretions."

"You think Melissa seduced him?"

"It would hardly be the worst thing she did and how better to punish her lover who would not leave his wife than to get pregnant by his brother?"

I wrinkled my nose.

"And if it wasn't him," Sophia said as she traded her bacon for the fruit bowl. "I imagine he knows who."

Nodding slowly, I turned that over in my head. "Jason Reed and Harper didn't get along."

"Absolutely not, whatever anyone saw in public was merely a pantomime for the masses. Jason and Harper loathe each other."

Then he might be willing to talk to us without torture. Maybe. Waldemar was after something specifically with Lainey, and she'd brought up King, Lainey's mother, and her father as well as her grandfather.

We were missing a piece, and I refused to let us be caught unaware again.

"You're planning something," Sophia said and at my raised eyebrows, she laughed. "I recognize that look in your eyes. I approve, whatever it is. I just want you to know that. Now, what else can I help you with?"

The funny thing was, she absolutely would approve. "Tell me about the shows you're going to see, then I need to excuse myself and yes," I promised, raising a hand. "I will bring Lainey with me next time."

THIRTY-ONE

LAINEY

" I 'm sorry, Mr. Reed is not available," his assistant said. "You'll have to call again another time." Then the call disconnected. Jason Reed had been avoiding all of us, including Adam. He hadn't been in to his office in the city, and they weren't taking messages at either his home in Westchester County or his apartment in the city.

"They're still covering for him," I told Adam. We were already on the way to the new Stork Club. It had only opened in the past ten years, but it had definitely begun to build its reputation on the past Stork Club.

Where the original had been exclusively a nightclub from 1929 to 1965, the new one catered more as both a gentleman's and lunch club here in the city. Still prestigious, it offered a cafe society for the elite and the wealthy whether they were movie stars, celebrities, or aristocrats.

I'd kind of wanted to see the new one since it opened, but it also fashioned itself a reputation as a men's only club.

Women, of course, had to be allowed in some areas. But since they were private and required a membership, they could easily decline ladies they didn't want.

Misogynistic dinosaurs.

The club's location was not advertised. You had to know someone who had been invited. Adam had been, and as irritatingly amusing as that was, I couldn't help but be grateful.

We'd taken a limo today. Bodhi's people were handling security and the driving. I'd given Wood the rest of the month off unless Marlene needed him for something. I missed them, but for now, it was safer for both of them if I was away from them.

The limo pulled into the drive in front of the velvet canopied opening. "Don't go far," Adam told the driver as the doorman moved over to open the rear door. I stepped out, with Adam following me.

He showed his card to the doorman and the man nodded, admitting us. The lobby was tiled black with its gold appointments. My heels clicked as Adam moved with me. Today I was in a dark blue sweater dress that hugged my body but didn't require a belt to smooth the lines.

The heels were the perfect color, and it coordinated with Adam's tie. I also had the microphone clipped in place to my bra. It was flat, pressed against the skin, and didn't move. It let the guys hear everything.

They had staff in the elevator who took Adam's card and swiped it before swiping their own. Then we were taking the elevator up several floors to where the club held court. You couldn't just wander in off the street.

Adam offered his arm as the doors opened, and I rested my hand on the inside of his elbow. "Ready to go make some trouble?"

I grinned. "You think very highly of my plans."

"Correction," he murmured, nuzzling a kiss to my temple. "I think very highly of you. Your plans, however, well, let's just say you don't always choose predictable paths."

"That's what makes life with me so interesting," I reminded him and he snorted. It was soft, but genuine.

"Not the word I would choose."

I'd never been so tempted to pinch him, but I was thinking about it. A host strode forward to welcome him. They shook hands, and the man practically fawned over Adam without giving me a second look.

Yeah, women were only brought here for the entertainment and pleasure of the men, whether it was a mistress, a wife, or a stripper.

Somehow, I rather doubted daughters were included. Then again, considering Harper's disgusting behavior, maybe the ones who were would not enjoy the experience at all.

I could barely suppress the shiver of revulsion. Adam shot me a questioning look, but I shook my head. Not important right now. We were here because Adam had a source at Reed that said Jason preferred to take meetings here when he could, specifically to avoid Harper and Hamilton.

Odd location for a man I never quite pictured as gross as his brothers, but then what did I really know about him? His wife Sable had never had the time of day for me or my mother. In fact, she treated my mother like trash and barely noticed me unless my grandfather was there.

Fletcher, on the other hand, was one of my favorite humans and he was their son. So—maybe everything redeeming about them had escaped in the form of their child?

"A table for two," Adam was saying. "Someplace quiet and relaxed."

"The lounge isn't that busy at the moment," our—well, Adam's host said. "If you'll come with me."

We followed him past the dining room which also didn't seem that busy. What tables were occupied were few and far apart. The hallway was done up in real wood and beautiful light fixtures. The paintings were also classics, with at least one Van Gogh and Rembrandt on display.

Interesting.

No expense had been spared.

The carpet muffled my heels as we stepped into the lounge. Like the darkened hallway, the room had thick carpet, lounging areas spread out from tables and chairs to sofas and spaces clearly meant to afford more intimate company.

As our host guided us through, I caught sight of Jason on the far side near bookshelves. It almost looked like he'd found himself the most comfortable space in a university library and had settled in to do research while drinking coffee.

"Oh darling," I said in my best fluttery voice. It halted Adam dead in his tracks and he stared at me. The absolute lack of expression was a dead giveaway cause his eyes were dancing.

"Yes," he said slowly as if he needed every ounce of control to keep his micro-expressions in check, "dear?"

"I see someone we know."

At the slightly aghast look from the host, I was so tempted to add a little bounce to my delivery. But frankly, I didn't care what he thought, and since I could see Jason, I'd rather ditch him and go find our answers. I motioned toward his uncle and Adam nodded.

"Absolutely, let's go say hello." He turned us in that direction. When the host started to follow, Adam snapped his fingers. "No," he told him. "Stay."

The dismissive glance coupled with the command halted the host in his tracks. Lips pursed. "You enjoyed that," I murmured.

"I did. If only you were so obedient." The sensuous whisper teased over my skin, and it was my turn to snort.

"You would never like me if I were that cooperative."

"We could always test it," he dared me, and I rolled my eyes.

Jason chose that moment to notice us, and he frowned. He lowered his pen as he started to stand. "We don't have an appointment," he warned in a low voice that he clearly didn't want to carry.

"Since when did we need an appointment, Uncle?" Adam moved his hand to my lower back and offered me a seat opposite Jason.

"Adam..." Jason half-growled the words. "This is highly inappropriate. You know better."

"Of course he does," I said as I took my seat and crossed one leg over the other. Adam took the seat next to me, and Jason sat down slowly. "But here's the thing, Mr. Reed— you can talk to us here and now, keeping this ever so pleasant. Or I can make a scene, then you'll talk to us after. The only thing on the line is your reputation."

"If you make a scene, you think that's going to damage my reputation?" Jason eyed me like I'd sprouted a second head.

Adam reached forward and picked up a couple of salted nuts from the dish.

"Everyone goes through a wild phase. I'm twenty-one, just into the first part of my inheritance, and my mother—well, we all know how she earned her reputation. I'm fairly sure I'll be just fine." Head tilted, I gave Jason a once over. "You on the other hand... you don't like controversy or the spotlight. I understand, it can be very uncomfortable to have everyone talking about you—*again*."

The corners of Adam's lips tipped upward in a smile. When Jason shot him a look, Adam shrugged. "Talk to the lady. At least, she is asking nicely. If I take over, it won't be nice...and I won't be asking."

It was the most pleasant threat. I glanced at Adam, met his gaze, and we both smiled as we faced Jason again. He shook his head in absolute disgust.

"Fine, what do you want?" He focused on me again.

"Did you ever have an affair with my mother?" The silence that greeted the question detonated like a bomb, muting the whole room.

When Bodhi returned with that rumor, Adam had been apoplectic. Years he spent thinking I was his sister, now was I his cousin?

The sex was already out of the bag, if we were cousins, well, we were gonna be kissing ones. To hell with everyone else. I didn't *feel* related to him other than he was my family.

He would always be my family. I wasn't giving him or any of them up.

Jason, though, his expression transformed. From annoyed to appalled, he gaped at me. "Are you...are you *insane*?"

The answer was so scandalized, I almost laughed. There was nothing manufactured about it. Jason had even *paled* before he flushed in embarrassment. Adam, however, did laugh.

"Melissa's a beautiful woman, and as much as I dislike her," Adam said, "one could hardly fault you for finding her appealing."

"That's disgusting," Jason said, real anger in his tone along with revulsion. "I would never cuck my brother. Harper might be a jackass, and a sleaze, not to mention a backstabbing asshole. *I*, however, am none of those things. Even if Melissa had been with someone else, I would never have treated *Sable* that way."

The fury in his eyes blazed, and he gave me a look of such dislike, I actually felt a bit guilty for the question. "Then why does your name come up in conjunction with the identity of my father? Or I suppose I should rephrase that as sperm donor?"

The shock in his expression shuttered and his face drained of emotion. "I have no idea. Nor do I care to know. I don't gossip about family, and I don't trade in the salacious details of what women do or don't do or who they do them with. You can excuse yourselves now, or I can ask security to excuse you."

The utter shutdown was so profound that it almost felt like a door slammed shut in my face. Adam stared at Jason for a moment, but Jason had returned to his papers and ignored our very existence.

After another long minute, Adam rose and offered me a hand. Agreed. Whatever this was, the bridge had been fire-bombed before we could even breach it. Jason knew something, but he wasn't sharing.

Ignoring the host who waited for us, Adam directed us toward the exit and the elevator down. I couldn't blame him, I didn't want to stay either. Once we were in the elevator, he said nothing.

The car was waiting for us before we even reached the front. Once we were back inside, Adam said, "Take us around the block." Then he closed the privacy window and dialed something on his phone.

A moment later, I caught the sound of Fletcher's voice. Adam blew out a breath, "I need a favor. Your father knows something about Lainey's parentage. He won't share. In fact, he acted like we'd just committed murder right in front of him and shut us down."

He listened for a beat and then nodded even if Fletcher couldn't see him.

"I'd never ask if it weren't important, but it's for Lainey." Adam glanced at me and I slid my hand onto his thigh. "Thanks. I'll be here."

Then he ended the call.

"Fletcher is going to reach out to Jason."

I grimaced. "How long has it been since they talked?"

"Years," Adam said, rubbing the top of his phone against his lower lip. "If anyone can get a secret out of Jason, it's Fletcher."

I almost hated to ask him to. "If Fletcher wasn't willing, he would have told you no."

Adam nodded, but it was a distracted type of nod. His mind was clearly elsewhere.

"I'm turning off for a couple of minutes, guys, we're in the car," I said, then worked my hand into my purse and shut off the transmitter. Adam had already secured the privacy window between us and the driver. Twisting on the seat, I reached for Adam's hand. "I'm here."

Shaking his head, Adam said, "It's not important right now."

"It is important. We've had so much going on and no time to talk really. Not without someone else there. Not even after our time with Ezra." I hadn't asked if they'd found a way to be together without me there. It wasn't my business, and if they wanted me to know, they would tell me.

Frankly, my sex life with Milo and Bodhi wasn't something I advertised either. We were all entitled to our privacy and our secrets. I trusted them to not hurt me. Everything else would sort itself out.

He sighed, turning my hand over and tracing his fingers against the lines there. I gave him the length of two full blocks as our driver cruised in the traffic.

"It's about Ezra," I said finally and Adam lifted his gaze to me.

"Kind of obvious, I suppose," he admitted and I lifted my shoulders.

"To me, yes, but then I've been watching you both these past few months. The way he feels about you and the way you feel about him—it's not easy."

"Ezra," Adam said in a tone that was as affectionate as it was annoyed, "has *never* been easy."

"True. You wouldn't take easy if it walked up to you and offered to suck your cock." Crude, perhaps, but his flash of a smile said he didn't disagree with me. "I know I've never been easy for you either."

"No," he said in agreement. "You haven't. But you've always been worth it."

I smiled and reached up a hand to cup his cheek. "So are you."

"How did I not know that I was—I guess bi is the word," he admitted.

I shrugged. "Maybe you're more pansexual than

bisexual."

He frowned. "What's the difference?"

"The difference is you're attracted to people, not a gender. You love Ezra—you have loved him for years, and you find him mentally attractive, and you're discovering he's physically attractive too. That doesn't mean you're bisexual because him being male isn't what attracts you, just like me being female isn't it."

Adam eyed me for a long moment. "It's because you're Lainey."

I nodded. "And he's Ezra. You were attracted to me when you thought I might be your sister."

He grimaced. "Not my proudest moment."

"If you'd acted on it with willful disregard, and tried to groom me or act like I was there for your pleasure no matter my age—sure. But you didn't do that. You never acted like that, you handled it, maybe with anger, but you kept it appropriate between us. Period. Again, it wasn't my age or my gender... the age kept you away."

"I'm kind of fucked up," he admitted, and I laughed.

"How does it go? We're all a little bit fucked up?" I slid my shoes off as we circled the block again. "But Adam, here is the thing...You love Ezra. You want desperately to protect him, and you're trying to figure out how to do that while maintaining the relationship you already had. That relationship is going to change, just like ours has. As much as you crave being in control, you have to remember—Ezra needs it too."

Stroking my hand, Adam said, "I'm not good at giving up control."

"No, but you have been letting Bodhi take point. Ceding to Pretty Boy when he has a good idea. You have let Liam take over before too, depending on the situation. I get that, it's all situationally based. But Ezra is willing to go down on his knees for you. He will give you control. That's trust. Can you do the same for him?"

"Not likely to bow to anyone, Lainey," Adam admitted. "Not sure how I'd be on my knees or if I can even suck a cock."

The last held just the barest elements of uncertainty. Adam wasn't sure he'd be good at something. "You know," I told him as I slid down on the floor, lifting my skirt to keep it clean before moving to between his legs. I smoothed down his pants, very aware of the sudden rigid line of his cock. "Being on your knees isn't so bad, when you're the one who chooses to do it and it's for someone you want."

His eyes burned as I locked my gaze on his. With care, I unzipped his pants and worked off the buckle and button until I could slide my hand in. His cock was eager, twitching against my palm as I glided down it from base to tip.

Dipping my head, I wrapped my lips around the head of his cock and never looked away.

"Fuck," he said on a harsh breath.

"Later," I promised, then nibbled along the length of his cock before tracing the vein on the underside with my tongue. "I'm on my knees for you Adam, and I want you to take all your pleasure in my mouth. Let me give you that control..."

I could almost see the moment his control snapped and then he threaded his hands into my hair. I relaxed as he thrust past my lips and sighed. It was another few loops around the block and a good fifteen minutes before he came, and I swallowed every drop.

When he dragged me up for a kiss, he whispered, "I love you so fucking much."

"I know," I promised him. "I love you too... we can make this work, you can."

He kissed me again and then his phone began to ring. "Thank you," he said. "I'll think about it..."

"Hmm...and I can give you more lessons on cock sucking anytime you want."

Real laughter snorted out of him and he shook his head before he raised the phone to his ear.

"Did he tell you anything?"

CHAPTER

THIRTY-TWO

ADAM

We had a name.

Yuri Leistung.

When I repeated it to Lainey, she'd looked bewildered. The name meant nothing to her.

"I'm going to do a deep dive," Fletcher said. "I told my dad I'd have dinner with him and Mom. So this lead better pan out."

"Thanks," I told him. "I know that's not high on your list of things to do."

"It's fine, I'll introduce them to Drew. She'll protect me. Talk soon." Then Fletcher was gone. That had been some thirty-six hours earlier.

Now we had a full dossier courtesy of Fletcher. Yuri Leistung had gone to university with one Harper Reed. They'd actually been roommates in their freshmen years. It spurred a rivalry that continued for another decade.

According to Jason, after Melissa couldn't persuade my

father to leave my mother, she proceeded to tackle a number of different affairs. Her goal? Rub his face in it. None of them gave her the reaction she wanted until Yuri appeared at a function.

They struck up a conversation, and Harper reacted. He made the mistake of ordering her not to speak to the man again. She left with him that night and apparently they were in the Caribbean the next day. Whatever happened, Melissa's affair with Leistung persisted on and off for months.

Melissa made sure Harper knew about it. Then she turned up pregnant and Yuri was nowhere to be seen. She returned to New York, eventually had Lainey and resumed her place, but no one brought up Yuri—not even Melissa.

"So why keep him a secret though?" Lainey asked. "I get if he were an embarrassment for Harper. I suppose she didn't tell Grandfather because of the lack of pedigree. Though I doubt he would care about that."

Maybe not now, but then? I imagined old man Benedict definitely cared about pedigree. Even now, he wanted nothing to do with me because of mine. Still...

"Yuri Leistung died not long after you were born, Lainey," Fletcher said from where he was on the speaker phone. "Reports are sketchy. I've found a couple of obituaries that say he died in a car accident. A couple of incident reports filed with NYPD stating he'd been in a bar brawl on the same day. There's more—apparently there was a huge turnover in power with some of the Bratva transplants, old grudges. One report says he was probably a victim of that."

"Is he dead for sure?" Lainey asked, her brow furrowed. "I mean, if it indicates different ways he died, are they sure he's dead?"

"I've got a grave listed here, I suppose we could go dig it

up and do some tests. You like that ghoulish shit, Bodhi, don't you?"

For his part, Bodhi merely shrugged. "Someone has to be able to clean up the messes."

"As Rick is fond of saying, if you make the mess, you should be the one to clean it up."

"Gentlemen," Milo said, pinching his forehead. "I appreciate the snark and on another day, I might make popcorn and listen, but right now, can we stay on topic?"

"Of course," Vienna's voice came over the speaker, soothing and calm. "Fletcher's been working diligently to build the information. Cash and I are both trying to build a profile—but there's conflicting information."

"Conflicting like inconsistent?" I asked.

"Conflicting," Cash said, joining the conversation, "like Yuri Leistung was one person for a few years and then became someone else entirely."

"Someone took over his identity?" Lainey shook her head. "Why?"

"Could be a lot of reasons," Cash said. "The trick is, I can't tell exactly when the switch happened. You have a pattern of behavior that's reckless, but not irrational. Then in the last two years of his life, including the affair with your mother, the recklessness ratchets up and we add increasing violence on all fronts."

"In fairness, if there is mental illness in his family," Vienna picked up the thread. "He might have been exhibiting signs of schizophrenia, paranoia, psychosis... any number of conditions. Again, all speculative. But the age would have been right, sometime in his mid-twenties."

I raked a hand through my hair and stared up at the ceiling. "What does this name give us?" I asked. It wasn't quite rhetorical and yet, we'd been looking for this nugget of information.

"It's Eastern European," Fletcher supplied. "Eastern Europe keeps coming up."

"There's criminal ties," Milo added. "We're looking at Bratva by some of the reports, human trafficking for others. Whether Yuri was directly involved or not, it ties back to this."

"We know my father was involved in human trafficking." That made me sick. It also made me wonder if that was another reason Jason and Harper despised each other so much. If so—what had Harper done to Jason to keep him silent?

I pinched the bridge of my nose again. A hand landed on my shoulder, the grip tight and firm. An offer of support. Lifting my head, I met the sympathy in Ezra's gaze. He knew.

Of course he knew.

We'd really drawn the shit straws on terrible fucking parents.

"Is it possible that Leistung had any other ties to the Bay Ridge families?"

"Not that I'm seeing," Fletcher said. "The only people we can ask are not necessarily available for consultation. What other names I can link to him also appear to have died at some point. So there's almost no one we can ask."

"That's not true," Lainey said and Bodhi pivoted sharply. He got it a split-second before I did.

"You do not have to do that," I told her.

"Of course, I do," she said, rubbing her arms as though chilled. Milo was closer and he wrapped his arms around her. "Mother may not ever improve, but she was the one who had the affair. She has to know something about him."

The secret had been kept from everyone. Clearly, Harper had to have known who her father was, but he said nothing. They didn't tell Leopold either. They'd buried this secret and kept it buried.

Yuri had been buried not long after her birth. To keep the secret? To keep him from claiming her? Something else altogether?

"Does Leistung have family?" I might be reaching here. "I mean, connected family. We're saying Bratva, but was he just a foot soldier or someone higher up?"

Considering Dad went to Harvard, I didn't think a foot soldier would be getting that kind of education.

"Records from Europe are a bit harder to get and need to be translated. I'll stay on it and let you know." Fletcher blew out a breath. "I'm never sleeping again. Talk soon." Then the call ended.

"You know," Bodhi said. "If he does have family, another reason to keep the secret is to keep the family from coming to take Lainey."

"Depends on the family," Ezra said. "I've seen a few of those groups. Women might hold power, but they don't display it publicly, at least not for outsiders. No offense, Koyonok, penises are still more valuable for heirs than vaginas."

"None taken, I like penises too," Lainey said. The dry remark pulled smiles from all of us.

The laughter helped to dispel some of the tension. Not all of it, clearly, but some. It was like a mental palate cleanser, and I focused on the problem.

"Everything takes us back to Eastern Europe. You need a passport, Hardigan. If you don't have one, we need to get you one fast."

"I'll take care of it," Bodhi said. "We need a specific area to go to...Eastern Europe is still large. The contacts PPG has will help. Narrowing those locations by the numbers Fletcher tracked will help. But Waldemar has more."

The last sentence summed up my own thoughts. She'd given us enough information to be useful, to get a feel for *where* Andrea was heading. We still needed to find her. To get her and bring her home.

"Well, we know what the cost of the information is," Milo said pointedly.

"That would be killing your father," Ezra pointed out. "Not a great place to be."

"The man has *never* been a father," Milo said in a flat tone. Lainey rubbed her hands against his where they rested over her stomach. She leaned with her back against his chest. "Ever. All he ever did was inflict misery. Now that he's back in my life? He's doing it again."

I studied him for a long moment. "I can do it." The offer was not one I made lightly. I'd wanted to kill King for years. Ever since the first time he threatened Lainey. Then the first time I saw Ezra dragged into that hell with me. Yeah, I had zero problems killing King. "She gave me the job once. You and Bodhi took care of my father. I can take care of yours."

"Not alone," Bodhi said bluntly. "If we do this, we do it together. King has his own security and he has to know his days are numbered. Every move he's made has been to try and secure allies and instead of adding to them, he's been losing them."

"My heart really does bleed for him." Lainey shook her head. Sarcasm laced every word. "We know he has connections, and more. We also know he leverages people. When we take him, we need to take him somewhere no one will see or hear him."

"I know a place," Ezra said. "It's a drive. But we could take him up to the Catskills. Lots of places up there."

"Do we want to take that kind of time? If we do, we could be with him for a while to extract everything." Bodhi didn't sound opposed. "We need to weigh the risk versus the reward. Every day is a day longer than we want for Andrea."

"It is," Milo said. "But King has been holding onto the cards and the information. It's time we stripped it out of him. If we need to go, we can turn him over to the Vandals."

"Can Em handle that?" I asked. Emersyn Sharpe O'Connell was a tough girl. But no one should have to deal with torturing and killing their father.

"She'll be fine," Milo said, surprising me. "The guys will look after her, and trust me, after everything else, he's actually the least of her evils when it comes to shitty family."

True.

Too true.

The quiet stretched between us. We needed to interrogate King and to get answers from him swiftly. We also needed to be able to trust the answers. Then we needed to eliminate him.

"Give me a couple of hours," Bodhi said. "I may have somewhere closer we can use, but I have to check some things out. Stay close."

He paused to give Lainey a kiss then strode out of the room. She closed her eyes in his absence and leaned on Milo. Ezra stuck with me.

"Are you really okay?" I asked, focusing on Milo. Maybe we'd never have the kind of friendship he had with the Vandals, but he was Lainey's. By extension—that made him ours too. "I thought—I've dreamed of killing my father. Of beating him to death with my bare hands. When the moment came, I hesitated. My stomach churned, and I don't know if it was fear or regret or some misguided sense of loyalty, but I didn't want to be the one who did it even though I wanted him dead."

"The difference," Milo said. "The real difference—your father beat obedience into you. Obedience and compliance. It made those loyalties—to yourself, Andrea, and Lainey conflict with the loyalty he forced on you. I get it. I don't owe King that. Do I want to put a gun to his head and just end it? Yes. The thing is, from the moment he returned, I've had to be restrained to get what we need out of him."

"You've done a hell of a job," Ezra admitted.

"Thanks—cousin." The faint smile pulled one from Ezra, and then Milo shrugged. "The moment I don't have to be restrained with him anymore? I'm not going to be. You two want to kill him for the shit he did to you? Respect. But for what he did to Ivy? For what his actions did to my mom? I have no trouble ending him."

Everything he said was true. Twisted and dysfunctional as it was, there was still some micro-sized piece of loyalty still burning inside of me for the Reeds. But now it was for *my* Reeds.

Fletcher.

Andrea.

Lainey.

Ezra.

Fuck, might as well add Milo and Bodhi to the list.

"Come on," Lainey said, starting to move. "We need to eat. Then decide if we're going for a soft or hard approach with King."

"Hard," Ezra said without hesitation. "My dear uncle and I deserve some quality time, and I would be more than happy to knock him on his ass."

With a glance at me, Ezra raised his brows. I nodded. "We should call Liam, even if he doesn't need to be here." The slow, cold smile on Ezra's face seemed to mirror the one on my own.

Liam had his own axes with King.

"Definitely," Milo said, and then we let Lainey usher us to the kitchen and we figured out food. We almost had it together when Bodhi rejoined us.

"I have a place," he said. "We can access it tonight. When do you want to get started?"

CHAPTER

THIRTY-THREE

LAINEY

We had a plan, and we were getting ready to execute it. Before that happened, though, I had to speak to my mother. The facility she'd been moved to was still in Manhattan. A private clinic with personal doctors. Grandfather had sent in the best.

The security at the facility was also top tier. Ezra and Milo came with me, while Adam and Bodhi worked on finalizing the next step for King. Milo had called Em, and she'd given her blessing as it were. Liam was on his way to the city, along with a couple of other friends.

This would be a group effort. The nurse who showed me to my mother's "suite" briefed me on her current care regimen. Her kidneys were failing, and the damage to her liver was significant. They were keeping her on a regular regimen of dialysis to ease the pressure on her body.

More tests. More speculation. More tempered optimism. Hope for the best, prepare for the worst. Despite how nice the facility was, it seemed darker somehow after the briefing.

"The doctor has been in today, and we have evening rounds in a few hours, but if you want to speak to him—I can have him paged to come in."

I shook my head. "No, I am certain your briefing was thorough. It also matches the report he sent earlier today." My grandfather made all the arrangements, but I didn't think he'd come to see her, nor was he planning on it.

Instead, all the reports came to me. I could hardly blame him just as I knew he wouldn't blame me if I washed my hands of her. I couldn't do that. I also hadn't asked him about Yuri Leistung yet.

"You okay?" Ezra asked, rubbing my back as I looked at the door to Mother's suite.

"No," I said, squeezing Pretty Boy's hand before pressing upward to kiss Ezra's jaw lightly. "But I will be."

"We'll be right here," Pretty Boy promised, dropping a kiss on my lips before he let go of me and opened the door to let me in.

The room was done in earth tones with hints of pink and softer mauve accents. It offered a lot of comfort, including large chairs, a television, a huge bed, and the illusion of being at home.

The beeping of some machines along with the lock and whir of others created a kind of rough symphony. There in the bed, looking somehow smaller than she ever had, was my mother.

I left my purse in a chair and moved over closer to the bed as I pulled another chair next to it. I studied her pale features. Even lying in a hospital bed, gray with fatigue and wearing no cosmetics, she was a beautiful woman.

There was a peacefulness to her at the moment that had never been present in our life. At least not where I could see it. I glanced at the various pieces of equipment, mentally identifying them before focusing on her again.

Maybe Grandfather was right not to come and see her. Maybe. I blinked rapidly, fighting to keep my reactions contained. Crying with Em had really helped, but every day seemed to contain some new blow. Fortunately not something that would destroy us. Yet, each sliver of information we carved off turned out to be one shock after another.

The king trying to kill Milo all those years? A man named Julius King who was also his *father*. The same father who abandoned him.

Julius King also tried to have Adam killed. I had no idea how many people he sent Adam and Ezra to kill over the years. Ezra, who was also his nephew, had been used to do the crime to set up his son—and it turned out they were cousins.

Neither had ever known.

The details were filthy with the grimy muck they'd been dug out of. In addition to his crimes as a drug dealer, King was also into child slavery and blackmail, human trafficking, murder, extortion and so much more.

He wanted respect and power. He wanted control. For some reason, after decades of not giving a damn, he wanted his children back. To love them? Somehow I suspected not.

It was just another power play for him.

Then there were the Reeds. Harper was now dead, but only after he sold his own child and set up my mother to die. We still had to take care of making his death "public." Hamilton was out there, but he had no power at the moment, and he was a thorn we would deal with eventually. Jason? Jason seemed to have morals.

That was something.

The Grahams.

I curled my fingers into my palms. Wallace Graham was King's brother. I would bet he knew. It seemed like something sleazy he would do. His abusive cruelty toward Ezra all these years would not go unpunished.

At least Bodhi's family seemed relatively sane. Except, he, like me, was also missing a sibling. A hunt he'd been on for years. A hunt he was setting aside to help us find Andrea.

Then there was the so-called third King child. Were they real? Or another ghost story?

So many ghost stories...

"Lainey..." Mother's voice was weak and she pulled me to the present with the wheeze. "You're here."

"I'm here," I told her. "I've been trying to see you as much as I can, but... you need a lot of rest."

"The doctors won't tell me when I can go home. No one will call Harper. Will you call him for me?"

"Of course, I'll take care of it. Right now, don't worry about calls or anything else. Just rest."

She frowned, then licked her lips. "Thirsty."

I moved to get her some water and held the cup carefully so she could sip from the straw.

"The food here is terrible," she complained with a hint of a smile. "Maybe you could have Harper send over the chef? Or at least get my meals delivered?"

"I'll see what I can do." I put the cup down and then moved to sit on the edge of the bed. This close, I could study her reactions and she could see mine.

"You look worried, don't frown so much," she informed me. "It leads to wrinkles."

A snort of laughter escaped me. "Not too worried about those right now."

"You will be," she said, then seemed to try and pat my hand. "No frowning. Smooth features. Keep you nice for when you get older. Like this."

"You're always beautiful," I told her, and she smiled for real. She did like to be complimented. "I guess I'm lucky that I look like you. Means I'll be pretty too."

"That's very sweet of you to say. Promise me you won't frown so much."

"Of course, frowning leads to wrinkles." I studied her. "Mother...I need to ask a question, so I need you to focus on me."

She opened her eyes to look at me then squinted. The room wasn't bright at all, but her eyes seemed a little dilated. The pain medications might be making her a little loopy. "What question?"

I took a deep breath. "I need to ask you about a man named Yuri Leistung." I barely finished speaking and her closing eyes snapped open. The pupils swelled so big they drowned out the color.

"Do not mention his name," she told me, some of the fogginess leaving her voice. "Ever. Forget you know it."

"You know him?" I asked, studying her.

"It's not important if I do or not. Forget his name. Don't mention him. Don't speak of him. Just—forget. Promise me."

"I wish I could," I said. "But his name came up, and there's a lot going on. They say he might be dead."

"Lainey," Mother said, failing when she tried to sit up. She did manage to latch onto my arm. "Don't look for this man. Just don't. I know you hate me most of the time. I deserve it. But stay away from Yuri Leistung."

"I just told you, he's probably dead. That's what the reports were saying."

"Reports can be exaggerated," she said, and her heart rate leapt on the monitor. "Lies can be told. People will believe anything if you pay them enough. Yuri might be dead, and if he is, good. But his family isn't. You have no idea how dangerous they are. Don't pursue this."

His family.

She dug her fingers into my arm. "Promise me, Lainey."

"Mother..."

"*Promise* me!"

Her pulse jumped again then her grip on my arm went slack. Alarms went off. The doors opened and a medical team poured in. I let them hustle me back, running into Milo who'd followed the team in. Ezra was on my other side.

The doctors and nurses worked to stabilize her, but the alarms kept going.

Stay away from him.

Don't mention him.

Don't look for him.

But he's dead? Even if he wasn't...

"His family isn't. You have no idea how dangerous they are. Don't pursue this."

Her words echoed inside of me as they tried to restart Mother's heart. That was the alarm. The flatline of her heart. She'd gotten upset and then...

Yuri Leistung, whoever he was, might be my father. His family was out there. My family was here.

Everything came down to family.

Everything.

Milo kept an arm around me and Ezra held my hand as

the doctors slowed finally. It had been thirty minutes. Had it really been thirty minutes since the first alarm went off?

"Time of death..." the doctor said, and I closed my eyes.

The thud of my heart was like a hammer driving in the nails on the coffin. She'd been dying, but...

"I'm so sorry, Miss Benedict."

A litany of sympathies. Then an oh my god from a nurse, and the news was on. A tale of a plane crash involving Harper Reed. At this time, there were no survivors.

That part had gone well, even if the timing was a little coincidental and uncomfortable.

It wouldn't be long before that story was running everywhere. Then the news would break about Mother. At some point, Milo walked me out of the room with her and down the hall.

He found a quiet spot and we sat. "I'm here, Mayhem," he whispered, keeping an arm around me and holding me upright.

Ezra joined us a little while later. "They're on their way," he said. "I've also taken care of the notifications. What else can I do, Kotyonok?"

I shook my head. I hadn't expected her death to hit me so hard, and at the same time, I was relieved. That—that twisted me inside and out.

"We have a plan," I said softly. "But before we do this, I need to talk to Margareta Waldemar."

"Not yet," Milo said. "After."

I nodded. After was fine. My phone buzzed and I took it out to look at the screen.

Bodhi.

He and Adam were on their way, but he had more bad

319

news though. The photo that followed stabbed at me. I'd been right about Tally.

Her secret was King.

It was the last puzzle piece I needed.

The last clue before we took the whole damn thing apart.

∼

The Bay Ridge Royals will return in the epic conclusion, Desperate Victory.

AFTERWORD

I can't believe we're here, all the pieces are in place, and the war that has been surging around them is ready to exploded. Lainey is going to stop at nothing to keep her new family together and to find her sister.

Milo, Adam, Ezra, and Bodhi have her back every step of the way. The long-kept secrets of the Royals are about to utterly shattered and let out into the light.

Desperate Victory is coming.

xoxo

Heather

P.S. Yes, I'm in my corner with coffee, snacks, and my laptop.

Reader group:
facebook.com/groups/heatherspack
Spoiler group:
facebook.com/groups/teammadatheather

DESPERATE VICTORY
BAY RIDGE ROYALS BOOK 6

Grandfather tried to prepare me for everything...

Yet, how could anyone prepare me for this?

Kidnapping.

Blackmail.

Deception.

Grief.

Vengeance.

The Royals have always been about blood. Blood lines, blood relations, and the spilling of blood. I didn't ask for this war. I didn't go looking for it.

But I will let nothing and no one keep me from the men I love and we will find what was taken from us. No one will ever steal from us again.

They say desperation makes for strange bedfellows, fortunately, the men in my bed are far more dangerous to everyone else.

It's time for a change in leadership, one way or another, the Bay Ridge Royals are going down in flames. Once it's all ashes—then we can rebuild.

BENEDICT FAMILY

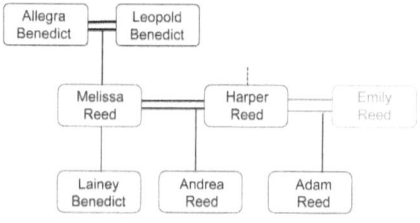

HARDIGAN FAMILY

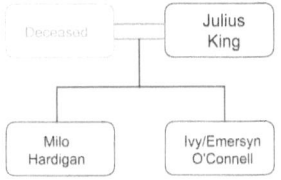

REED FAMILY

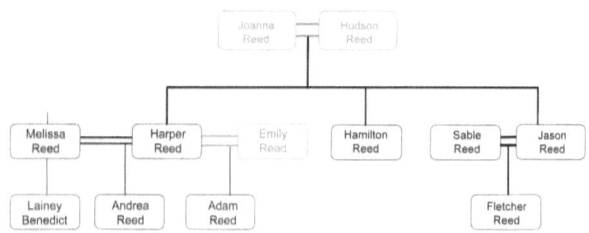

GRAHAM FAMILY

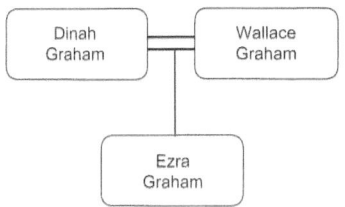

CAVENDISH FAMILY

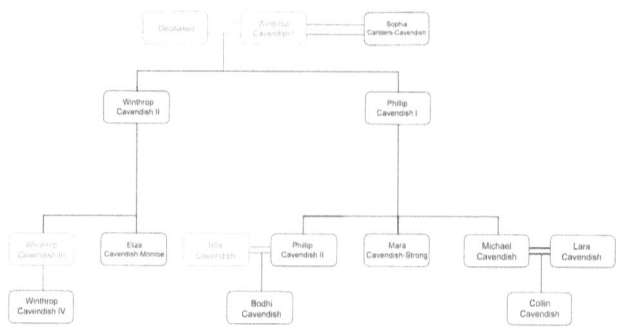

MARLOWE FAMILY

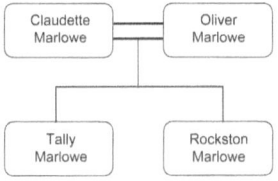

About Heather Long

I *love* books. Not just a little bit, but a lot. Books were my best friends when I was growing up. Books didn't care if I was new to a town or to a class. They were always there, my trustiest of companions. Until they turned on me and said I had to write them.

I can tell you that my own personal happily ever after included writing books. I've always said that an HEA is a work in progress. It's true in my marriage, my friendships, and in my career. I am constantly nurturing my muse as we dive into new tales, new tropes, new characters and more.

After seventeen years in Texas, we relocated to the Pacific Northwest in search of seasons, new experiences, and new geography. I can't wait to discover what life (and my muse) have in store for me.

Maybe writing was always my destiny and romance my fate. After all, my grandmother wasn't a fan of picture books and used to read me her Harlequin Romance novels.

Follow Heather & Sign up for her newsletter:
www.heatherlong.net
TikTok

Also by Heather Long

82nd Street Vandals

Savage Vandal

Vicious Rebel

Ruthless Traitor

Dirty Devil

Shamelessly Loyal (Novella)

Brutal Fighter

Dangerous Renegade

Merciless Spy

Reckless Thief

Fierce Dancer

Bay Ridge Royals

Shamelessly Loyal (Novella)

Battle Lines

Deceptive Truce

Wicked Surrender

Violent Chaos

Desperate Victory

Blue Ivy Prep

Problem Child

Mad Boys

Party Crashers

Money Shot

Bravo Team Wolf

When Danger Bites

Bitten Under Fire

Cardinal Sins

Kill Song

First Chorus

High Note

Last Word

Chance Monroe

Earth Witches Aren't Easy

Plan Witch from Out of Town

Bad Witch Rising

Fevered Hearts

Marshal of Hel Dorado

Brave are the Lonely

Micah & Mrs. Miller

A Fistful of Dreams

Raising Kane

Wanted: Fevered or Alive

Wild and Fevered

The Quick & The Fevered

A Man Called Wyatt

Heart of the Nebula

Queenmaker

Deal Breaker

Throne Taker

Lone Star Leathernecks

Semper Fi Cowboy

As You Were, Cowboy

Shackled Souls

Succubus Chained

Succubus Unchained

Succubus Blessed

Shackled Souls (Omnibus)

STANDALONES

Kiss of Fate (w/Blake Blessing)

Taste of Karma (w/Blake Blessing)

I'll Be Home... (w/Tate James)

Untouchable

Rules and Roses

Changes and Chocolates

Keys and Kisses

Whispers and Wishes

Hangovers and Holidays

Brazen and Breathless